AMAZON SLAVE

She was lifted from her feet and pushed roughly against the hard wooden mast. Before she could raise a word of protest, Emily found herself tied to the huge round pole. Her hands were behind her back, well and truly secured by a long thin rope wound tightly around her wrists.

The captain was glancing over his shoulder and Emily saw Laura approach, offering him his cane. He thanked her and turned to face Emily. He studied her slowly for a moment, his gaze taking in her exposed breasts, and the skimpy, soiled bikini bottoms she wore. A wry smile twisted his lips.

'Undress her,' he snapped.

A NEXUS CLASSIC

AMAZON SLAVE

Lisette Ashton

This book is a work of fiction.
In real life, make sure you practise safe, sane and
consensual sex.

This Nexus Classic edition 2004

First published in 1998 by
Nexus
Thames Wharf Studios
Rainville Road
London W6 9HA

www.nexus-books.co.uk

Typeset by TW Typesetting, Plymouth, Devon

Printed and bound by Clays Ltd, St Ives PLC

ISBN 0 352 33916 0

One

Emily was awoken by the scream. The shrill cry carried
easily through the still night air, chilling her semi-naked
body. Too scared to move, Emily stayed hidden beneath
the tarpaulin cover of the lifeboat. She strained her ears
for sounds in the dark but after the scream there was
only silence. Aside from the lapping of the river against
the hull of the slow-moving boat, there was nothing to
be heard. The only other sound she could discern was
the gentle rustle of a cool breeze in the clipper's tall
white sails.

The moments ticked slowly by and her fear began to
ease. As was usually the way with Emily, the emotion
was replaced by curiosity. She considered moving from
her hiding place to see what was happening. The idea of
offering assistance pricked her conscience and she tentatively stretched her aching limbs, preparing to move.

A second scream stopped her.

Gooseflesh erupted on her bare arms and Emily knew
it had nothing to do with the inclement tropical night or
her lack of proper clothes. For the first time since her
ordeal had begun, Emily realised how vulnerable her
situation was.

Is this nightmare ever going to end? she wondered
miserably. First the argument with Roddy, then getting
stranded; alone and penniless. Now this! It was turning
into a memorable holiday, she realised but for all the
wrong reasons. If I ever get home, I'm never leaving

1

England again, she decided firmly. The next holiday I have will be no more adventurous than Mablethorpe.

Sliding the harsh tarpaulin slowly from her body, Emily risked a wary glance at the world. Illuminated by pale silver moonlight, the tropical night was refreshingly cool. The gem-encrusted waves of the river sparkled brilliantly against the rich black waters. The uninhabited shores were shrouded by an impenetrable sable jungle. Above, the mackerel sky went on forever around a huge gleaming moon.

It isn't Mablethorpe, Emily thought, a wry smile breaking across her lips, but it does have some benefits. She climbed carefully from the lifeboat and stretched each aching limb before moving.

This morning, when her world had been so different, she had been planning to spend the day reading a book and working on her tan. Ruefully studying her bikini and loose silk kimono, Emily realised she was still dressed for that excursion. She shivered as a cool night breeze brushed her legs, and cursed the skimpy costume.

Pulling herself to her full height, she was aware of each grumbling muscle in her body. She had been curled up in the lifeboat for what seemed an eternity during the last twelve hours. Bursting to pee, longing to move and hardly daring to breathe, Emily had felt like the victim of some particularly cruel captor. How she had managed to fall asleep in those circumstances was still a mystery to her. Now, every pore in her body rejoiced at this unexpected taste of freedom.

She was blessed with long coltish legs and a narrow waist. Her slenderness was accentuated by full breasts that pushed forcefully against the scant confines of her bikini top. Every inch of her skin was sun-bronzed and beneath the light of the moon her long dark locks sparkled with glistening silvery highlights.

She shivered and glanced warily around the ship.

The deck was deserted and she wondered if the

bone-chilling scream could have come from somewhere else. Her knowledge of the wildlife in the tropical rain forests was severely limited. She supposed the scream could have been the harrowing cry of some wild nocturnal creature on the shore – or the mating call of some over-loud parrot. Either option seemed preferable to the images her mind had conjured up. Grasping hopefully at the idea, Emily carefully moved away from the lifeboat. Walking on tiptoe, she made her way slowly along the deck to investigate.

'I should never have suggested we have this blasted holiday,' she whispered angrily to herself. She cursed her own stupidity for trying something this adventurous. Things had gone wrong from the very beginning. Quickly, they had become worse and she could think of no one to blame but herself.

The first problem had been Judy, Roddy's step-sister. She had invited herself on the vacation and then moaned about every loss of luxury they had encountered. A cock-up in the booking office, a flat tyre on the rented car and a loose cap on the bottle of sun lotion in her luggage had all contributed to the catalogue of disasters.

When Emily's handbag went missing, it had been the final straw. At least if they had gone to St Tropez she would have been able to handle the language a little easier. In St Tropez there were authorities who could deal with things like missing handbags. Here, in the barely charted depths of South America, she had learnt it was her problem. The fact that it contained her passport, credit cards and all her money was unimportant. It was her handbag, she had lost it, and she could deal with the problem herself.

Roddy had shouted at the village official who explained this to them. Then he had shouted at Emily for causing the problem. His words had been hateful, vitriolic and severely cutting.

3

Emily's retaliation had been worse. She dragged up every personal insult and slur she could think of. She screamed her anger at him and vented her spleen until her voice went hoarse. By profession she was a corporate financier and seldom had the chance to argue with such ferocity. That morning, she had made up for lost time. She and Roddy had argued passionately, allowing their tempers to colour the words.

'Fuck you, Roddy!' she had screamed into his face. 'If you hate this holiday that much, why don't you fuck off home?'

'If that's what you want,' Roddy had screamed back at her, 'I will.'

Ten minutes later, as she watched the rented jeep drive furiously away down the dirt-track road, Emily realised she was on her own. Judy had thrown her own things into the car with Roddy, and together the pair had deserted her.

'Bastards,' she had cursed softly.

The memory was still fresh and no sweeter.

Another scream broke the night's still silence. A torrent of heart-wrenching sobs followed.

It was the sound of a woman crying.

She swallowed nervously. Words, English words she realised distantly, could be heard beneath the tears. Summoning all of her courage, she bravely walked towards the sound. Her bare feet were cooled by the hard wooden planks of the decking. She continued on, reminding herself that as long as she was barefoot she was silent.

'I'm sorry, Captain Wilde . . .'

Emily heard the words as a whisper. The woman's voice was strained and broken by gasps. Motivated by curiosity and concern, Emily moved stealthily towards the sounds.

'. . . I'm sorry. It was an accident. The boat swayed and I . . .'

4

The sound of a sharp blow stopped her words. Her apologies were replaced by a low, guttural moan.

Emily stopped, shocked by the noise.

'Thank you, Captain Wilde,' the woman's voice whispered softly.

Shafts of golden light spilled on to the deck and Emily froze. She cowered in the long black shadows and tried to reassess the situation.

The windows in the pilothouse were aglow with warm yellow light. Unsecured, the main hatch swung lazily open and closed. That was where the sounds were coming from, she realised. Fear held her in the shadows and she struggled valiantly with the emotion.

'Harder, you worthless tosspot. Harder!' It was a man's voice, angry and threatening.

Emily sank lower in the shadows.

'This hard, you fucking idiot!' The words were followed by three swift whistles. It was the sound of a cane cutting air. Each swipe was punctuated by the crack of wood biting flesh. 'This hard.' Again, Emily heard three swift blows.

Curiosity bettered her fear, and she eased herself slowly from her hiding place. Moving cautiously along the deck, she crept bravely towards the pilothouse.

'Sorry, Captain Wilde.' This was a man's voice, chastened and mumbling.

Emily pressed her face against the hatch, trying to see what was happening. It took a moment for her eyes to adapt to the bright light inside. When her vision had finally adjusted, she stifled a gasp of surprise.

There were three people inside: two men and a woman.

The woman was naked. Bent over one of the consoles, she had her back to Emily; every curve and contour of her frail figure was on display. The cheeks of her arse were striped with angry red lines. They burnt brightly against the pallid colour of her wan flesh.

5

Emily realised these marks were fresh.

She had not needed to be woken by the woman's scream to guess this much. Nor had she needed to hear the chastened aftermath of her punishment. Seeing the two men standing over her, each one boldly brandishing a cane, was sufficient for Emily to work out exactly what had been happening.

The pair of them had been caning her arse.

Emily stared at the woman's buttocks, amazed by the marks that had been inflicted. Beneath these welts she could see the fading bruises of previous punishments.

She glanced warily at the two men. The taller of them was dressed in a pair of loose black trunks. A mop of tousled black hair covered his brow, complementing his swarthy complexion. He had a broad build that looked muscular and capable without being affected. Emily considered his type of body to be a natural shape. She had never cared for the aesthetic perfection of professional bodybuilders, preferring the allure of an unfeigned physique. His olive complexion lent a rugged charm to his appearance. Judging by his dark frown and the arrogant set of his shoulders, Emily guessed he was the captain.

Her gaze shifted to the man standing next to him. With his fair hair and pretty-boy looks, Emily did not think this man looked half as formidable as the captain. He looked a little more muscular, but he lacked the commanding air of authority that seemed to come naturally to the dark-haired man. She wondered if that could have been to do with his nudity. From personal experience she knew that people seldom looked commanding when they were naked. As she watched the three, she wished the blond man would move so she could get a proper glimpse of him. He had his back to her and she could only see the side of his face and his pert, tight buttocks.

'Do you think she's had enough?' the captain asked.

He grasped the woman's arse and squeezed one cheek with a merciless hand. The tips of his fingers brushed dangerously close to the rising mound of her sex. His touch was hard and uncompromising, forcing a gasp of surprise from the woman.

Emily drew breath. She was mesmerised by the scene.

'Laura's basque could have been ruined by your stupidity,' he growled. His fingers tightened against the bruised flesh of her backside, pressing hard against the reddened skin. 'I suppose you were lucky she was in a forgiving mood and asked me to punish you while she changed.'

The woman moaned, a soft forlorn cry. 'I am lucky, Captain Wilde,' she whispered.

Emily had to strain to hear her words.

'And I am sorry.'

The captain spat, a harsh dismissive sound. 'You haven't even begun to be sorry, yet,' he told her menacingly. He turned his attention to his blond colleague. 'Stripe her cheeks,' the captain snapped sharply. 'Do it well,' he added pointedly. 'Or I'll make up the shortfall on your arse, do you understand, Vincent?'

Vincent swallowed and nodded. He raised his cane and brought it down forcefully on the woman's bare arse. Her cheeks quivered beneath the onslaught. Her pleasured cries of despair echoed through the night.

Emily watched as he rained blow after blow on to the woman. Her earlier thoughts of helping were now forgotten. Even if she had seen the boat was on fire, Emily doubted she would have found the strength to move.

As Vincent shifted position to get a better swing of his cane, Emily caught sight of his cock for the first time. Long and hard, it stood proudly before him. He had no pubic hair, she noted, and this seemed to accentuate his length. His testicles were a small tight pouch at the base of his shaft.

Peering closer, Emily realised there was a small, tight

7

silver chain separating his balls. It was connected to a loop of metal around the base of his cock and, although she could not tell for certain, this appeared to be keeping his shaft hard.

His foreskin had peeled back to reveal a swollen purple head. Vincent's erection throbbed eagerly and seemed to twitch with each blow he administered.

You cruel bastard, she thought incredulously. She did not know who the insult was directed at, and the accusation carried no real weight. She could not blame Vincent for his arousal. A tingle of dark excitement was sparking between her own legs, and she rubbed the heel of her palm gently against the crotch of her bikini bottoms. There was something so intimate and personal about the situation that Emily felt a yearning to be part of it.

'Madness,' she told herself angrily. The pair of them were gratuitously beating the woman, and she was enjoying the spectacle. Not only was she enjoying the whole incident, she was actually wanting to participate. 'I've been out in the sun too long today,' she told herself. 'It's starting to effect me.'

'You've made Vincent get all excited,' the captain noted. There was a trace of good humour in his voice. He grabbed the woman's hair and pulled her from the console.

For the first time, Emily saw her face. She was a pretty brunette with pale blue eyes and a doll-like face. Her lips were parted in a gasp of surprise as she tried to free her hair from the captain's grip. Watching intently, Emily barely noticed the woman's face. Her attention was caught by the pair of silver loops that pierced her nipples. Her gaze was riveted on the body jewellery, and she tried to come to terms with what she was seeing. She had heard people talk about getting their nipples pierced before now. One or two of her more gregarious colleagues had joked about doing it but so far as Emily knew, none of them had dared. And here she was staring at a pair of tiny metallic ball closure rings penetrating the flesh of this woman's breasts.

Unconsciously, Emily shifted position, leaning forward so she could get a better look.

The brunette's breasts were small and pert with large dark areolae. They rose and fell softly, her breathing made heavy by the punishment she had endured. Her nipples stood hard and proud, penetrated on either side by the curved silver loop.

Not aware that she was doing it, Emily rubbed her hand harder against the warm cleft between her legs. Almost accidentally, her fingers slipped inside the warmth of her bikini bottoms.

Like Vincent, Emily saw the woman had no pubic hair. Her slender flat stomach was of a milky complexion that went down to the bare depths of her sex. At first, Emily thought it was a trick of the light. A sparkle of silver seemed to glisten between the woman's legs. Incredulous, Emily realised the woman did not just have pierced nipples. The lips of her pussy were pierced as well.

'What are you going to do about his excitement?' the captain demanded. His voice sounded cheerful, but there was a threatening note to it that Emily found wholly unnerving.

'I'll do whatever you tell me, Captain Wilde,' the woman said quietly.

He smiled, a hard and bitter expression. 'Do you think you can please him?' the captain asked.

The woman shrugged. She glanced coyly at Vincent, then turned her gaze away. 'I don't know,' she ventured. 'I guess so.'

The captain's smile darkened. 'And do you think I've punished you enough for your accident?'

Again, she shrugged. 'I guess so,' she told him. She dared to turn her face up and glance hopefully into his dark, foreboding face.

9

The captain's smile was predatory. 'We'll have an arrangement,' he said eventually. 'Get down on your knees, and suck Vincent's cock. I'll cane your arse until you've made him come. Then we'll consider you properly punished.'

'Thank you, Captain.' With eager anticipation, the brunette knelt down on the floor of the pilothouse. She reached forward and took hold of Vincent's bare length in one hand. Lovingly, she caressed his cock before stroking it against the side of her face. Her fingers rolled it languidly back and forth, tugging the foreskin over the tip, then pulling it back down again.

With a sly smile, she glanced up at Vincent and traced her tongue along his length. She opened her mouth, her lips pursing eagerly, the corners wrinkling into a smile as she moved towards the end of his cock.

Vincent groaned.

Emily shuddered. Her fingers had found the lips of her labia. As she watched the trio, she teased herself slowly open, drawing the soft pad of her fingertip against the soft warmth of her sex. There was a burning heat between her legs. As she rubbed the tender folds of her pussy lips, Emily noticed for the first time how excited she was. The wetness of her arousal coated her lips. Barely aware she was masturbating, Emily continued to play with herself as she watched the events in the pilothouse.

'Is she doing that satisfactorily, Vincent?' the captain asked.

Vincent nodded. His lips were split by a broad grin. His eyes shone brightly with appreciation. 'Perfectly satisfactory, Captain Wilde.'

The captain's smile was a thin, cruel line. He raised his cane and held it high above his head. With a viciously sharp swing, he brought it down against the seat of the woman's arse.

She gasped loudly. Every muscle in her body seemed to tense.

Vincent moaned excitedly.

Emily shivered and rubbed herself harder. Her fingers toyed with the lips of her pussy, stroking the skin and teasing the tip of her clitoris. With her other hand she had eased one breast from the confines of the bikini top. Slowly, deliberately and with just a little more pressure than was needed, she rolled her nipple between her finger and thumb. The nub was hard, tight and delightfully responsive. A wealth of sparkling sensations erupted from the taut bud, thrilling her with their intensity. Her breathing had deepened to a ragged gasp. She tried to stifle the sound, wary of giving herself away.

Vincent's broad grin was almost splitting his face. His hands had fallen to the sides of the woman's face and he held her against his rigid cock. The woman sucked eagerly on his length, her lips sliding slowly up and down his shaft. She reached her hand under Vincent's balls and teased the shaven sac with her slender fingers.

From her position at the main hatch, Emily could see the woman's fingers catch on a small, shiny padlock beneath Vincent's balls. She instinctively knew that this was attached to the silver chain and the sight intrigued her.

Captain Wilde brought the cane down again. Repeatedly, he struck one cheek, then the other. The grin on his face was proof enough of his enjoyment as was the bulge at the front of his black shorts. He delivered blow after blow to her backside, each one harder than the last.

The brunette stiffened beneath every cutting stroke. She sucked harder with each vicious impact and seemed determined to end her punishment by making Vincent climax. The glimmer of excitement that shone in her eyes indicated her own enjoyment of the situation. Emily was in no position to tell for sure, but she guessed the woman was receiving more pleasure than pain from her beating. Her pierced nipples jutted hard from her small breasts, and the lips of her pussy glistened with dewy moisture.

'This will teach you not to do it again,' Captain Wilde growled. He punctuated each word with a blow from the cane.

The brunette pressed herself hard on Vincent's cock. She swallowed the end to the back of her throat and glanced happily up at him.

'Spill one drop of his come,' the captain threatened, 'and I'll have Vincent stripe your arse while you suck me.'

Excited by his words, Emily stifled a groan. Her fingers were rubbing furiously at her swollen clit, rolling soft circles around the nub of eager flesh. She could sense an impending climax as it welled deep inside her. The strength of her arousal sent shivers to every muscle of her body. It took a massive effort of will-power to control her fingers so they could continue with their important work between her legs.

As she watched, a dark part of her mind envied the woman in the pilothouse. The idea of being used in such a way should have been abhorrent. She had always believed that good wholesome sex could only come from mutual understanding. Sex was the bonding of two like-minded adults pleasing one another. What she was witnessing was not sex. It was barbarism.

Excited beyond belief, she yearned for it. The idea of spanking someone, or being spanked, thrilled her immensely, bringing her orgasm even closer.

She splayed the lips of her labia wide apart and slid a finger deep into the wet depths of her pussy. Her climax was a whisper away: so close she could almost taste its sweet electric taste. She released her other breast from the bikini top and squeezed the nipple. Continuing to rub at herself furiously, she shivered as the first thrill of pleasure washed over her.

In the pilothouse, Vincent groaned a soft growl of

elation. His hips bucked forward with the force of his climax and he pushed his length deep into the woman's mouth.

She continued to suck hard on his cock, holding her buttocks high for the captain to strike them. He delivered a final, stinging blow and she screamed euphorically. Continuing to lick at Vincent's flagging cock, the brunette smiled fondly up at him.

'Let that be a lesson to you,' the captain said, a smile twisting his lips. 'I trust you won't be so clumsy in future.'

Still aching from her ordeal in the lifeboat and quivering with the strength of her orgasm, Emily fell heavily to the deck. She neither knew nor cared if they had heard her in the pilothouse. Her satisfaction was so overwhelming it went beyond consequences.

A sound above her made her glance upwards. At first she thought it was the breeze filling the clipper's sails.

The tall blonde woman stared down at her. A frown creased her lips. With her gaze fixed on Emily she called into the pilothouse. 'Captain Wilde! I think you'd better come out here.'

The captain's voice rose from inside. 'Laura? What's the problem, honey?'

The woman continued to glower down at Emily.

Embarrassed beneath her stare, Emily realised how dreadful she must have appeared. Her breasts had spilled from the top she wore and she still had one hand inside the pants of her bikini. The fact that the pants were now soiled with the cream of her climax only made Emily feel more uncomfortable. She tried to think of an explanation or an apology that would suit the situation but nothing came to mind.

'I can't decide what it is, Captain,' The woman called back to him. 'It's either a stowaway or a peeping Tom. Do you want to come and help me decide what to do with her?'

Emily swallowed, nervously. She knew she was in trouble. Now, she just had to wait to find out how bad it was.

'I know she's in trouble,' Roderick said with forced patience. 'I just wish I knew how bad it was.'

Judy smiled sympathetically at him. 'Are you worried about her?'

He nodded. 'I was stupid leaving her alone,' he told her. 'We should never have argued.' He sat heavily on the bed and rested his head in his hands. 'What the hell has happened to her?'

Judy sat down next to him and put a comforting arm around Roderick's shoulder. She gave him a reassuring squeeze and smiled encouragingly at him. 'Don't start blaming yourself, Roddy,' she said quietly. 'Emily's a big girl. We both know she can look after herself.'

He snorted derisively. 'In the boardroom she can look after herself. Out here she's alone. She's got no change of clothes, no money and no passport.' He glared despondently around the room, desperately searching for inspiration.

It was the same hotel room he and Emily had shared the previous night and that fact alone made him uncomfortable. The room was slightly cleaner and a little more hospitable than some of the places they had stayed during the last week but it was nothing spectacular. Emily had described it as a prison cell with a mozzy net.

Judy put her hands on Roderick's shoulders and began to massage him carefully. 'You're too tense,' she told him earnestly. 'Lighten up a little. We've done all the searching we can do for one day. We'll carry on looking for her tomorrow. I doubt she'll have gone far from the village.'

Reluctantly, Roderick nodded agreement. After the argument he had driven out of the village like a lunatic. Judy had remained silent in the passenger seat as he

14

drove, save for the occasional hint about which road to take. An hour later, when they had used up all the dirt-road and were travelling along one of the more hospitable stretches of blacktop, Roderick's conscience had pricked him.

'We have to turn back and see if she's all right,' he had told Judy.

Silently, she had nodded agreement.

Roderick had done a smart U-turn on the road and headed back. The return journey had taken a little longer, but Judy had helped him with her usual level-headed grasp of the terrain. When they returned to the hotel, he discovered Emily was no longer there. They had scoured the town, interviewed every one of the natives who they had been able to speak to and shouted themselves hoarse calling Emily's name.

All their efforts had proved fruitless. Emily was still missing.

Sitting in the hotel room, Roderick began to wonder what had become of his fiancée.

Judy applied her fingers skilfully to his neck. She moved from his side and climbed on to the bed so she had better access to him. She had just finished showering in her room and her body still held the subtle fragrance of lightly perfumed soap. The towelling robe she wore hung loosely on her body. Had he bothered to look, Roderick would have noticed she was naked beneath the garment and making no attempt to conceal the fact.

'That feels good,' he said absently as Judy rubbed the stiff muscles on his neck. He was dressed only in a pair of jeans, having discarded his shirt because of the tropical heat. He rolled his shoulders into her deft fingers, allowing Judy to tease the knotted flesh. 'That feels bloody good,' he encouraged. He tensed for a moment as she tugged his hair, then realised she was releasing the band from his ponytail. As his long dark locks spilled over his shoulders he shook his head gently, flicking a little body into the mane.

'Why don't you lie down?' Judy suggested. 'You look like you need an all over massage.'

He turned to face her, a grateful smile twisting his lips. 'I can't tell you how good that sounds,' he said honestly. 'It's been a bitch of a day.' He started to move on to the bed and then turned a concerned frown on her. 'You don't mind doing this, do you? I mean, I'm not keeping you from going to bed or anything, am I?'

Judy grinned at him and pushed him easily on to the bed. 'I wouldn't have suggested it if I minded,' she said practically. 'Now lie down while I relieve all your tensions.'

He grunted dry laughter into the pillow. 'I could do with that,' he agreed, shifting centrally on the bed. He tried to free his mind of the day's fraught legacy as she worked the heels of her hands into his shoulders. He had not realised until Judy began her massage just how badly he ached. Anxiety, worries and tension had knotted the muscles of his back into painful tight pockets.

Her hands worked slowly down his shoulders, stroking his slender back and kneading each hard bubble of tension. With his face buried in the pillow, he was unaware that her robe had fallen open.

Judy worked her hands further down his body, concentrating the tips of her fingers on the small of his back. She caressed his pale flesh, working the muscles beneath the skin until they were in a state of almost blissful relaxation. Continually, she moved her hands over him, touching, stroking and reassuring him.

'You need to take your jeans off,' she said quietly. 'I can't get to your back properly.'

Roderick stiffened. He half turned on the bed and stared up at her. Because she was his step-sister, he had never bothered to consider her properly and it felt as though he was looking at her for the first time. She had

16

a pleasant face, he noted. Her sparkling green eyes always hinted at an air of cunning that was simultaneously frightening and exciting. Without the peroxide blonde highlights, her hair would have been a drab mousy colour but this did not trouble Roderick. He found her over-the-top appearance reassuringly glamorous. Staring up at her, he frowned uncertainly, trying not to let his gaze rest on the open folds of her gown.

'I can't take my jeans off,' he said quietly. 'I'm not wearing any shorts.'

She raised her eyebrows and smiled lasciviously at him. Laughing softly at his bashfulness, she put her hands on his torso and began to gently knead his body again. 'If I'm going to do this massage properly, I have to get your jeans off,' she explained patiently. 'I'm not interested in seeing your dick,' she added quietly. 'I just want to make you feel better.'

Roderick stared at her doubtfully. He felt sure she was telling the truth. Judy was not just his step-sister, she was also his friend and he doubted she would lie to him. Staring into the emerald depths of her sly green eyes, he noticed the glimmer of cunning there and wondered if he was imagining it.

'Besides,' Judy went on quickly. 'You're my step-brother, and that's so close to being family there's no real difference. Normal brothers and sisters see one another naked all the time and that doesn't mean anything.'

He considered her words for a moment, aware that she was right. There was still something about the situation he did not trust but he put that down to his own tiredness and his fears for Emily. With a slow nod of agreement, he reached for the button at his waistband and began to ease the metal stud from the denim.

'Let me,' Judy said, brushing his hands away.

He began to protest, then realised he was being stupid. Judy was not trying to seduce him, Roderick

17

reminded himself. She was only trying to help. He lay back on the bed as she teased the buttons of his fly open. She moved her head down to study the buttons, her fingers fumbling awkwardly with the stiff denim. Her long yellow hair fell over her face and spilled against his bare stomach. As she tried to see what she was doing, the ends of her hair tickled his skin softly.

It was the sort of gentle stimulus he was used to experiencing before oral sex. On those joyous occasions when Emily had gone down on him he had enjoyed the sensation of her fringe brushing over his abdomen. It was an erotic precursor to one of the most intimate acts of foreplay.

Roderick swallowed thickly, aware that Judy's hair on his stomach was having a familiar effect. He could feel his length slowly rousing within the loose confines of his jeans and he blushed furiously, wondering how much embarrassment his erection would cause.

Judy tugged the buttons open one by one, making sure she unfastened all of them before moving her head away.

Roderick lay perfectly still as she did this. He would normally have only opened three or four of the awkward rivets, before sliding the jeans off over his narrow hips. Opening all six of the buttons, Judy seemed to take a great delight in prolonging the moment. Her fingers brushed innocently against the hardening flesh of his length. Her skin was cool against the rising heat of his arousal and he struggled against an involuntary twitch of his cock.

'You're blushing,' Judy noted as she tugged at his jeans. 'You shouldn't be embarrassed,' she told him cheerfully. 'I've seen dicks before you know.' Leaning conspiratorially close to him she whispered in his ear. 'I've even been known to play with them from time to time,' she giggled.

Roderick felt the jeans being tugged from his legs. His

skin was momentarily cooled and to conceal his stiffening member, he rolled quickly back on to his face.

'There's no need to be so shy,' Judy told him earnestly. 'You have a really nice body. Your arse is lovely. Those cheeks are so tight and pert.' She placed her hands on his buttocks and kneaded the pliant flesh gently.

Roderick sucked in a deep breath. His erection pressed furiously hard against the mattress. It was wrong to be getting aroused he told himself. This was Judy, his step-sister and she was only giving him a tension-relieving massage. His body was responding to signals that he knew were not there.

Her hands worked their way from his buttocks and began to stroke at the tops of his thighs. Her fingers pressed tightly into the muscles of his legs and she ran her hands slowly down them.

Roderick tried not to writhe on the bed. His erection was throbbing urgently now and he felt desperate to conceal it.

'Stop stiffening up,' Judy told him suddenly. 'You're not letting me massage you properly when you go all tense like that.'

Roderick mumbled an apology into the pillow.

Judy smiled down at his back. 'You're still embarrassed, aren't you?' she observed. 'I can tell. Is it because you're naked?'

Not daring to tell her the real reason, Roderick nodded and agreed.

She sighed happily. 'Well, if that's all it is, I think I can help you.'

He felt her shift position on the bed and was left wondering what she was doing. He realised exactly what she was up to a moment later, when he saw her towelling robe fall to the floor.

'There,' Judy said cheerfully. 'Now we're both naked, so there's no need for either of us to blush, is there?'

19

Roderick's cock twitched with renewed urgency. He felt her shift position again. This time she moved herself around so that she had straddled his back and was facing his feet. She began to massage his calves with slow deliberation. Her thighs were pressed firmly against his hips. As she rubbed her hands against his flesh, Roderick realised she was exciting him even more than before. Gently, with an almost imperceptible slowness, she lowered herself on to his back. Roderick felt the heated wetness of her labia pressing against his spine. The cheeks of her arse seemed to separate, allowing the warm dewy lips of her sex to spread against him.

He did not know if it was deliberate or unconscious, but he felt her writhing slowly against him. The lips of her sex seemed to caress him with their lewd, intimate kiss.

'You still feel tense,' Judy observed unhappily. 'What do I have to do to make you relax?' she teased.

With his face buried in the pillow and his erection burrowing into the mattress, Roderick said nothing.

'Turn over,' Judy said suddenly, as though she had been struck by inspiration. 'I should massage your front as well if you want to feel all the benefits.'

'No!' he exclaimed quickly.

His words had no effect. She moved off his back and tried rolling him from his stomach. 'Come on, Roddy,' she encouraged. 'It's going to make you feel better.'

'I can't,' he declared unhappily. His cheeks burnt crimson as he risked a glance into the sparkling warmth of her verdant eyes.

Judy frowned, not seeming to understand his dilemma. 'You can't?' she repeated. 'Why on earth not?'

Roderick closed his eyes and ground his teeth together with helpless frustration. 'You've excited me,' he explained coyly.

Judy sighed. 'Is that all?' she asked. 'Turn over, Roddy. I need to massage your front.' Her words allowed him no chance to refuse. She placed her hands on his side and gently turned him on to his back.

Roderick lay there, painfully aware of his arousal. He tried to take his mind from the urgent pulse in his cock by staring at Judy. As his gaze fell on her naked body, he realised it was a mistake. It was the first time he had seen his step-sister naked, and he had to admit she was a sight to behold. Her long, bleached blonde curls framed her face and spilt over her shoulders but he was not looking at her face. She had a slim, waif-like frame with a narrow waist and unassuming hips. Her breasts were small and pert, tipped with rose-hued areolae and hard, thrusting nipples. He considered them for a moment, wanting to raise a hand and touch one of them. He dared not, after all Judy was his step-sister, but that did not make the longing go away. If anything, it made his sudden desire for her even more urgent. He wanted to take both her breasts in his hands and fondle them passionately.

Casting his eyes down, before the enticing sight of her tits could drive him beyond temptation, Roderick found himself studying the dark curls of her pubic triangle. None of his previous girlfriends had ever bothered to colour their hair. For the first time he was faced with the sight of a woman whose pubic bush was a different colour to the hair on her head. Beneath the forest of dark curls, he could see that her pussy lips were already moist and he wondered hopefully if she was as excited as he was.

His cock twitched eagerly.

'You are excited aren't you?' Judy observed cheerfully, smiling at his hard cock.

Roderick shrugged nervously. There was something not right about this whole situation he realised. Although he knew he should be trying to work out what was troubling him, Judy's nudity seemed far more relevant. He had almost forgotten his fiancée and the

21

desperate search he had been conducting for her. Similarly, he had come close to forgetting that he and Judy were virtually siblings.

'I shall have to call you my 'big' brother from now on, won't I?' Judy teased. She drew the tip of her finger slowly along his cock, traversing the length from his balls to the swollen end.

Roderick closed his eyes and groaned softly.

'That's right,' Judy said, as though she had suddenly come to a decision. 'I have to finish your massage don't I? You sound as though you're really struggling with all that tension.' She climbed easily back on to the bed, straddling him again in one fluid motion. As before, she had her back to him but this time she was concentrating her massage on his shins and knees.

Roderick thought of making some protest. Things were going too far. He did not know how much longer he would be able to resist her delectable charms but he knew he could not tolerate much more. He glanced up and found himself staring at the moist wetness of her pussy. The puckered ring of her arse nestled just above the lips of her labia and he strained to stop his cock from shivering. Bent over him, her backside looked magnificently large, and he longed to place his hands on her hips and guide her sex towards his face. It was another thought, too exciting for him to contend with and he breathed deeply, trying to suppress his yearning.

His nostrils were filled with the clean sweet fragrance of her arousal. He could sense the musky aroma of her pussy and this time, no amount of effort in the world could have stopped his cock from twitching furiously. He felt his shaft brush against the cool flesh of her body.

Judy giggled softly. 'You're enjoying this massage, aren't you?'

'You're very adept,' he replied quietly.

'You're dick just jumped up and brushed against one of my tits,' she said. 'You can be quite saucy when you try, can't you?'

'I didn't mean to,' Roderick mumbled. 'It was an accid –'

'I'll bet you didn't mean to,' Judy laughed, a knowing touch to her voice. She glanced over her shoulder and smiled at his embarrassed face. 'You wanted your dick to touch my tits, didn't you?' she asked suddenly.

'No!' Roderick exclaimed, shocked by her words.

'You've wanted to feel it pressing against them all evening, haven't you?' Judy said, ignoring his protest. 'You probably wanted this all along.'

Without another word, she stopped massaging his legs and moved her hands to her breasts. Placing one on either side of his stiff cock, she squeezed the two orbs together and slid them slowly up and down the length of his shaft.

Roderick was in no position to see that she was manipulating her nipples as she did this. He lay back on the bed, groaning elatedly. When he dared to raise his head a moment later, he realised that Judy had shifted down on the bed a little. Now her arse cheeks were mere millimetres from his face. The scent of her arousal was a strong and heady perfume. He inhaled deeply, relishing the intoxicating fragrance. Her labia were glistening with wetness, and for the first time he realised she was just as sexually excited as he was. When they had been touching his back, he realised the lips had spread open. They were still open and he stared longingly into the dark depths of her inviting warmth.

Pressed between the haven of her pert young breasts, Roderick wondered how much longer his cock could endure such divine treatment. He could feel his balls tightening and his stiff cock seemed to quiver continually. Slowly, Judy kneaded her orbs into the pulsing shaft of his dick. She pressed hard against him, unmindful of her own comfort. The tips of her fingers teased circles across the sensitive tips of her nipples and she thrilled to the tingling stimulation.

Roderick leant forward on the bed. All his previous reservations were now gone. Emily was forgotten and he could easily overlook the fact that Judy was his step-sister. He moved his mouth dangerously close to the lips of her pussy and paused. For a moment he was happy to inhale her sweet bouquet. He did not know if she would be angry or upset but he suspected it would be neither of those two emotions. If the excited scent of her sex was anything to go by, Roderick guessed that Judy would squeal with delight when his tongue pressed into her hole.

She moved away from him. Striding off the bed, she snatched her breasts away from his cock and smiled apologetically at him. 'I'm sorry, Roddy,' she began awkwardly. 'That really wasn't fair of me, was it? I know you weren't trying to perv off with me, or anything like that. I shouldn't have teased you like that.'

'I wasn't complaining,' Roderick pointed out, more than a little breathless.

She shook her head. 'You're just being kind,' Judy told him. She picked up her robe from the floor and began to wrap it around herself.

Roderick watched, horrified that she was taking the splendour of her body away from him. He struggled to find the words that would make a suitable argument or protest and force her to stay.

'I only wanted to give you a massage,' she said softly. 'I guess I went a little too far.' She smiled slyly at him. 'I blame you,' she added cheerfully. 'You're just too irresistible.'

Roderick frowned unhappily into her face. He watched as she bent over and kissed his forehead chastely. He then watched as she went to the adjacent room and slid through the communicating door. It was only when he heard the click of the latch falling into place that he realised he had watched all of this in complete silence.

Alone, he remembered his unsatisfied erection. Without a second thought, he took the organ in his hand and quickly began to roll the foreskin back and forth.

As she closed the door on Roderick's room, Judy clasped a hand over her mouth to silence the gales of laughter that had been welling inside. She could not believe it had been so easy to manipulate him. His expression, when she climbed off his body, had been so forlorn it looked hilariously comical. He was even more malleable than she had dared hope. She guessed that before the end of the week she would have Roderick eating out of the palm of her hand – or for that matter, anywhere else she chose.

Her plan to get rid of Emily had worked splendidly so far. It had gone far better than she had expected. Tempers between Roderick and Emily had been fraught from day one of the holiday. The theft of Emily's handbag had been the final straw and Judy had only to stand back and watch her plans come to fruition.

After the argument she had travelled with Roderick and deftly guided him on the swiftest route away from the village. On the return journey, she had warned him about driving too fast and suggested the occasional 'detour' that would hasten their arrival.

They returned six hours after leaving and Judy had not been surprised to discover that her rival was gone.

'And it's all thanks to you,' she said, walking over to the handbag on her bedside cabinet. She glanced at Emily's initials, monogrammed in silver on the clasp. Her lip curled into a sneer and she snatched the bag open. Without bothering to look at them, Judy tipped the contents into the waste-bin at the side of her bed. She glanced at the rubbish, noting the passport and foreign currency that lay there. Reaching into the bin, she pulled out a half-used pack of cigarettes and a gold-plated cigarette lighter. Then she dropped the handbag on top of the rubbish.

Lighting one of the smokes, she lay back on the bed and inhaled deeply. As her fingers toyed idly with the lips of her pussy, she lay back and blew tiny smoke circles towards the ceiling. Waves of pleasure began to emanate from her clitoris and she smiled happily. Things were working out just perfectly.

Two

Things happened in such a whirl that Emily was left dizzy and terrified. Captain Wilde appeared in the main hatch, a thunderous expression darkening his face. He still held his wicked-looking cane and his black shorts bulged with the swell of his erection. Emily stared apprehensively at him. A flock of butterflies began to flap their wings in the pit of her stomach.

'Who the fuck is she?' he demanded.

Laura, the statuesque blonde, shrugged. 'I have no idea. She speaks English.'

He grunted humourless laughter. 'She would. Hold this.' He passed his cane to the woman and reached down for Emily. 'You're coming with me,' he told her firmly. Ignoring her cries of protest, Captain Wilde dragged Emily away from the pilothouse and towards the main deck.

'Stop,' she hissed. 'Don't. You can't do this to me.'

Effortlessly, he picked her up and carried her over his shoulder. He did this so casually she felt like nothing more than a rag doll in his arms. Beating his back with her fists and kicking her legs wildly in the black night, she cursed and screamed angrily for him to put her down.

He laughed darkly, untroubled by her insults.

'You can't do this to me, you bastard,' Emily sobbed, striking her hands against his broad muscular shoulders. 'You can't do this to me.'

'You're a stowaway aboard my vessel,' he growled softly. 'I can do whatever I fucking want.' With a whisper of dark merriment he added, 'Would you like to stop hitting my back before you hurt me? I've already decided to punish you. You don't want to make it worse for yourself by upsetting me.'

His words were spoken so calmly that Emily felt chilled by the subtle threat. Five minutes ago she had watched this man beat a woman's bare arse, striking blow after blow with careless disregard for her feelings. As she watched, she had wondered how exciting it would feel to endure such an episode. Now, on the brink of finding out, she realised the appetite of her curiosity was not quite so ravenous.

He hurled her from his shoulder and threw her against the mast. Like mythical creatures of the night, the brilliant white sails of the clipper rustled all around them. For an instant she was lost in a strange world of her own rising panic. There was no light on the upper deck and aside from the natural luminescence of the sails, she was shrouded in darkness. Her terror increased when she felt the captain's hands on her body.

She was lifted from her feet and pushed roughly against the hard wooden mast. Before she could raise a word of protest, Emily found herself tied to the huge round pole. Her hands were behind her back, well and truly secured by a long thin rope wound tightly around her wrists. She could move her feet, but that did not help in any way. Unused to the tilt and roll of the boat, she needed to keep them firmly on the deck to stop herself from toppling.

She was firmly bound and unable to escape. As her eyes got used to the darkness, she could make out the captain's silhouette before her. Fear and apprehension clouded all other thoughts. Her breathing quickened and her body shivered uncontrollably. She stared angrily at the captain.

He was glancing over his shoulder and Emily saw Laura approach, offering him his cane. He thanked her and turned to face Emily. He studied her slowly for a moment, his gaze taking in her exposed breasts, and the skimpy, soiled bikini bottoms she wore. A wry smile twisted his lips.

'Undress her,' he snapped sharply.

Laura walked over to Emily's side and quickly obeyed the captain's instructions. She released the clasp at the back of the strapless bikini top. Her hands encircled Emily's torso and brushed almost casually against the swell of her breasts. Then the garment was being moved away from her.

Emily watched as Laura tossed it overboard. The flimsy piece of fabric was visible for an instant, flying towards the rails at the starboard side. Then it was gone, snatched into the black velvety waters of the night.

Emily swallowed uneasily when she felt the woman's hands on her hips. Warm fingers reached inside the tops of her bikini bottoms. The woman hooked her thumbs into the pants and slowly slid them down to Emily's ankles. As they were drawn down, Emily was aware of Laura's fingers stroking slowly against the cool flesh of her legs.

'Don't do this to me,' Emily gasped, her cheeks burning bright red with a mixture of fury and embarrassment. 'I'll apologise. I'll say I'm sorry and you can throw me overboard but don't do this to me.' Her words tapered off helplessly, tinged with a pathetic note of desperation.

She saw the captain exchange a glance with Laura. Then he turned and smiled at Emily. 'Which tabloid do you work for?' he asked crisply.

Emily blinked and shook her head, wondering if she had heard him correctly. 'Tabloid? I don't work for a tabloid.'

He raised his cane and slowly stroked the tip of it across her bare breast. It was almost a seductive movement but Emily still tried to flinch away from it. She stared down at the wicked length of the implement as it touched her exposed orb. Her heart was pounding quickly and she could feel her tired and aching arms trembling with fear. Distantly, she realised that her nipple was standing erect as the cane passed against it.

'Stop with the play-acting and tell me why you're here,' Captain Wilde snapped. 'I'm not renowned for my patience, and I don't think you want to see my unpleasant side, do you?'

Emily shivered. A cool breeze touched her naked body but it did not chill her. She was staring at the source of her tremor as he raised the cane above his head. 'Untie me,' she hissed. 'I don't work for a tabloid. I'm here accidentally and I'll happily go away if you just untie me.' This time she heard her words come out as a ragged plea.

He lowered his cane and for an instant, Emily wondered if he was going to release her. He moved slowly towards her, his cruel lips grinning broadly. She could feel his naked chest brushing her breasts as he pressed himself close against her. His face was next to hers and his warm breath blew softly on her cheek. The swell of his erection pushed at her stomach through his shorts. She was simultaneously chilled and excited by his nearness.

Captain Wilde pressed his mouth over Emily's and kissed her.

She tried to move her mouth away but the binding on her wrists was secure. His body was hard and lean against her. His hands held her hips and stroked the tops of her thighs. Then he was pulling her pelvis and rubbing himself against it. Distantly she realised he was simulating intercourse.

Emily realised she should have been shivering with

revulsion. She was tied to a mast, being manhandled by the brutal bastard who had thrown her there. She should have been screaming for him to release her and get his filthy hands away.

Instead, her treacherous body responded eagerly to the captain's touch. Her nipples were hardened buds that yearned for him to touch them. The tingling between her legs was a dull throb that begged to be satisfied. She tried to move her mouth away from his, unhappy with the vulnerability of her situation. Her breathing had deepened and she could taste the erotic flavour of her own arousal. Conflicting emotions whirled inside her. She wanted to be away from the man – a million miles away. At the same time she wanted to be a lot closer.

'What's your name?' he whispered quietly.

She drew a ragged breath. 'Emily.'

He nodded, his lips rubbing gently against her face. His hands moved up her body and began to stroke the soft flesh of her breasts. His thumbs pressed against her nipples, teasing them casually beyond the point of erection. Then he was tweaking the flesh playfully between the tips of his fingers. 'And why are you here, Emily?'

She moaned softly. 'I was alone and stranded in that last village you stopped at,' she said quickly. Her words were broken by the heady depths of her arousal. 'I needed to get out of there, and I had no other way of doing it. I saw your boat, climbed on board and stowed away in the lifeboat.'

He nodded, his fingers teasing the flesh of her nipple to a state of pleasure she would never have anticipated. His lips caressed the soft flesh of her neck, just below her ear. 'Is that the best story you can come up with?'

She gasped miserably. 'It's the truth,' she told him. Emily desperately wanted him to believe her and release her from the mast.

He moved slightly away from her. His hand fell from her breast and brushed casually against the thick swatch of her dark pubic bush. His fingers rubbed slowly against the lips of her sex.

She groaned excitedly. His touch inspired an explosion of pleasure that left her trembling with desire.

'I'm not wholly convinced that it's the truth,' he told her. 'And I'm in a bit of a quandary as to what I should do.'

Emily stared at him. The lids of her eyes were half-closed with pleasure, but she saw no reflection of her emotion on the captain's face.

'I don't have the time or the inclination to try and deal with the local authorities,' he said briskly. 'And I don't believe your story. Now, I would appreciate it if you could start telling me something that I do believe.' He took a step backwards, away from her.

'I am telling the truth,' Emily insisted.

The first blow of the cane struck the top of her left leg.

She shrieked, stung by the welt of fire that burnt her skin. Her cries echoed softly in the night but she doubted they travelled any further than the enveloping folds of the sails. A choked breath hitched in her chest and she strained against the ties on her wrists. A second blow struck her right leg. This one stung even more furiously than the first and she sucked in a noisy breath.

'Bastard!' she screamed angrily, wondering how the man could dare to do this to her. He had just been exciting her with his kisses and caresses. Now he was striking her with a passionate fury. She tried not to think of her arousal, unhappy with the fact that it had not dissipated. Her nipples were still rock hard nubs and the avaricious yearning between her legs was an urgent drumbeat.

'Who are you? And why are you here?' he demanded. The cane whipped through the air. The sound was lost amongst the rustle of the stiff sails. Emily felt two blows strike her in sharp succession. The tip of the cane bit cruelly against her inner thighs. It was a mere whisper away from the lips of her vagina. She held herself still, not daring to think of the pain she would have experienced if his aim had been a millimetre higher.

'I've told you who I am,' she said stiffly. 'And I've told you why I'm here. Why don't you believe me?'

This time the cane struck her nipple. She moaned loudly, torn between conflicting sensations. The pain was intense. A fire of unprecedented proportions burnt furiously in her breast. Along with the pain, she could feel an exquisite explosion of pleasure beginning to spread through her body. Shivers of excitement tingled in every pore. The combination was so extreme it thrilled and terrified her.

He moved closer and kissed her again.

She responded to him eagerly.

Inside, she could feel a dark cloud of self-loathing beginning to develop. She hated herself for enjoying his punishment yet still she pushed her tongue into his mouth and explored him. She heard herself gasping with pleasure and realised how close she was to orgasm. When his fingers touched the aching tip of her bruised nipple, she felt the orgasm tear through her. Waves of delight washed over her body and she shrieked loudly, engulfed by a torrent of ecstasy.

Emily closed her eyes tightly against the pleasure-pain coursing through her body. When she opened them, he was smiling broadly into her upturned face. She glared angrily at him.

'Captain Wilde! Captain Wilde!'

The urgent voices were calling him from the stern and he turned to face them.

Emily followed the direction of his gaze and saw the man and woman running along the deck. She recognised them as the blond man and the dark-haired woman who had been with the captain in the pilothouse. They were both dressed in loose robes, but she knew they were naked beneath the garments.

Emily watched as Laura moved from her side and approached the couple.

'Nothing to report, Laura,' Vincent told her. His words carried easily in the night.

The captain took a step toward him. 'Nothing?' he barked sharply.

Vincent shook his head. 'We've searched from bow to stern. There's no one else on board and she has no baggage of any description.'

The captain turned to Emily and smiled at her. 'Well,' he grinned. 'It looks like you may have been telling the truth after all. Perhaps I should untie you.'

She glared at him, despising his indifferent tone. 'That would be a nice idea,' she said through clenched teeth.

He shrugged. 'I'm tempted to leave you tied to the mast,' he said. 'But I suppose you've been punished sufficiently for stowing away.' He studied her silently, his black eyes glaring contemptuously at her. Without another word he turned away and nodded a silent command at Laura.

Emily felt a wave of relief washing over her as the woman untied her wrists. She glared hatefully at the captain while Laura did this. 'You had no right to do that to me,' she told him angrily.

He laughed. 'I'm the captain of this boat,' he said crisply. 'And you'll soon find out that I have the right to do whatever the hell I want.'

Emily swallowed and tried not to shiver beneath his commanding glare. She did not doubt that the man would be capable of a lot worse than she had already experienced. The idea unsettled her. In spite of the fact that she had found dark enjoyment from his punishment, Emily had no intention of submitting to him again.

She rubbed her aching wrists, conscious of her nudity but unembarrassed.

'Take her down below,' Captain Wilde snapped.

Emily glanced up and realised he was talking to the dark-haired woman who had been punished in the pilothouse.

'Get her cleaned up and prepared for dinner,' he continued. Then, glancing at Emily, he told her, 'We'll talk over food.'

Emily bit back an angry retort, glaring furiously at the captain's unreadable black eyes.

The captain met her gaze, his lips twisted in a smile of contempt. His disapproval for her was obvious as he boldly studied her naked body. The curl of his sneer could not have been more pronounced. Without another word, the captain turned and marched away.

As the shower's spray poured over her, Emily tried to get the memory out of her mind. The cool water should have a cleansing effect, she thought. Just as it removed the light trace of sweat from her naked body, it should have been able to purge the unwanted recollections from her mind.

Using the soap on her breasts, Emily massaged the two orbs until they were coated with a rich, creamy lather. Her nipples still ached from the punishment they had received earlier. She felt them tingle with pained excitement as she soaped herself. Each time her hands made a circle against the yielding flesh, she felt her breath deepen to a ragged gasp.

Her arousal was made worse by the recurring memory of Captain Wilde brandishing his cane. Her body was marked with stripes and her bruised nipples ached when she touched them. The fact that she had enjoyed the beating was confusing to say the least. The memory of her experience kept recurring to her like the melody of a popular tune. In spite of the humiliation and

35

discomfort, the most poignant thing she remembered was the intense pleasure.

'Stop it!' she cautioned herself, aware of the way her own lascivious fingers were stimulating her. 'You don't want to start doing that again, do you?' Her hands made one last circle on her breasts and then she bravely moved the soap away. She took comfort from the thought that the experience had left her with no psychological damage, even if the physical pain still lingered. It would have been easy to let the memory of this evening spoil her appetite for pleasure permanently. Wanting, but not daring to touch herself again, she held her chest beneath the shower's spray and allowed the water to rinse her clean.

It was easy enough to soap the rest of her body and she was beginning to feel more confident when another mental picture came to her.

She closed her eyes and could see the captain in the pilothouse with the dark-haired woman, Dawn. He was standing over Dawn's raised arse, his cane held high in the air. With her eyes pressed shut, she saw him bring it down again and again with malevolent ferocity. The thin strip of wood burnt bright red lines across the pale flesh of her gorgeous backside. The dark cleft of her sex was visible, the soft folds of her pussy lips pouting between the cheeks. Dawn squealed gratefully with a mixture of pain and pleasure. Enjoying the beating, she held her arse higher for him to strike her again.

In the shower, Emily pressed the soap between her legs and began to gently rub it against the swollen heat of her sex. The cool water continued to pour over her breasts, exciting myriad tingling explosions of pleasure from the taut nubs of her aching nipples.

Between her legs, the soap slid easily against the wetness of her labia. Emily caught her breath, amazed by the tidal wave of pleasure coursing through her. She had considered the image to be arousing in a dark sort of way but she had not realised it excited her to such an extent. After the humiliating experience she had endured at the captain's hands, she had doubted she would ever feel dark longing like this.

She pressed a finger against the soap-slippery wetness of her hole and allowed the tip to tease the sensitive skin of her pussy flesh. Suppressing a groan of elation, scared that someone outside the shower might hear her, Emily teased the lips of her labia apart and began to finger her clitoris. The bud of her sex was already hard and erect, as though it had been waiting for her touch. She brushed the pad of one fingertip gently over the aroused pearl, then squeezed it playfully between finger and thumb. The wealth of sensations that thrilled her was incredible. Slowly moving her hands lower Emily gently pushed a finger into her wet hole. Her desire was now so great it was almost palpable. In a frenzied rush she began to finger-fuck her pussy. Before she knew what was happening, she felt the blissful haven of an orgasm encompassing each of her body's nerve-endings. Without realising she was doing it, Emily sighed loudly. The explosion of delight erupting between her legs was so great she briefly forgot her resolution to remain silent.

'Are you all right in there?'

It was a woman's voice, concerned and just outside the shower's Plexiglas door.

Emily pressed a hand over her mouth to stop herself making any more sounds. 'I'm fine,' she said quickly. 'Just fine.'

'I have your towel here,' the woman's voice replied. 'For when you're finished.'

Emily put the soap down and allowed the shower's spray to cool her body for one final time. Stepping out of the cubicle, she was surprised to see Dawn still waiting for her.

Again, she was treated to the memory of Dawn's punishment in the pilothouse. It brought with it a fleeting taste of her earlier arousal and she dismissed the recollection nervously.

'Your towel,' Dawn said, holding out a large bath sheet. She was dressed in a loose navy blouse and a short wraparound skirt that showed her shapely legs to perfect advantage. She smiled warmly at Emily's naked body, not disguising her open admiration. Her gaze flitted appreciatively over Emily's figure and her soft smile broadened.

Emily could feel herself blushing. 'Thank you.' She took the towel and studied the woman, uncomfortable with the rigorous scrutiny she was being given. Emily could not understand why Dawn was staring at her and after a few moments her discomfort turned into nervousness.

'I can take care of myself now, thanks,' she said tightly.

The woman nodded. Without another word, she turned and made for the door. With her fingers on the handle, she paused and turned to face Emily. 'You have a very attractive body,' she said quietly.

Emily swallowed, uncertain as to what she should say in response to this. 'That's kind of you to say,' she stammered nervously.

Dawn grinned. She took a step back towards Emily, her hand outstretched as though she was going to do something.

Emily wondered how things would have progressed if Captain Wilde had not chosen that moment to call her away.

'Dawn. In here, now.'

Even through the inner walls and partitions of the boat, his commanding voice still carried a powerful weight.

Emily glared angrily at the wall, hating the sound of the man's voice.

Dawn smiled sadly into Emily's face. 'I'd better go to

38

him,' she said quietly. 'He'll only make it worse if I don't.'

Again, Emily was left wondering what she could possibly say. It was a bizarre situation and she already had a better understanding of it than she would ever have wanted. Bitterly, she nodded agreement with Dawn. 'I'll see you later,' she said after a moment's thought.

Dawn seemed to brighten at these words. 'Yes!' She said excitedly. 'We'll see one another later. Good idea.' Before Emily could stop her, Dawn had slipped out of the shower room.

Emily watched the door close behind her and slowly began to towel herself dry. 'They're all strange on board this ship,' she told herself unhappily. 'What have I got myself into?'

Ten minutes later, Emily sat down with the captain and his wife. 'That was a lovely shower,' she said, speaking to Laura. Plucking at the side of the silk robe she wore, she added, 'And thanks for the loan of this.'

Laura waved her compliments away. She was a beautiful woman: tall, blonde with full breasts, a slender waist and long, shapely legs. Even though she was still dressed in dark stockings and a black figure-hugging basque, she did not seem embarrassed by her attire. It seemed like it was the most natural thing in the world for her to dress like this and then attend supper with a complete stranger. She settled herself in the seat opposite Emily and placed her hand on the captain's leg. With an indulgent smile for her guest, Laura said, 'Vincent and Dawn are preparing a little supper for you. I'm sure you must be ravenous by now.'

Emily nodded. She considered thanking the woman again, then stopped herself, aware that Laura had been in attendance when the captain was punishing her. Not wishing to appear rude, she contented herself with simply nodding and smiling.

'Why did you stow away on board the *Amazon Maiden*?' Captain Wilde asked sharply.

Laura squeezed her hand tightly around the man's leg. 'No darling,' she cautioned him patiently. 'We agreed we would talk about that after she'd had a chance to eat and rest a little.'

The captain frowned darkly but his wife was unintimidated.

'The *Amazon Maiden*?' Emily asked curiously. 'Is that the name of this ship?'

'Boat,' the captain corrected absently. 'She's a fifty-foot clipper, a formidable vessel, but she's not a ship. She's a boat. And yes, she is called the *Amazon Maiden*.'

Emily thought it was a pretty name, but she would never have told him this in a million years.

He glowered at her coldly. 'It's written on the side of the boat, clear for any stowaway to see.'

'You're being contentious again, Captain,' Laura told her husband calmly. She had a musical voice. It managed to soften the atmosphere in the saloon in spite of her husband's bad mood and Emily's loathing for him.

'As I told you before,' Emily said, 'I'm sorry I stowed away. I was stranded back in the village. My boyfriend had driven off. I had no money, and I'd lost my passport. I'm so unfamiliar with the language here that I was scared to approach anyone. If I'd known you spoke English I would have told you my predicament before I came aboard your ship.' She glared defiantly at him, daring him to challenge her story again.

'It's not a ship, it's a boat,' Captain Wilde corrected. He returned Emily's insolent glare until she eventually looked away. 'You sound like you've been through rough waters,' Captain Wilde said stiffly. 'We'll talk more while you eat.' He snapped his fingers and said crisply, 'Dawn. In here please.'

Dawn entered the saloon at his command. 'Captain Wilde?'

Emily glanced uncertainly at the woman, remembering her forward appraisal in the shower. The most prominent image she had of Dawn was the sight of the woman's naked body. Emily recalled the feeling of erotic excitement she had experienced when she saw Dawn's pierced nipples. Without realising she was doing it, Emily studied the contours of the woman's breasts through her blouse.

She had a slender figure and a petite frame. Her long, lank locks and pale expressive eyes leant an air of mystery to her appearance that was attractive in a vulnerable sort of way. It seemed hard to believe the woman wore such intimate body jewellery. Studying the misshapen thrust of her pierced nipples, Emily realised she could not have imagined the sight.

'A glass of Bacardi for our guest,' Captain Wilde instructed. 'And I'd prefer it if you could serve her meal before she dies of malnutrition.'

'Vincent was just completing the side salad, Captain Wilde,' Dawn said, taking a glass from the cupboard. She filled it with a generous measure of Bacardi and added a couple of ice cubes. Placing the drink on the table in front of Emily, Dawn smiled slyly at her.

Emily was aware of something dark and unfathomable in the woman's eyes. She could not quite read the meaning in her glance, but she knew there was some sort of intimation in the expression. When Dawn winked discreetly at her, Emily guessed exactly what the meaning was.

Blushing furiously, Emily turned away.

Her hand found the drink she had been given and she took it eagerly. Unless she was very much mistaken, Dawn had been trying to make a pass at her. Considering what she had seen the woman doing, Emily would have thought Dawn got enough pleasure from the men on the boat. Thinking about the highly charged passion in the pilothouse and the undercurrent of sexual tension that pervaded the saloon, Emily realised just how wrong her first impressions had been. Dawn obviously got her pleasure from both men and women and Emily found the idea unsettling. Remembering the way the woman had been looking at her in the shower, she realised it all made sense.

She suppressed a shiver of revulsion, not wanting the others to see how she really felt. Trying to steady her nerves, she took a sip at the Bacardi and glanced around the saloon.

The boat had a subtle air of opulence that was beautifully understated. The vessel had been decorated tastefully in pale blue colours that lent an air of spaciousness. The light teak woodwork was polished to a dull lustre as were the framed photographs on either side of the companionway. It was a luxurious room with just enough homely charm to make it feel hospitable. If she had been there under other circumstances, Emily felt sure she would have had a marvellous time.

Sitting beneath the imposing stare of Captain Wilde, she did not feel her time on board the *Amazon Maiden* would be anything like a pleasure cruise.

Her thoughts were interrupted by the sound of the galley door opening. Dressed in a pair of tight-fitting jeans, Vincent appeared carrying a tray with a single plate on it. He quietly served her meal, then waited by Laura's side for his next instruction.

She glanced at the freshly cooked seafood platter he had presented her with. The fish was succulent and cooked to perfection. The vegetables in the side salad were crisp and tasty, lightly coated with a spicy garnish that she found exquisite. It was not until she was halfway through the meal that Emily realised they were all watching her eat.

She glanced up from her plate, wondering if she had transgressed some other maritime rule.

Laura smiled at her. 'Please, carry on,' she said quietly.

Emily took a sip of her Bacardi and followed it with another forkful of food. As she watched, Emily saw Laura place her hand over Vincent's groin and rub the swollen bulge between his legs. The shape of his hard cock was clearly visible through the denim and he smiled gratefully as the woman toyed with him.

Shocked, Emily turned away and discovered the captain was grinning at her lasciviously. She suppressed a shudder and drained her glass in one. This was all getting too weird, Emily thought. She had no idea what to make of it all. There was a heady sexual tension in the saloon. Emily felt the atmosphere like a tight band across her chest.

'You two can go and keep an eye on the pilothouse,' Captain Wilde said crisply. He glanced sternly at Vincent. 'But while you're up there, you will remember my rules.'

'Yes, Captain,' Vincent said obediently. He and Dawn moved quickly out of the saloon, climbing up the steps of the companionway to the pilothouse. Emily watched as the blond man ascended, followed by Dawn.

She could sense Captain Wilde watching her, waiting for a reaction. Emily remained nonchalant beneath his shrewd gaze, not daring to show any of the emotions that raged inside her. Not trusting herself to return his gaze, she glanced at Dawn and Vincent as they made their exit.

As Dawn moved higher up the ladder, Emily realised she could see beneath the hem of her skirt. She wanted to snatch her gaze away. She had already proved herself a peeping Tom and she did not want to compound her guilt. Memories of the retribution she had suffered still burnt in her aching nipples.

The dark cleft between Dawn's legs was clearly visible. As she rose further up the ladder, Emily realised she could see the small ball closure rings that pierced the woman's genitals. The discreet glimpse of pink flesh was an exciting sight and Emily felt herself flush with the mixture of emotions that swirled inside her.

She had been repulsed by Dawn's come-on but at the same time she had been darkly excited. Catching a discreet glimpse of the woman's shaved pussy with its intimate body jewellery, Emily felt those dark, unexplored feelings return. She wondered what Vincent and Dawn might be getting up to in the pilothouse.

Quickly, she stopped herself from following that train of thought. There were enough erotic distractions on the boat without filling her mind with such torrid ideas. She turned her attention back to the remainder of her meal and picked at the vegetables with her fingers.

'You've put us in a bit of a predicament,' Captain Wilde said quietly.

Emily frowned and swallowed a mouthful of food. 'A predicament? How so?'

Laura smiled sadly. 'We're running on rather a tight schedule,' she explained. 'We had planned for most delays and eventualities but we hadn't planned for a stowaway.'

Emily shrugged easily. 'If you just pull over to the shore, I'll make my own arrangements and stop troubling you.'

Captain Wilde and Laura exchanged a glance.

'This is your first time in the Amazon Basin, isn't it?' Laura asked patiently.

'Is it that obvious?' Emily grinned.

Captain Wilde replied. 'It's obvious when you make damned fool comments like that,' he snapped angrily. 'This is a fifty-foot clipper sailing along a notoriously treacherous stretch of uncharted water. It is not a Mini Metro pulling into a layby on the A1.'

Emily tried not to quiver beneath his rising voice. 'I just thought –' she began.

'You didn't think,' he broke in. 'Unless you're an experienced crocodile wrestler, I don't think you gave it a moment's thought.'

Emily felt deflated. She stared unhappily at the captain. 'I didn't realise there were crocodiles here. I suppose I –'

'Furthermore,' he went on, speaking angrily over her. 'You have already told us that you have no money, no passport, no command of the language and no knowledge of the locale. Do you really expect us to leave you to the mercies of whatever you may encounter out there? I may have a harsh way of doing things, but if I left you on the shore, I'd be signing your death warrant. I might just as well have left you tied to the mast.'

Emily blushed, wishing he had not reminded her of that. Stroking her fingers sullenly through her hair she stared miserably at the remainder of her meal. Half of the plate's contents remained but her hunger had now disappeared. 'I could just walk back to the village where I was staying,' she said quietly. 'It was a port on the river so I shouldn't have any difficulty finding it. It's just a matter of following the water back to where we started.'

Captain Wilde tilted his head back and laughed heartily. 'That's a good one,' he said cheerfully. 'Oh, Jesus! Which planet are you from? You've obviously never visited Earth before.'

Laura leant across the table and placed a comforting hand on Emily's arm. 'We're about a hundred miles from where you joined us,' she explained. 'It would take a team of experienced trackers the best part of a week to do the journey. I really do think you would be heading for trouble if you tried that option.'

'Does that mean I'm stuck here?' Emily asked.

'You're not stuck here,' Laura said carefully. 'But we do have other problems to deal with. I'll explain and you can decide what suits you best.'

Emily studied the woman warily.

'We're sailing down to Havalaña,' Laura explained carefully. 'It will take us another week if we continue at our current rate, and when we arrive we have a business meeting planned. On the way there, we will be stopping at two ports for the odd supplies we might require.'

Emily nodded patiently.

'Our feelings were: we could either drop you at the next port, or take you with us down to Havalaña.'

'That's a fairly major port, isn't it?' Emily asked. She recalled seeing the name in one of the holiday brochures she had studied.

Laura nodded. 'They have a couple of hotels and a small airport. It's still a pissant little hole, but it's as close to civilisation as we're likely to get in this part of the world. Most importantly from your point of view, they have a British Consul.'

The words conjured up so many welcome images that Emily could not stop herself from grinning. A British Consul would be the answer to all of her problems. Her lost passport would be dealt with, she could organise plane tickets and sort out travel arrangements to go back home. 'They really have a British Consul?' she asked. 'I didn't realise. I mean –'

'Slow down,' Captain Wilde's words broke into the conversation softly.

Emily stared at him, puzzled. She felt his dark words colour the rosy hue of the image Laura had built up.

'This business meeting is fairly important to Laura and me,' he explained. 'The whole point of our journey there by boat is to prepare for it.'

Emily shrugged, unable to see what he was driving at. 'I can help if you like,' she said quickly. 'I have my own business back in England; I'd be happy to help sort out a presentation or run through any proposals you may have.'

The captain and his wife smiled indulgently. 'I don't think you understand,' Laura said patiently. 'When we have this meeting, we won't be discussing business.'

Emily frowned, wondering if she had missed something. 'If you're not discussing business, and you need to prepare before the meeting, then what will you be doing, and how do I fit in?'

Captain Wilde grinned broadly. 'Remember what you saw in the pilothouse earlier,' he said quietly. He leant across the table and stroked his hand against her cheek. It was a gesture that was far more intimate than Emily felt comfortable with. After being tied to the mast and manhandled by the man to the point of orgasm, she felt a bitter loathing for Captain Wilde. She flinched away from his touch before she could stop herself.

The captain glared at her, his smile replaced by a look of the darkest fury. 'What we shall be doing,' he said tersely, 'is preparing Vincent and Dawn for the meeting. We know from previous experience that our clients like to play corporal punishment games. As a sweetener for this deal, Laura and I have decided to entertain these two men by letting them use our slaves.'

Emily's eyes opened wide.

She stared at Captain Wilde, her features strained with disbelief. 'Slaves!' she repeated. 'Is this some sort of joke? Slaves? Corporal punishment games? You can't be serious?' She turned helplessly to face Laura. 'Is he kidding me?' she asked.

It was obvious from Laura's face that the captain's words had been said in earnest. 'He's not kidding,' Laura said quietly. 'We thought you'd be a little shocked by the situation, which is why we're prepared to give you a choice.'

'That's right,' Captain Wilde said quickly. 'If you don't want to stay on board until we reach Havalaña then we can drop you off at Port Maga in two days time. There's no British Consul there but I'm fairly sure they do have a telephone exchange. With a bit of luck you should be able to phone someone and organise your own help.'

'All that we would ask,' Laura said quietly, 'is that if

47

you chose to get off at Port Maga, you stay in your cabin until we arrive there. We wouldn't want to offend you with the things we do, and we can't afford for you to inadvertently interfere with our training programme.'

'Not that you'd be likely to be offended,' Captain Wilde said with a broad grin. 'You seemed to get something out of your punishment at the mast,' he observed wryly.

Emily blushed. She stared into his dark eyes and glared at his hateful smile. Turning to Laura, she asked, 'What if I wanted to stay aboard 'till Havalaña?'

'I don't think you'll want to,' the captain replied. 'I was going to suggest that in return for our taking you that far, you could show your gratitude in the same way that Vincent and Dawn show theirs. If we take you to Havalaña, we'd want you to be our slave for the week.'

Emily glared at him, unable to put her disgust into words. She turned to Laura, trying to find confirmation of the captain's dastardly suggestion.

'Take the night to think it over,' Laura said generously.

Captain Wilde smiled at her silent fury. 'We wouldn't want to rush you into a big decision like this. You can tell us what you've decided over breakfast.' He grinned lasciviously at her. 'I hope you decide to take us up on the offer,' he said. 'You seemed very responsive on the main deck.'

Sickened by the suggestion, Emily turned her pleading gaze to Laura.

'You'd better get yourself off to bed,' Laura said gently. 'The captain and I have our work to do now.' The heavy emphasis of her words left Emily with no doubt about her meaning. She did not know what work Laura and the captain would be doing but she felt certain it would be sexual. She nodded curtly to the pair of them and made her way to the cabin they had given her.

'Pleasant dreams, Emily,' Captain Wilde called after her. 'I'll see you at breakfast.'

With the hateful sound of his words ringing in her ears, Emily left the saloon.

The sanctuary of sleep had entwined her in its dark blanket-like folds. She lay in the single bunk beneath a thin cotton sheet and her dreams transported her away from the nightmare of the waking world.

Asleep, she was back in the hotel room with Roddy. The day had not been as bad as she had imagined, and they were drifting off together. His arms were around her, and she could feel the reassuring warmth of his body pressing against her naked skin.

In her dream, she could tell that Roddy was in a playful mood and eager to do more than just sleep. His hand caressed her breast fondly and she was surprised to feel him tweak her nipple playfully. The gesture inspired a thrilling response and she shivered happily beneath his touch. Aroused by his foreplay, she turned over in the bunk, eager to accept his advances. She embraced his slender body and held him tightly for a moment. Her mouth searched hungrily for his and, when they met, their kiss was electric.

She slid her tongue hungrily inside him and was pleased when he responded by fondling and caressing her breasts. His touch was firm and confident – a sure sign that she was dreaming, Emily thought.

In reality, Roddy was a cautious lover and his cuddles and caresses were seldom very stimulating. On those rare occasions when he did take the initiative and touch her, he always treated her like a fragile glass ornament. His hands whispered against her skin, but there was rarely enough pressure from his touch to properly excite her.

Tonight, her dream lover was not behaving like Roddy.

The kiss was broken and she felt tiny appreciative kisses being delivered to her neck, shoulders and breasts. Her nipples were kissed, sucked and teased until they stood hard, like soldiers on parade.

'Oh! Roddy,' she whispered. 'Please go on.' She placed her hands on his head as he continued to work his kisses down over the flat of her stomach to the thick swatch of her pubic hair. She felt a kiss being placed on each inner thigh before he nuzzled gently against the tender bud of her clitoris. Squirming happily beneath his touch, she allowed him to lap hungrily at the delicate folds of her pussy lips.

His mouth licked softly against her inner folds, teasing her and exciting her in ways that the real Roddy had never dared to try. Coupled with the soft roll and sway of the *Amazon Maiden* as it sped along the river, Emily revelled in the euphoria of the moment.

The river lapped gently against the hull in the distance, and with a sigh she realised the noise had woken her. She opened her eyes and stared at the square of star-speckled sky visible through her cabin's upper hatch. Even under these bizarre circumstances, she had to concede that the view was splendid.

Between her legs, the tongue continued to lap.

Emily froze, trying to work out what the hell was happening to her. If that bastard Captain Wilde had broken into her cabin she was going to . . .

'You taste lovely.' It was a woman's voice.

The words cut through her thoughts like a knife. She tried to compose her emotions into some semblance of order but it was an impossible task. A mixture of tiredness and arousal had turned her thoughts into a chaotic jumble. Emily knew she should be pulling away from the woman but the sensations she was enjoying were too good to relinquish.

Knowing it was wrong was one thing. Finding the will-power to stop it was another.

She allowed the woman to continue tonguing her cleft, and she breathed more deeply as the pleasure overwhelmed her. She wondered briefly who it was. The woman's voice had come as such a surprise Emily had not been able to recognise to whom it belonged. The dark silver rays of the moonlight made it impossible to discern whether the woman between her legs was a blonde or a brunette. With an air of dark, carnal abandon, Emily decided she did not care who it was. As long as they continued to please her for the next few minutes, she was willing to overlook their identity. Unable to believe her own acceptance of this promiscuity, Emily pushed her hands down and caressed the head nestling at her pussy. Her fingers ran through the long hair that stroked against the inner flesh of her legs. She tugged it gently and was pleased to hear a soft moan of appreciation from the woman who was licking her.

Emily could feel herself falling into a sea of ecstasy. Warm waves of delight washed over her as the unknown lover continued teasing with her tongue. A warm wet mouth delivered soft, gentle kisses to the heat of her sex. Her clitoris was tongued and nibbled by the mysterious woman who had chosen to share her bed. Emily could feel the hot, dark wetness of her arousal mounting. The climactic tingling sensations that welled within her were building to monumental proportions. Breathing hard, she clenched her fingers tight into the thin cotton sheet on the bunk and braced herself for the enormity of her impending orgasm. Every muscle in her body shivered in accord. Her climax felt so close it was almost unbearable. She released her hands from the sheet and lovingly caressed the woman's head.

The realisation of what she was doing was brought home to her as she caressed the woman's ears. Emily could feel her fingers brush against a pair of feminine drop earrings. Incredulous that she was being tongued by another woman, she bucked her hips forward and

51

groaned with triumphant elation. The strength of her climax was tremendous, filling every pore with an explosion of delight.

When her muscles finally stopped quivering, she realised the woman had slid a pair of fingers inside her. The lips of her labia were being spread wide apart by one hand while the woman eased a pair of fingers into the dark haven of Emily's pussy. Her inner muscles clenched greedily at the digits and she wriggled herself eagerly on to them. With a gentle pull, the woman started to ease her fingers out before pushing them back in again. She used them slowly and deliberately, following the same tempo as the boat's dip and sway through the river.

Emily sighed.

Then the mouth was being pressed against her. The tongue worked its way around the fingers, teasing the sensitive folds of her delicate pink lips. After licking her labia softly, the tongue returned to her clitoris.

Her sigh turned into a groan of pure delight. Without realising she had started to do it, Emily saw she was fondling her own breasts. She rolled the nipples gently between her fingers, exciting the hardened tips with a combination of playful tweaks and gentle caresses.

This time, when the orgasm struck her, she released a guttural roar of satisfaction. Her jubilant cry echoed through the boat and out into the night. Wave after wave of excitement rolled over her, transporting her body to an ethereal plane. For an instant she was so elated the world did not seem to matter. She was lost in the heady indulgence of whole and total satisfaction.

As the waves subsided and reality began to encroach on her bliss, she realised the woman was kissing her mouth. Emily allowed the woman to explore her. She could taste the musky scent of her own juice on the stranger's lips and found the flavour intoxicating.

She reached out a hand, eager to explore the woman's

body. Her fingers traced along the smooth dip of the woman's waist then up towards her breast. It felt so unusual to be caressing a woman in this way that Emily felt her longing increase. She could not recall experiencing such intense desires. Since she had first glimpsed the events in the pilothouse, she had been victim to a boundless sexual appetite. Stroking her hands against the woman's bare flesh, Emily's craving did not abate.

She realised it was Dawn when her hands cupped the woman's breasts. Her fingers touched the metal piercings which penetrated the delicate flesh of her nipples. Unable to resist the temptation, Emily drew her finger around the sensitive flesh of Dawn's areolae. She allowed her finger to tease the hardened nub by stroking it, then tugging gently on the silver ring.

Dawn sighed happily. She reached over to embrace Emily, her hands stroking, touching and caressing.

Emily stopped her with a kiss. She pushed Dawn back on to the bunk and held her against the mattress. There were no lights in the cabin, save for the trickle of starlight that filtered down from the hatch above. Both their bodies were held in shadows; the flesh was coloured almost navy in the midnight light.

Emily glanced down at Dawn's body, an appreciative smile breaking her lips. She was excited by the svelte slenderness of the woman's figure, and even more aroused by her own intentions. She swallowed nervously, trying not to think about what she was doing, then placed her mouth over Dawn's bare breast.

Dawn groaned happily.

Emily explored the pierced nipple with her lips and tongue. She sucked gently on the hard nub and teased the ring between her teeth.

Dawn's moaning increased. She rolled from side to side writhing her hips together. Softly, she encouraged Emily with warm, reassuring words. The light touch of her fingers stroked against the cool flesh of Emily's neck.

Moving her mouth from one breast to the other, Emily grinned happily. She licked the orbs, enjoying the salty taste of Dawn's sweat. Tracing her tongue downwards she licked over the flat of her stomach and moved her mouth to the bare mound of Dawn's shaved pussy.

Her mouth found the woman's hole, and she licked furiously at it. She had never dreamt of doing such a thing before, but her appetite for Dawn's heated sex seemed unending.

Emily had noticed the woman's labia were pierced before. Actually teasing the rings with her tongue was a pleasure she had not anticipated. She licked the folds of flesh gently, savouring the flavour and enjoying Dawn's guttural, appreciative moans. Her tongue slid easily into the warm wet confines of Dawn's hole and Emily shivered excitedly. She continued to lick, nibble and tease until Dawn was gasping helplessly, on the brink of a cataclysmic orgasm.

Emily smiled up at her. She pushed her fingers between Dawn's legs and found herself enjoying the feeling of fingering another woman's hole. It would have been exciting enough without the added stimulus of Dawn's pierced labia. But with the two sensations combined, Emily felt dizzy and exhilarated.

She changed around on the bed and straddled Dawn's supine body. Adopting the position as though it was second nature, she thrust her pussy into Dawn's face and buried her mouth against the wet mound of the woman's sex. Before, the excitement had seemed unbearable. Now, it was more than she could cope with.

As Dawn's tongue entered her pussy, Emily felt an explosion of pleasure fill her body. She kissed hungrily at Dawn's wet hole, lapping up the woman's juice and pushing her tongue against the hardening pearl of her clitoris.

Beneath her, Dawn growled happily. She was experiencing her own climactic thrill as Emily kissed her.

Moaning softly, she probed her tongue deep inside Emily's hole.

At the same time, Emily pressed her face hard against Dawn's wet lips. She kissed passionately the slick heat of her sex. Using the tips of her fingers to spread Dawn's lips apart, she ran her tongue gently over the exposed nub of her clitoris.

Emily lost count of the number of orgasms that coursed through her body. She was lost in a blissful paradise of pleasure. Her body ached with the dull satisfied throb of pure elation. Inhaling the heady scent of Dawn's arousal, Emily screamed delightedly. Her mouth was filled with the succulent sweet flavour of the woman's pussy cream, and she tried to recall if she had ever experienced so much pleasure in one day before. She could not recall ever feeling so satisfied. As the clouds of euphoria swept around her, Emily wished that the moment would go on for ever.

She did not know how long she and Dawn played together. The delight she received from exploring the woman's body was so intense, Emily could have endured it all evening. Her fingers were no longer content with just exploring the woman's shaved pussy lips. Occasionally she would tease a digit around Dawn's tightly puckered arsehole. As she did this, she could not decide which aspect gave her the most pleasure. Actually enjoying such intimacy with another woman was a thrilling experience, as was the sound of that woman's ecstatic cries of gratitude.

When the final climax tore through her, Emily rolled off Dawn's body and lay in blissful silence on the bunk. Dawn lay still for a while, obviously as sated as Emily after their shared passion. She was the first to move after their love-making, and that was only to reach for Emily's breasts so she could tease them again.

'No more,' Emily begged. 'I don't think I could take any more.'

Dawn shrugged. 'Don't you want to try?'

Emily grinned. 'Maybe later,' she said, shifting position so she could lie next to the woman. 'I wish I had a cigarette,' she said quietly. The craving was only mild and she had almost discounted it before the words had formed. She was reminded of the half-used pack in her handbag and this touched on a wealth of memories she did not want to explore.

Dawn frowned in the darkness. 'The captain doesn't allow smoking on board,' she explained, unaware of the thoughts tumbling through Emily's mind. 'It's a punishable offence.'

Emily shook her head, smiling softly to herself. 'He rules this ship with a rod of iron, doesn't he?'

Dawn nodded. 'It feels like iron sometimes, but it's made of cane. And remember, it's not a ship. It's a boat.'

Emily grinned in the darkness and repeated the word.

'Will you be taking the captain up on his offer?' Dawn asked. She put her hand against Emily's breast and casually toyed with the nipple as they spoke. It was a gesture made more intimate by its subtlety, and Emily allowed her to continue, enjoying the attention.

'Which offer is that then?' Emily asked coolly.

'He wants you to stay with us until we reach Havalaña,' Dawn explained. 'Why don't you do that?' There was a childlike eagerness in her voice. 'You and I could spend most of our evenings together, like this,' she coaxed. Her fingers tightened softly around the bud of Emily's nipple, adding encouragement to her plea.

'It's a tempting proposition,' Emily told her. 'With you as the enticement, it sounds almost too tempting,' she added softly.

Dawn giggled and kissed Emily lightly on the corner of her mouth. 'Once you get used to the captain, you find he's not so bad,' she explained. 'He can be very cruel, but that's not always as unpleasant as it sounds.'

Emily smiled, not wholly convinced that this was true. The scene in the pilothouse was vividly imprinted on her memory. As she recalled the situation, she knew whose position she would rather have occupied. The sight of Dawn, on her knees, being forced to suck one man's cock whilst another beat her, had been intensely arousing. Dawn had looked delightful being subjugated to such a humiliating punishment. However, Emily had thought the captain's position looked far more exciting. To be able to brandish the cane, to be able to have someone do her bidding when she told them, was a stimulating notion. She envied the captain's good fortune and his position of absolute power.

She smiled quietly to herself, surprised by the sudden appetite for sexual power. A thought occurred to her and she brushed Dawn's hand away crisply. Turning to study the woman's face in the darkness, she asked, 'Why did you come here, Dawn?'

'I wanted to do things with you,' Dawn replied coyly.

'Was that the only reason?' Emily asked, sensing there was something else in the woman's voice.

'Does it matter?' Dawn asked, unable to meet Emily's gaze.

Emily nodded. 'Yes,' she said. 'It matters to me.' She put her arm around Dawn's shoulder and held her naked body. Still unused to holding another woman like this, she felt the warm embers of her desire being rekindled between her legs. Almost unconsciously, she rubbed her fingers against the pierced nipple closest to her hand. 'Did the captain send you?'

Dawn nodded, unhappy at having to admit this.

Emily was not particularly surprised by the revelation. 'Did he say why?'

Dawn nodded again. 'He wants you as one of his slaves on the boat,' she began. Her words were a soft, reluctant whisper. 'He and Laura are having a bet as to whether or not you stay.'

In the darkness, Emily grinned. 'Why did he send you? Was I supposed to fall in love with your charms and decide that I couldn't bare to be parted from you after this night?' It was a fanciful idea, she supposed but it was the only plausible one that came to mind.

Dawn shook her head. She caressed Emily's breast as she spoke, allowing the woman to tease her own piercings at the same time. 'He said I had to give you a wink at dinner,' she explained. 'He wanted to see how you responded.'

Emily frowned, remembering the incident. 'As I recall,' she said quietly. 'I was so scared I probably looked revolted.'

Dawn nodded. She smiled fondly at the memory. 'Captain Wilde said that it was enough for him to know what you really wanted. He said if you reacted like that to a come on from a woman, you were obviously fighting your own real feelings.'

Emily's smile was perplexed. 'He's quite the psychologist, isn't he?' she remarked.

Dawn shook her head. 'He's a good captain. You could enjoy your time on this boat with us if you wanted.'

Emily shook her head sadly. 'I'm sorry, Dawn,' she said quietly. 'But I don't think I can now. I wouldn't feel right with myself if I thought I'd been manipulated by someone.'

Dawn stopped caressing Emily's breast and frowned at her unhappily. 'You're going to leave the boat. You can't!'

Emily kissed the dark-haired woman gently on the lips. 'I am, and I can,' she said cheerfully. 'There is nothing on this planet that could possibly make me submit to Captain Wilde.' First thing tomorrow, she decided, she would tell the captain of her plans. He could drop her off at the first port they came to, sooner if it was possible. She was determined to do whatever it took to get off the boat and get away from the man.

Staring upwards and glancing at the star-studded sky, she repeated the words, like a chant to ward off evil spirits: 'There is no way that I'm ever going to submit myself to Captain Wilde again.'

Three

Vincent watched as Laura and Captain Wilde tied Dawn to the wheel. She was stark-naked save for the ropes around her ankles and wrists. Her body glistened in the morning sunshine. The flesh was slick with an oily layer of sun tan lotion that Vincent had applied earlier. Her hands were outstretched and her legs were spread wide apart, revealing the pouting lips of her pussy. The pose accentuated her slender figure. It also put her in a distinctly vulnerable position. Her arse still sported the fading stripes of her punishment from the night before, and Vincent knew, just looking at her, that fresh marks would replace them before the day was out.

A hazy South American sun beat down on the boat, warming her bare flesh.

Laura moved in front of Dawn and tweaked the woman's pierced nipples. 'Should I clamp these to the wheel, Captain?' she asked wickedly.

Captain Wilde shook his head. 'That would give her an unfair advantage.' He grinned broadly and slapped a cheerful hand against Dawn's bare arse. The woman trembled beneath the blow. 'You've got a good day for your maiden voyage,' he said happily. 'Do you think you're up to it?'

'Yes, Captain Wilde,' Dawn whispered softly. Her breathing was already ragged from sexual anticipation.

He laughed darkly. 'Clear waters ahead,' he told her. His eyes shone with the wicked light of black mirth.

Vincent followed the captain's gaze to the bow of the boat and beyond. The Amazon was a tranquil ribbon of azure, stretching for miles until it reached the horizon where it shimmered in the day's heat. Huge purple and white water lilies lined the shores of the river, languishing in the shadows of the over hanging shrubbery.

They weren't just clear water's ahead, Vincent thought. The sky was cloudless and unbroken as well. The brilliant white sails of the clipper's rigging rustled gently beneath the unending cerulean canopy. He felt his chest swell with affection as he admired the day's beauty. It was a glorious day to be on the river, and he was determined to enjoy every last moment of it, if the captain would allow.

Vincent checked his watch and calculated how long Dawn had to endure on the wheel. It was eight o'clock in the morning. Breakfast had just been completed, and Vincent knew that Dawn would be tied to the wheel for the next three and a half hours. Captain Wilde was a cruel bastard, but even he was not so cruel as to keep Dawn tied naked beneath the treacherous rays of the Amazon's noon sun.

Captain Wilde picked up his cane and tested it in the air. It whistled smartly on its downward arc.

Dawn flinched instinctively. Even though she had only heard the sound, she released a small gasp of terror.

Both the captain and Laura laughed at her nervousness. They kissed one another passionately. His hands went to her breasts and gently squeezed the rounded orbs. She embraced him tightly, squeezing his buttocks through his shorts. The intimacy of their kiss was so strong that the naked girl between them was temporarily forgotten.

Captain Wilde broke the kiss and beamed happily at his wife. 'Are you ready to begin, honey?' he asked.

Laura nodded cheerfully. She took the cane from his

61

hand and tested it through the air. Again, Dawn flinched from the sound. The clipper jostled on the waves, veering ever so slightly to starboard. The captain and his wife laughed happily together.

Vincent knew the game they were planning. He could not suppress his own smile as he watched them prepare. It was a simple game, one of the typical challenges that the pair gave one another. Dawn was tied to the wheel, effectively in charge of the boat's direction. Her every movement affected the course of the *Amazon Maiden*, and she was the crux of the captain's challenge.

Captain Wilde stood on the port side of the boat, Laura was starboard. They were each intending to beat, caress, tease and arouse Dawn as she stood at the controls. If she veered the vessel towards the port shore, Captain Wilde was the winner of the challenge. Laura won if the vessel headed towards starboard.

Vincent had already been the centrepiece of this particular game, and he knew perfectly well what Dawn could expect. He smiled indulgently at her naked body, envying her the good fortune of being used by the pair.

'I'm ready when you are,' Laura told her husband. She smiled fondly at him. 'Are you going to begin the proceedings as Captain Nasty?'

He laughed indulgently. 'It is my turn,' he reminded her. 'You started off as Madame Whiplash the last time we played this.'

Laura smiled broadly and returned the cane to him.

Vincent nodded in rueful agreement. The couple were great game players and adhered to their own rules with a meticulous eye for detail that bordered on being pedantic. Whenever the two had a victim tied to the wheel, they each had to adopt an opposite role. If Captain Wilde was being his usual tyrannical self, Laura had to be all sweetness and light. Similarly, if Laura was playing at being the cruel vindictive bitch, Captain Wilde had to treat the slave with gentleness and cordiality.

Vincent could not see the point to their challenges. He did not know if they had money or forfeits wagered on the outcome. He simply knew that the couple extracted every last gram of pleasure from the games. Thinking practically, he supposed that was enough for them. The couple continually invented new contests for one another, Dawn and he had been piggy-in-the-middle for most of them.

'What's our heading, Vincent,' Captain Wilde called gruffly.

Vincent checked the pilothouse console and quickly noted the readings on the dials. 'Southward bound at eight knots, Captain,' he replied.

Laura grinned at her husband.

The captain smiled back. He raised his cane and brought it down against Dawn's left buttock. The slap of the wood against her bare flesh cracked across the deck.

Dawn gasped as the red hot wire of pain tore into her.

Captain Wilde delivered a second blow, harder and closer to the warm cleft between her legs.

Dawn shivered but remained still. The boat ploughed evenly through the gentle flowing waters of the Amazon without veering to either side.

Standing close, Laura smiled fondly at Dawn. She placed a hand on the woman's right breast and gently stroked the orb with the tips of her fingers. Teasing the hardened nub of her nipple, she toyed with the silver ring of metal that pierced the flesh.

Dawn's breath deepened. She half-turned to face Laura, an expectant expression pouting her lips.

The captain's cane burned sharply against her bare backside. Dawn stiffened uncomfortably.

'Eyes towards the prow, woman,' he growled angrily. 'You're at the helm, remember.'

Dawn straightened awkwardly, the movement made difficult because of her tethered limbs.

Laura moved her fingers from the woman's breast and placed her mouth there. Teasing the nipple gently, she inspired soft moans and sighs of appreciation with delicate flicks of her tongue.

From his position in the pilothouse, Vincent smiled at Dawn's predicament. He knew what she was going through, and he envied her the privilege of being used by the couple. His practical nature told him that he could not be the sole recipient of their punishment, but he still wished he was the one tied to the wheel. He knew that after the challenge was over, the loser would be allowed to punish Dawn for costing them the game. The prospect was so arousing he felt the stirrings of an erection flicker in his loins.

'Do you want to check on our guest, Vincent?' Laura called to him. She had moved her mouth away from Dawn's breast and was brazenly fingering her pussy. Her other hand caressed the woman's right hip, with loving, tender strokes.

Vincent nodded and headed below deck. It was cooler down below and he took a moment to breath in air that was not sun-parched and heady with the omnipresent scent of the rain forest. Dawn's voice could still be heard from above. She would occasionally moan with dull appreciation, then cry out softly, shocked by another bite of the cane. Beneath the sounds, Laura's gentle coaxing and the captain's passionate threats continually cajoled her.

Listening to the voices, Vincent smiled happily. He did not dare to hesitate for too long, scared of incurring Laura's wrath. Briskly, he went about his duties. Having walked through the saloon, past the galley and straight up to the forward cabin, he knocked smartly on Emily's door.

'Who is it?' Emily called.

Vincent swallowed nervously. 'Laura wanted to know if you required anything,' he explained.

Emily barked dry laughter and threw the door open. 'I'd like a little sanity,' she said sharply. 'But it seems like that commodity is in rather short supply on board this boat.'

Vincent shrugged, unsure of what to say. 'I think she meant a drink, or a snack, or a book or something,' he told Emily patiently.

Emily shook her head. She stepped away from the cabin door and moved back to her bunk. 'You can come in and chat with me for a while,' she told him. Glancing up at the hatch above her she added, 'I need something to keep out that noise.'

Vincent grinned and followed her into the cabin. He considered her to be an attractive looking woman. She did not have a full feminine figure like Laura, but her breasts were large and her figure was shapely. With the silk robe wrapped tightly around her body, he was aware of each and every delectable curve. He could not help but feel enchanted by her statuesque build and quiet air of authority.

'It's a gorgeous day out there, Vincent,' she said, sitting on the bunk. She crossed her legs beneath herself. It was a slow, calculated movement intended to attract his attention to the easily visible expanse of her bare thighs.

Vincent realised this as soon as he saw it. A smile surfaced on his broad, sensuous lips. 'By midday it will be intolerable,' he told her. At her invitation, he sat down on the bunk and frowned. 'I heard you telling the captain your decision this morning,' he said. 'He's not happy about it.'

Emily smiled tightly. 'I suppose that's some consolation,' she replied.

'Wouldn't you be better off travelling down to Havalaña?' he asked. 'Port Maga is a shit-hole. It's got a bad reputation.'

Emily studied him with a thoughtful expression on her face. 'How long before we get there?'

'At our current rate, we should be there by breakfast tomorrow.'

She grinned. 'It's not soon enough for me. As much as I'd like to stay on board and travel to Havalaña, I'm not prepared to pay the price that your captain's demanding. Shit-hole it may be, but the residents of Port Maga can't be any worse than Captain Wilde.'

Vincent shrugged, already having his own opinions about this matter. He stood up, preparing to leave the cabin. 'I suppose, if you think the captain is going to let you ashore, then I shouldn't try to disillusion you. I'll go back to the pilothouse if you don't need anything.'

'Disillusion me?' Emily looked shocked by the suggestion. 'But he said he'd let me off at the next port if that's what I wanted.'

Again, Vincent shrugged. 'I suppose I'm in no position to judge him. I answer to Laura. Dawn is the captain's slave. Perhaps she could tell you if he's a man of his word.' He made for the door again.

'Wait!' Emily stopped him.

She did not trust the captain, Vincent could see that much from her face. The sounds of Dawn's punishment and humiliation still filled the air and he knew the noise could only be adding to her doubts.

'How could I have been so foolish?' she muttered angrily.

'Excuse me?' Vincent asked, not certain he had heard her correctly.

Her face was a tortured mask of self-doubt and uncertainty. 'He's not going to let me off at Port Maga, is he?'

'He'll probably let you off,' Vincent replied carefully. 'If he's said that's what he'll do, you shouldn't doubt him.'

Emily glared angrily at the blond man. 'What the hell am I going to do?' she demanded impatiently. 'What the hell can I do?'

Vincent shrugged. He already knew what her next plan would be. As he watched a slow smile spread across her lips, he realised she had worked it out for herself. Patting the bed beside her, she beckoned for him to join her.

'Sit with me a moment, Vincent,' she encouraged. 'Perhaps we can help one another?'

Vincent stared at her uneasily. 'I can't help you,' he began. 'The captain wouldn't allow it.'

'The captain doesn't have to know about it, does he?' Placing her hand on his thigh, she smiled into his face. The warmth of her expression did not reach her eyes.

Vincent swallowed nervously. He could feel his cock stirring between his legs and realised exactly what Emily wanted from him. 'We shouldn't be doing this.'

Emily stopped his words with a kiss. 'The captain shouldn't be keeping me here against my will,' she murmured. 'But it's happening.' Tenderly, she stroked the side of his cheek.

Vincent started to place a tentative arm around her shoulders, then thought better of it. 'He might come down here and catch us,' he said, suddenly moving away from her.

Emily smiled and pulled him back to her side. She glanced up at the open hatch and they both listened to Dawn's occasional guttural moans punctuated by the whip-crack of the captain's cane. 'It sounds like the others are going to be occupied for a while now,' she told him. 'We should have plenty of time to get acquainted.'

Unable to resist her any longer, Vincent pressed his mouth against Emily's. He squeezed her in his arms and pushed her back on to the bunk.

Emily gasped, surprised by his sudden passion. She stared up into his face as he towered over her and asked, 'Will you help me? When we get to Port Maga, will you help me get off the boat?'

Vincent nodded. 'I'll help you,' he said quietly. The words came more easily than he would have imagined. Not wanting to waste any more time on conversation, he reached for the silk robe she wore and tugged it quickly open. Her naked body was revealed to him in an instant. Her bare breasts fulfilled the promise that their outline had intimated. Vincent reached for the magnificent orbs. He carefully kneaded them with his fingers while his thumbs rubbed gently around the large brown circles of her areolae.

Emily's groan was a sigh of soft appreciation. She reached up to him and ran her fingers over the skimpy cropped top he wore. A flat expanse of sun-bronzed stomach was on display and she drew the pads of her fingertips over the hard muscle. His broad chest pushed at the light fabric and she traced her fingers over the outline of his well-defined muscles. Between her legs, the urgent swell of his arousal pressed against the tight denim of his jeans. 'Take it off,' she whispered, tugging at his top.

Vincent glanced down at the garment and pulled it quickly over his head. As he removed it, Emily shivered beneath him. He realised the chain he wore had brushed against her bare breasts and he exercised an apologetic smile. Attached to his well-formed pectorals, biting into the sensitive flesh of his nipples, was a pair of sturdy clamps, linked by a thin silver chain.

Emily gasped as she stared at it. 'Nipple clamps!' she exclaimed, her tone a mixture of disgust and awe. 'Doesn't that hurt?'

Vincent smiled and shook his head. 'Laura has had me wearing them all morning,' he explained. 'I can barely feel them now. It only hurts when the chain gets caught or pulled,' he added.

Emily grinned and curled her finger under the silver links. Tugging him playfully towards her, she caused an expression of breathless delight to cross over his face.

Vincent tried to resist her. He watched as she tugged on the length of chain, stretching his nipples away from his chest. A series of white-hot explosions shivered through his body. His excitement was so great he could feel his chest glistening with sweat.

'That looks like fun,' she breathed, rubbing her hand against the rock hard length between his legs. She smiled salaciously. 'You were enjoying that, weren't you?'

'Very much,' Vincent told her. 'You wouldn't believe how good they can feel.'

Emily considered him for a moment. She reached for one of the clamps and unfastened it from his breast.

Vincent sighed softly as the clamp was released. He glanced down at his nipple and saw that the jaws had left teeth marks in the tender flesh of his pale areola.

'That looks sensitive,' Emily observed.

He nodded ruefully. 'It is.'

Before he could stop her, Emily had placed her mouth over his exposed nipple and was sucking greedily at it. Her tongue flicked over the sensitive nub and she teased it between her teeth with gentle nibbles.

Vincent groaned quietly. The bulge in his trousers felt as though it were on the point of bursting. The wealth of incredible pleasures emanating from his chest was far too exquisite for him to endure.

Emily removed the second clamp and treated his freshly exposed breast to the same delicious torment. She sucked hard on the flesh, teasing the aching nub with the tip of her tongue. At the same time she used her fingers on his other nipple, rolling it lightly from side to side and occasionally squeezing it.

Vincent's breathing was a ragged pant. He stared at the woman with a newly found appreciation, unable to believe she had excited him so much. His erection was a furious powerhouse, longing to be released from the confines of his jeans.

Emily moved her lips from his tortured breasts and

smiled up at him. She offered him the clamps and said quietly, 'Put them on me.'

Vincent stared at her uncertainly. 'Are you sure?' he asked. 'They hurt like a bastard.'

Emily smiled. 'That's why I want you to put them on me. Quickly, Vincent,' she added stiffly. 'You wouldn't hesitate if Laura had told you to do it.'

Vincent needed no further instructions. He touched her left breast, then her right, trying to decide which nipple to clamp first. Sucking the right one, he drew his tongue over her areola in lazy circles. Before he had finished, Emily was breathing deeply and wriggling impatiently on the bed. Her nipple was a tight, hard bud that begged to be bitten by the clamp.

With infinite care, Vincent pressed the handles together, opening the jaws as wide as they would go. He placed them on either side of Emily's right nipple and studied her face. 'Are you sure you want me to?' he asked warily.

She grinned into his concerned face. 'Do it to me, Vincent,' she hissed urgently. 'I want to feel them now.'

Slowly, he released the spring clip and allowed the clamp to fasten on her breast.

Emily drew in a shocked breath. Her cheeks coloured bright red as an explosion of divine pain swept through her chest. Her breath came in ragged gasps and she growled words of tortured elation. She grinned happily into Vincent's face, panting softly as she neared her orgasm. 'The other one,' she gasped breathlessly. 'Put the other one on me.' She reached for her own breast and pointed the nipple at him. The hardened nub pushed eagerly towards him, as though it was desperate to feel the intense stimulation that the clamp would inspire.

Knowing it was what she wanted, Vincent applied the clamp.

The teeth bit slowly into her breast and he watched as

Emily suppressed a shriek of pure joy. She rubbed her hand hard against the cleft between her legs, her fingers moving faster as the pleasure intensified. When she touched the hardened nub of her clitoris an orgasm tore through her body. Emily's screams of joy echoed around the cabin. A broad grin of elation split her face.

The sight of Emily laying naked beneath him was more than Vincent could tolerate. He unfastened his jeans and withdrew his rock-hard shaft.

Emily stared appreciatively at his length and reached for it eagerly. As her fingers stroked and caressed his cock the rigid muscle hardened beneath her sensitive touch. She moved her hand to the base of his length and squeezed tightly.

Her fingers stopped suddenly and he realised they had brushed against the silver chain around his balls.

'What the hell is this?' she asked. Her finger stroked the chain and went below the tight sac of his balls. Her curious expression deepened as she tugged at the small metal padlock that secured the silver links.

He grinned, not bothering to look at the device. 'I suppose you'd call it a sex aid. When it's fastened tight, it keeps me constantly erect. Laura makes me wear it all the time,' he explained. 'But it's on loose now.'

Emily tried to run her finger between the chain and his skin but found she was unable. 'It doesn't feel very loose,' she told him.

Vincent grunted humourless laughter. 'Trust me, it's on loose. When it's on tight, I stay hard but I can't climax. That way I can please her for as long as she wants.'

Emily grinned. 'I could understand how that would come in handy. How do I tighten it?'

Vincent shook his head. 'You need to unfasten it first, then tighten it,' he explained. 'And only Laura has the key.'

Emily sighed, stroking lazily at his rock-hard length.

'What a shame,' she whispered softly, genuine regret tingeing her words. Her fingers encircled his shaft, squeezing it firmly. As she lay back on the bed she guided him slowly between the sodden lips of her wanton hole.

He entered her easily, the wetness of her excitement lubricating his entire length.

As he began to slide slowly in and out of her warm velvety depths, Emily gasped happily and encouraged him with soft words of praise.

The clamps continued to bite into her nipples. Vincent could see she was struggling against the relentless pain of the jaws. From his own experience, he knew the joy that the clamps could create. He watched her tease the chain between her fingers and knew she was inspiring a new burst of tortured pleasure.

He grinned down at her, a broad smile twisting his lips.

Staring up at him Emily reached for the clamp on her right breast. She unfastened it quickly and her face contorted with gratitude as relief washed over her. The inner walls of her vagina tightened hungrily around his length. Still holding the clamp, she attached it to Vincent's left nipple allowing it to bite sharply into his flesh.

Vincent groaned excitedly, forcing his cock deep inside her.

Inside the velvety wetness of her pussy, his length stiffened with mounting excitement. She gripped him tightly with her inner muscles and pulled herself away from him. As she moved, the chain tugged tightly between the two clamps. Myriad prickles of pleasure erupted in his chest.

He could feel the climax beginning at his balls. His cock was deep inside her and his entire length shivered with the dull throb of his orgasm. His balls were tight and pressed against the lips of her pussy as he came. They pulsed against the delicate flesh of her labia as he began to ejaculate.

Vincent stifled a groan of enjoyment, then fell to the

bed at her side. The movement of the clamps forced another wave of pleasure to sweep through him and he was aware that Emily was trying to stop herself from shrieking with ecstasy.

He gently removed the clamp from her and replaced it on his own chest. He could not suppress the small grimace of pain that the action inspired. Pulling the cropped top back over his chest, he smiled across at her.

Emily leant towards him and placed a kiss on his mouth. 'Thank you,' she told him quietly. 'It's good of you to help me.'

Vincent's smile vanished, replaced by a look of dark consternation. 'I'll do what I can,' he told her. 'We'll work something out for Port Maga tonight, after Laura and the captain have retired.'

Emily nodded. 'I'll look forward to it,' she told him.

As Vincent made his way towards the door, he watched her lay back on the bed and smile up at the hatch above her. A thought pricked his conscience and he frowned darkly to himself. The sounds of Dawn's plight were still audible, but now it was as distant and unimportant as the animal cries from the shores.

He paused at the door staring at the soft smile on her face. He wondered if it would be right to tell her why he had come to her cabin, then stopped himself, knowing he could not say anything. His troubled thoughts were broken by the sound of her whispering voice.

'Port Maga,' she told herself happily. 'And then I can go home.'

Blushing, Vincent left the room.

'I don't think we're going to find her in Port Maga,' Judy said glumly.

Roderick nodded sullen agreement as he drove. 'She could be anywhere on the entire fucking continent,' he said gruffly. 'But we've exhausted everywhere in the village and Port Maga is just about our only lead.'

With his concentration focused on the road, Roderick could not see the sneer of contempt that etched Judy's features.

Angrily berating herself, Judy wondered why she had allowed Roderick to search the port. They had separated in their search for Emily and each tried interviewing different people, in the hope that they could cover more ground. Judy had suggested this only because she knew Roderick had a poor command of the Portuguese language. She had not thought he would be able to communicate with any of the natives. She had never dreamt he would end up talking to one who had seen a woman matching Emily's description. That on its own would not have been so bad, but Roderick's helpful friend also claimed to have seen Emily surreptitiously boarding a boat.

She cursed her own luck and she cursed the native who had imparted this information to Roderick. Her only hope now was that the idiot had been mistaken but she realised that was too much to hope for. She lit a cigarette and stared glumly out of the window, trying to think of a way out of the situation.

'Should I take over the map-reading?' she asked suddenly.

Roderick shook his head. 'Don't trouble yourself,' he said kindly. 'It's not like I'm trying to find some back alley in Central London. I think there are three junctions between here and Port Maga. Even I can't screw up something as simple as that.' He grinned reassuringly at her.

Judy returned the smile, hoping the expression did not look as plastic as it felt.

'Would you like me to take the wheel for a while?' she suggested.

He shook his head and smiled. 'No. I'm fine. I find this sort of driving quite exhilarating.'

Judy grinned at him and nodded easily. She turned

her attention back to the window and stared silently out of the vehicle, trying to think of another ploy.

The roads were nothing more than strips of dried mud, snaking treacherously through overhanging foliage. Driving through the leafy green tunnel provided some shade for the vehicle, but not nearly enough. The heat inside the hired jeep was phenomenal, and even with the windows wound down and the rickety air-conditioning on full Judy felt as though she were being roasted alive.

Unconsciously, she unfastened a couple of buttons at the top of her blouse. Staring down at the expanse of cleavage she was revealing, an idea came to her. She smiled, suddenly feeling pleased with herself. She wafted the top of her breasts with her flattened palm, wishing the motion would actually cool her. It was enough to draw Roderick's attention and because that was her intention, she was satisfied with the result.

He glanced nervously at her, then fixed his attention back on the road. 'It is hot, isn't it?' he remarked, mumbling the words awkwardly.

Judy smiled to herself. The fish is hooked, she realised triumphantly. Now it's time to reel him in. She unfastened another button, exposing her low cut bra and ample cleavage. The short skirt she wore revealed the long expanse of her shapely legs. Wriggling in her seat, she 'accidentally' raised the hem another couple of inches.

Roderick glanced sideways at her and swallowed uneasily. The tantalising glimpse of thigh was so enthralling he almost lost control of the jeep. As it bounced towards the edge of the road, he swiftly corrected the steering-wheel. With the accident avoided, he drove more slowly, continuing to snatch surreptitious glances at the enticing sight.

'I was wanting to talk to you about last night,' Judy said quietly. She tossed her cigarette out of the open window and placed her hand on his leg.

This time Roderick managed to keep the jeep on a straight course. It took a huge amount of will-power, but he did it with a concentrated effort. 'About last night?' he repeated nervously. 'I'm sorry about that,' he told her. 'I shouldn't have been so aroused. I must be some sort of pervert or something. I mean, you're my step-sister, aren't you? If I embarrassed you or upset you, then I can only say I'm really sorry.'

Judy raised her eyebrows with mild surprise. 'Have you been rehearsing that little speech?' she asked.

He grinned. 'The words had gone through my mind a couple of hundred times this morning,' he explained. 'I've been wanting to say them since we had breakfast. I've just been looking for the right moment.' He glanced shyly at her. 'I don't suppose I would have said it if you hadn't spoken first.'

'Why don't you pull over for a moment?' Judy suggested.

He glanced at the road ahead. 'We're only a couple of hours away from Port Maga. Perhaps we should push on until we reach there.'

Judy frowned. 'I need to talk to you now, Roderick,' she said, emphasising the words slowly. She moved her hand up his leg so that it was brushing against the crotch of his trousers. 'Please pull over for a moment,' she implored him. 'Please.'

Roderick bounced the jeep to the side of the road and stepped on the brake.

As soon as he cut the engine, Judy pressed her mouth over his. 'I should have done this to you last night,' she whispered, smothering his face with kisses.

Taken aback, Roderick allowed her to kiss him, aware that his arousal was increasing by the moment.

'You're gorgeous, Roddy.' She pulled his face towards her and reached behind his head. Unfastening the ponytail, she freed his hair and allowed it to spill over his shoulders. Then her hands were opening his shirt and working their way down to the waistband of his pants. She pressed herself close to his chest and sucked one nipple. 'I can taste your sweat,' she told him, a lecherous grin resting on her lips.

'I'm sorry,' he began. 'It's just so hot in here and –'

Judy interrupted his words with a kiss. Whispering into his ear she said, 'I wasn't complaining. You taste wonderful.'

He tried to hold her, the gesture made awkward in the confines of the jeep's front seat. Judy moved closer to him, continually smothering his face with kisses. As she did this, she was working on the buttons of his jeans, unfastening them with a furious urgency that was not wholly playacting.

'I wanted you last night,' she whispered. 'I should have done this then.'

Roderick was breathing heavily. 'I haven't minded waiting.'

She released his cock and pulled it out of his jeans, pleased to see that he was already rock hard and ready for her. Judy smiled fondly at his erection. Without a moment's hesitation she moved her head over him and took the entire length in her mouth. With slow deliberation, she worked her mouth up and down. Her tongue occasionally flicked the swollen head of his cock. Nibbling the head, she pushed her tongue into the tight hole and sucked gently.

Roderick groaned happily.

She moved her mouth away from him and smiled into his face. 'Even your dick tastes of sweat,' she said lewdly. 'I think that's a beautiful taste.' She moved close to him, and raised the hem of her skirt.

He stared uncertainly at her, wondering how she was going to manage straddling him in the confines of the jeep.

Judy pulled the skirt up so that he could see the crotch of her panties. She teased the gusset to one side, revealing the dark curly hairs around her pubic lips. With an agile kick of her leg, she was almost on top of him.

The tip of her toe caught the map he had been using and casually knocked it to the floor.

With one leg either side of his body, she leant closer.

Roderick moaned excitedly. She was so close to him that the scent of her arousal filled the air. His rigid cock rubbed stiffly between them. It was so hard they both knew he was close to a climax already.

Holding the panties with one finger, Judy spread the lips of her wet vagina apart and slowly lowered herself on to his length. She sighed happily as the length filled her. A broad smile illuminated her face and she moved her mouth over his. Taking as much of his cock as she could manage in this position, Judy used a finger to tease her clitoris. She rubbed the hardening nub of her clit slowly, delighted by the heady wave of pleasure that the action inspired.

Roderick pressed himself back in his seat, already on the point of climaxing.

Her heated wetness was wrapped around his length and she moved slowly up and down squeezing her pussy lips tightly around his shaft. She grinned as he moaned with soft appreciation. He studied her face lovingly as she leant over him. When he reached for her breasts, she allowed him to massage them softly through the fabric of her bra. His fingers found the fierce hard nubs of her nipples and he stroked his thumb softly over them.

Judy laughed, a low guttural sound. 'That's good, Roddy,' she told him. Her voice was an intimate whisper. 'That feels really good.' The excitement of a climax was building quickly inside her. She could feel the euphoria swelling in her abdomen like a huge balloon of pleasure just waiting to burst. Determined to extract as much satisfaction as she could from the moment, Judy slowed her clit-teasing finger. She halted her pace on

Roddy's cock and began to move more languidly up and down his shaft.

Roddy shivered in his seat.

Judy could feel the climax threatening to burst from his balls, and she realised he was fighting valiantly against it. She knew he wanted to please her and impress her with his stamina. She knew he wanted her to use his cock for hours until she could take no more of it. She knew he wanted all of these things. But more than that, he desperately wanted to come.

She traced lazy circles against her sex with one wet finger. The tip of her nail occasionally caught in the wiry hairs of his pubic bush and he flinched happily whenever she snagged them. If he had been sweating before, it was nothing to the way his body was now coated with wetness.

Judy too was perspiring freely. Her blouse was sodden and large glistening beads of perspiration clung to her forehead as she slowly rode his shaft. She leant over him and Roderick felt some of the droplets splash against his bare chest.

His orgasm surprised both of them. Judy felt his cock twitch spasmodically between her legs and she stared at him, her mouth agape.

Mortified by his hasty ejaculation, Roderick began to mumble an apology but Judy did not allow it. She moved her lips over his and began to probe her tongue in his mouth as she rode his failing member. Her finger rubbed furiously against the tip of her clitoris.

Roderick shifted uncomfortably in his seat. He slowly withdrew from her, continuing to kiss her as he moved. His hands stroked the eager swell of her breasts, his thumbs concentrating on the urgent pressing of her nipples.

Struggling in the tight confines of the car's front, Judy moved herself slowly backwards. The lips of her pussy brushed accidentally against the rounded tip of the jeep's gear lever, and she paused thoughtfully. Pressing herself against the wide leather tipped top, she began to lower herself on to the implement. It was wider than any cock she had ever had between her legs and she groaned loudly as it entered her. Her lips were fully spread, stretching the skin around her clitoris until it was furiously tight. Her fingers rubbed angrily over the pearl of pleasure, and she drew deep broken breaths of ecstasy. Using the gear-stick as a makeshift cock, she rode it with wild abandon. Her fingers continued to play with the hard nub of excited flesh.

As the orgasm welled deep within her, a broad grin of elation appeared on Judy's face. She smiled, the expression looking more like a sneer on her face. Moving her head down, she began to lick greedily at Roderick's limp dick. She could still taste the scent of her own arousal, coupled with the remnants of his spent seed. Mixed with the sweet flavour of his cock's sweat, the blend was an erotic cocktail.

She shrieked as the orgasm swept through her, bucking her hips purposefully up and down on the head of the gear-stick. The throb of pleasure seared from the tip of her clit, soaring to every nerve-ending in her body. She trembled uncontrollably, her hips continuing to grind every last piece of pleasure from the moment.

Roderick grinned at her as she dismounted the gear-stick and began to straighten her clothes. He reached behind himself and refastened the ponytail in his hair. Smiling fondly into her flushed face, he said, 'that was one of the greatest conversations I've ever had.'

Judy grinned back at him. She reached between his feet and picked up the map from the floor. So that her motives did not appear too obvious, she allowed her mouth to slide wetly against his flaccid cock. Sitting back in her seat, she licked her lips as he watched. 'Perhaps we'll talk more when we get to Port Maga,' she told him lewdly. Wafting the map at him, she added,

'I'll navigate. That way we'll get there that much quicker.'

He straightened his clothes and flicked the key in the ignition. The broad smile still filled his face. 'Perhaps we can make it a longer conversation, next time?'

Judy smiled and said nothing. She was thinking it unlikely they could have a shorter one. Roderick had climaxed just as she was starting to get properly excited. She still felt a bristling of annoyance with him for his early climax. Knowing this would not be a wise thing to say, she nodded quietly at him, maintaining her fixed grin.

With a glance at the map, she quickly began to work out the best route away from Port Maga.

'I could get used to this,' Emily murmured, pressing her back against the mast. The afternoon breeze cooled her naked body, a blessing following the blistering rays of the noon sun. She could see the prow of the boat cutting its way quickly through the fast-flowing waters of the river, headed towards a clear blue sky that stretched forever.

Kneeling before her, Vincent placed a hand on each thigh and delivered small, gentle kisses to the tops of her legs.

Emily held her breath, anticipating the wealth of delight he was about to administer. This was the part she could get used to, she reflected. The glorious tropical scenery was enjoyable but it did not satisfy her as fully as the control that she had over the submissive man between her legs. Vincent was so pliant; Emily revelled in his attention. He did exactly as she said, and in their brief afternoon together she had tried to discover how much he would obey. Already, she had begun to realise she was nowhere near the edge of his limits, and that thought excited her greatly. There was obviously a vast chasm of unexplored potential inside the man, and she wished she had the chance to use him fully. She had already decided that, when this entire episode was finally ended, she would try to discover if Roderick had the same inherent tendencies.

She closed her eyes as his tongue stroked over her labia. He slowly teased the rosebud of her sex until she felt her lips unfolding for him. Unhurried, just as she had instructed him to be, Vincent lapped slowly at the responsive flesh. There was no trace of urgency or eagerness and Emily smiled contentedly to herself. This was how life should be, she thought, gratified by the sparkling frisson of his tongue against her wetness. This was what being in control was all about. There was so much more she could do with Vincent, if only she had the time.

If she had asked him, he would have tongued her arse. She could have spread her labia in front of his face, and pissed on him. If she had done that and instructed him properly, he would have drunk every last drop. The idea of having someone so servile, acting on her every whim, thrilled Emily immensely.

When the fingers brushed against her nipple she enjoyed the subtle whisper of pleasure that the touch inspired. She had not told Vincent to do this for her, but she was not going to complain now that he was doing it. She murmured a soft word of praise and opened her eyes to see exactly what he was doing.

Captain Wilde smiled back at her.

Emily bit back a cry of surprise. Vincent was still working his tongue slowly between her legs, but those sensations were forgotten now. Even the captain's fingers, inspiring subtle flash-bursts of delight, seemed unimportant.

'I see you're enjoying yourself,' Captain Wilde noted wryly. He squeezed the tip of her nipple playfully between his fingers.

Emily slapped his hand away. She also shifted herself

away from Vincent's tongue, too angry to bother with the trace of reluctance that whispered at the back of her mind. After reaching for the silk robe she had dropped on the floor, Emily quickly punched her arms into the sleeves. She wrapped the robe tightly around herself and turned her angry glare on the captain. 'Can I do something for you?' she asked tersely.

He raised his eyebrows. His face was covered with a hateful smile of unconcealed amusement. 'Are you sure you don't want to stay until we reach Havalaña?' he asked. 'You look as though you've enjoyed your first full day on board.' His smiled widened. 'To be honest, you looked as though you enjoyed yesterday as well, once you'd climbed out of your lifeboat.'

Emily continued to glare at him. 'The sooner I can get away from you, the better I'll feel.'

He shrugged, indifferent to her harsh tone. 'Just so long as you remember I'm the one making you feel better,' he replied glibly. 'We'll be arriving in Port Maga at six o'clock tomorrow morning.'

Emily studied him uncertainly. She knew they were arriving at the port tomorrow, but she had thought he would try and keep it a secret from her. He was trying to keep her prisoner on board the boat, and she was suspicious as to his motives for telling her about the docking.

'I've had Dawn prepare a small case for you, with a change of clothes and some money. At least that way, you should be able to organise your own rescue party,' he said crisply.

Emily continued to stare at him uncertainly. 'You're really letting me go?' It was such a difficult fact to believe that she had trouble accepting it.

He laughed at her expression. 'You've been a joy to have on board, Emily,' he told her. 'I wish you had decided to stay with us to Havalaña. You really would have been fun. Both our slaves have said you were splendid company.'

Emily glanced at Vincent, then back to the captain. As his words sank in, she began to realise just how foolish she had been. All the time, when she thought she had been exerting her own will on to Dawn and Vincent, they had been playing her on the instructions of the damned captain. 'You sent them both?'

He grinned and nodded.

Emily knew Dawn had spent the night with her on the captain's instructions but she had thought Vincent was trying to help her. Thinking back to this morning, she saw that he had been the one who caused her to doubt the captain in the first place. She now realised this had been a subtle ploy to get her into bed. All the time, when she had believed she was in control, the captain and his slaves had been using her like a marionette.

'You hateful bastard!' she declared angrily.

Captain Wilde nodded. There was a note of steel in his voice when he spoke, and Emily could see that he was unhappy with her outburst. 'You're not the first person to call me that,' he told her flatly. 'Contrary to what you think of me, I will be putting you off this boat tomorrow morning at six o'clock sharp. I trust you will be washed and dressed by then, because even if you're not I'll be throwing you on to the dock.'

'It can't come soon enough for me,' Emily told him stiffly.

He nodded. Turning his back on her, the captain headed towards the pilothouse. He paused halfway along the deck and studied her with a grave frown. 'I truly hope you find your way back home, Emily. If you think that Laura and I will be on hand to offer you any more help, then you're gravely mistaken.'

Emily snorted rudely. 'I wouldn't take your help if you offered it with gold bars,' she said coldly.

Captain Wilde shook his head and smiled. 'I wouldn't be offering you any enticements,' he said tightly. 'If you ever need my help in the future, you are really going to have to beg for it.'

Emily stared angrily after him. There was something about his words that chilled her. She dearly hoped she would never have to meet the man again after tomorrow morning. He had to be the most hateful creature she had ever encountered, and if she never saw him again. . .

A nervous voice in the back of her mind broke into her thoughts, warning her that she wasn't off the *Amazon Maiden* yet. She remembered that she had stowed away on the boat to get out of one village. There was not much chance of Port Maga being any more hospitable.

Thinking of Captain Wilde's parting words, Emily hoped she never had the need to ask him for help. She could tell he would be unlikely to offer her free assistance. She also had a fair idea about the price she would have to pay.

The thought sent a shiver of revulsion coursing down her spine.

Four

'You really are a pair of hateful bastards,' Emily said calmly. 'If I had the time, I'd borrow the captain's cane and stroke your bare arses with it.'

Vincent continued to ride his cock in and out as she spoke. He was standing behind her with his hands on her hips. The long shaft of his cock filled her pussy and sent shivers of delight thrilling through her body. The padlock was fully tightened around his length, and Emily knew that he could continue to ride her for hours if she chose to allow him.

He mumbled an apology, his lips nuzzling gently against the nape of her neck.

Dawn was on her knees. Her tongue was working Emily's clit into a burning frenzy as she licked avariciously. The juices from Emily's pussy, inspired by Vincent's cock, coated her mouth and her lips. She murmured a brief apology, then continued with the task Emily had demanded of her.

Emily could not find it in herself to blame either of the slaves for her predicament. She had been the one who stowed away on the boat, and she had also lured Vincent into bed for her own ends. She did blame the captain for his part in the whole affair, but she could not put much weight behind her hatred. He had allowed his slaves to wish her a fond farewell this morning, and Emily thought that for him it was a magnanimous gesture.

She wriggled her pussy further on to Vincent's cock, enjoying the feel of his length inside her. Absently, she told him to play with her tits while he fucked her.

Vincent obeyed. His fingers found her nipples and he massaged the orbs. Playfully, he tweaked and pulled at the hard nubs.

Emily sighed contentedly.

They were standing on the prow of the boat. Emily had her hands on the metal rails of the pulpit, steadying herself as Vincent repeatedly entered her. The morning had not yet begun and the sky was a dusky purple, fading quickly as the new day prepared to begin. A gentle breeze ruffled her hair as the hull cut small white crests through the dark blue waters of the Amazon. She inhaled the florid fragrance of the river's air and tried to ignore the melancholy hue that coloured her thoughts.

Emily knew that Captain Wilde was watching them from his position in the pilothouse, but that did not trouble her. Only an hour away from getting off the *Amazon Maiden*, she felt a wave of relief rushing over her. She was going to miss Vincent and Dawn. They had taught her about a way of life that she would never have encountered in a million years back in England.

But still, she thought it would be nice to return to some semblance of normality, even without the luxury of a pair of servile slaves.

'Port Maga's just there, on the horizon.'

Emily turned at the sound of Laura's voice. Dressed in a powder blue basque with matching stockings and shoes, she looked as delightful and formidable as she had when they first met.

Emily grinned. She felt no shame or embarrassment at being talked to whilst she enjoyed the two slaves. At one time, she knew she would have been shocked by the notion of talking to a third person as she satisfied her carnal appetite. Now, it felt like the most natural thing in the world.

Her inner muscles clenched tightly around Vincent's cock. His huge length filled her, and she could feel the gently pulsing organ stretching her wide. At the same time, Dawn pressed her tongue against Emily's clit. The slippery wetness of the brunette's mouth was a delightful addition to the pleasure of Vincent's cock. It inspired a thrill of excitement that rippled through her body.

'I hope I haven't interrupted your journey too much,' Emily said quietly.

Laura shook her head, smiling. 'It's been an entertaining distraction to have you on board.'

'I doubt Captain Wilde sees it that way,' Emily said. 'I haven't upset the plans for your business meeting, have I?'

Again, Laura smiled and shook her head. 'Vincent and Dawn know what they're doing. Neither of them have let us down before. Will you be all right on your own?'

'I should be,' Emily said, after a moment's thought. 'It's been kind of you to help me so much.'

Laura leant close to her, her lips mere millimetres from Emily's mouth. 'I wish I'd had the time to get to know you a little better,' she whispered.

Emily felt her excitement heighten. Laura was a beautiful woman and one with such an innate air of authority that Emily could not help herself from feeling attracted to her. She needed no more incentive than the nearness of Laura's mouth. Moving her head slightly forward, she kissed the blonde gently on the lips.

Laura's hands caressed her sides as they kissed and Emily became lost in a wave of euphoria. The wind was blowing gently on her face; Vincent was riding his long cock forcefully between her legs; and Dawn continued to lap hungrily at her clitoris. Every nerve-ending in her entire body seemed to be revelling with a wealth of stimulation. She felt dizzy with the thrill of the climax that welled inside her.

As Laura cupped her buttocks, Emily passed over the brink of ecstasy and groaned delightedly. Tremors of pleasure continued to rack her body. She was distantly aware that Laura had stepped away from her, but Vincent and Dawn were continuing to lick and fuck her, making up for the woman's absence.

When the waves of pleasure had finally subsided, Emily pushed the two slaves away. She turned to Laura, who had watched her climax from a distance and smiled happily. 'I almost feel sorry to be going ashore,' Emily said honestly.

Laura linked her arms through Emily's and escorted her back to the pilothouse. 'I'll help you pack,' she said quietly.

It was a handwritten sign, black enamel paint on a sheet of battered white tin. There were knocks and dents in the metal, where debris from the road had flown up and chipped at the paintwork. In one corner, Judy saw there was a bullet-hole penetrating the top right-hand corner. She glared hatefully at the town's name: Port Maga.

'Fuck!' she snapped irritably. 'Fuck, fuck, fuck!'

Roderick stepped out of the jeep and joined her. He was wearing a broad grin and he draped an arm easily around her shoulder. 'I never thought we'd find the place,' he said cheerfully. He punched her playfully on the shoulder and said, 'You're nearly as bad as I am when it comes to map-reading.'

Judy forced her lips into an indulgent smile. 'I didn't realise I was so bad.' She tried to make the words sound cheerful through her clenched teeth. 'The place looks like a shit-hole,' she ventured casually.

Roderick nodded. 'We'll check out the dock, and if that's no good we'll scout round the town.' He walked back to the car and held the door open for her.

Judy smiled at him, pleased by his chivalry. She was unhappy about being in Port Maga, but at least she was with Roderick and that meant a part of her plan had worked out. If she kept a level head and played things properly, she knew she would have him as her own fiancé before the end of the holiday. These thoughts tumbled through her mind as they drove through the maze of roads leading towards the riverside. She ignored the ramshackle collection of shacks and huts that lined the roads. Her interest did not even pique when they passed a large unimpressive hotel that boasted en suite showers. Judy was lost in a world of her own schemes and plans.

Oblivious to the wiles and machinations of Judy's mind, Roderick drove into the village. He handled the jeep skilfully and parked it a safe distance from the riverside. The dock comprised of two small jetties and a large wooden hut. Roderick smiled sadly at its understated simplicity.

Judy could see that his hopes of finding Emily in Port Maga were slowly sinking.

'Is this it?' Judy sneered.

'I'm afraid so,' Roderick said glumly.

Judy rolled her eyes. Her disgust was apparent. She could think of no words base enough to express her contempt for the entire continent. 'I'll go down and check out the mud hut,' she said eventually. 'Do you want to book into that concrete dungeon of a hotel that we passed? I can catch up with you later.'

Roderick was already climbing out of the jeep. 'No need,' he told her. 'I'll go down there with you.'

Judy groaned inside and allowed him to escort her down to the riverside.

'We arrive in Port Maga in ten minutes,' Captain Wilde informed Emily stiffly. 'I could ask a few of my contacts on the shore if they can help you.'

Emily shook her head. 'I've had enough help from you already,'

His smile vanished. 'You really are an unforgiving little cur, aren't you,' he said softly.

Emily returned his angry frown. 'I'm not unforgiving,' she told him. 'I'm just not that willing to forgive you.' She studied him, annoyed that he had such a nice body, handsome face and despicable personality.

'I don't like to repeat myself,' Captain Wilde said quietly. 'But because I think you're too thick-headed to take this in a first time, I'll make an exception.'

'Go on,' Emily said quietly.

'We'll be docked in Port Maga for two hours,' he began. 'After that, the *Amazon Maiden* will be gone forever.'

'So?' Emily asked, haughtily.

'So,' he continued. 'I'm throwing you a lifeline. If you can't find a telephone in the port, and you think the natives look formidable and inhospitable, you have two hours to change your mind.'

'I thought you said I wouldn't be allowed back on board your ship?'

'Boat,' he corrected smartly. 'And I never said that. I believe I told you that if you wanted to come back aboard, things would be different. I think you know how I mean, don't you?'

Emily stared at him and shivered. 'I know exactly how you mean,' she said stiffly. 'But don't worry. There's no way I'm coming back.'

His smile was thin and cruel. 'We'll see,' he said quietly. 'We'll see.'

'Could you understand him?' Roderick asked helplessly.

Judy shrugged. 'I don't know. I thought I knew the language, but I'm not sure he does,' she explained. 'It must be a dialect or something.'

Roderick sighed and stared unhappily at the muddy banks. 'Did he say that a boat like that one had been through here in the last couple of days?'

Judy shook her head. 'He hasn't seen anything matching that description.'

Roderick stamped his foot on the floor. 'Damn and blast!' he exclaimed angrily. He glared at the fast flowing waters of the river and then glanced further up it. A movement on the horizon caught his attention and his bad mood seemed to dissipate. 'Could that be it?' he asked.

Judy squinted in the direction he was pointing. 'It could be,' she said calmly. Her thoughts were racing ahead. 'It could well be,' she told him with more conviction. 'Why don't you quickly go and find that hotel room. I'll wait here and see if she's on board.'

He shook his head. 'That won't be necessary, Judy. I'd better wait and make sure she's all right if she's on there.'

Judy smiled, a knowing expression on her lips. 'I think you'd better find the hotel room,' she insisted. 'While you're there you can either change your clothes, or think of an explanation for those stains and the lipstick marks around your groin.'

Roderick glanced down at himself and flushed furiously. He nodded agreement with Judy's plan and took a step towards the jeep. 'Are you all right here, alone?'

Judy nodded. 'I'll be fine,' she told him. She watched him rush back to the jeep then drive from the riverside. As soon he was out of sight, she marched briskly back to the docking clerk. Her command of the language was a lot better than she had let Roderick know. She chatted with the clerk idly about the boat that was heading towards them. He had already recognised it as the *Amazon Maiden*. He knew the captain and knew the man's habit for docking at Port Maga regularly.

Judy talked easily with the man for a couple of minutes. Once she had learnt that the boat would only be docked for two hours, she thanked him for his time. Walking swiftly from the riverside, she hurried off to join Roderick at the hotel. Another plan was already formulating in her mind.

'What's wrong?' Captain Wilde asked.

Emily shrugged and shook her head. 'Nothing,' she told him. 'I'm just being silly I guess. I thought I saw my step-sister on the dock. How crazy can you get, huh?'

His smile was understanding. It was an expression she could have almost liked. 'Are you so desperate to see a friendly face that you're imagining them now?'

'Perhaps it's not a friendly face I'm after seeing,' she said, thinking of Judy's quiet indifference towards her. 'Maybe I'm just anxious to see someone who doesn't want to take my clothes off and cane me.'

He grinned at her, taking in the contours of her figure in the short summer dress she wore.

The dress had been given to her by Dawn. Because of the height difference, it showed more of Emily's legs than she felt comfortable displaying. She wanted to cover herself from the captain's appreciative glances but she knew that doing this would only give him another reason to laugh at her. Feigning nonchalance, she continued staring over the port rails, her attention fixed on Port Maga.

'Looking like that,' he said quietly, 'you'll probably find a lot of men wanting to do a lot worse. At least with me, you know where you stand.'

She nodded bitterly. 'I knew where I was standing when you tied me to the mast,' she told him evenly. 'That doesn't mean I'm in a hurry to relive that experience.'

He shook his head sadly and turned away. 'It's too nice a day to play childish word games,' he decided. 'There are docking procedures to follow.'

From the corner of her eye, Emily watched him leave her side.

* * *

93

'Was she there?' Roderick asked quickly. 'Had they seen her? What's happened?' He had just stepped from the shower and was towelling himself dry.

Judy smiled approvingly at his naked body. 'It wasn't the *Amazon Maiden*,' she lied quickly. 'The crew were all Brazilian and none of them could help.'

Roderick cursed angrily. 'So what do we do now?'

Judy's broad grin was warm and inviting. On her way from the riverside she had decided exactly what they would do next. The *Amazon Maiden* was going to be docked for the next two hours. She had to keep Roderick in the hotel room for at least that long, and she knew exactly how to do it.

'Follow me,' she said softly.

He stared at her uncertainly.

Judy reached her hand towards his groin. His cock was flaccid but she grabbed it between her fingers and stroked it with the warm palm of her hand. Responding to her touch, the erectile tissue began to harden quickly.

'Shouldn't we be looking for Emily?' he asked, with no real conviction.

Judy guided him from the en suite bathroom into the bedroom. It was basic accommodation: plain walls, thin curtains and a small wrought-iron bed. The furniture was sparse and unimaginative. The only thing Judy had liked about the room was the huge window that dominated one wall. Now, she considered it unhappily, aware that it could spoil her plan. If she intended to have Roderick take her in every conceivable position for the next two hours, he might glance out of this window. However, it would be unlikely that he would see Emily from there, she realised. The chances were that she was not on board the *Amazon Maiden*, but Judy did not dare to take the risk. She had planned carefully and executed her ideas with clockwork precision. There was no sense in risking failure now.

'Lie down,' she told him. 'I'm in the mood for some fun.'

He frowned uncertainly. In spite of his doubts he sat on the bed and stared expectantly at her.

Judy glanced from his face to the window and realised he still had an adequate view of the world outside. 'I said lie down,' she reminded him. She pushed her fingers gently against Roderick's slender chest and made him lay on the bed. Glancing from his face to the window she saw that he was no longer able to see outside. 'That's better,' she said.

'What do you want to do?' he asked, grinning up at her.

Judy smiled. She unfastened the skirt she was wearing and stepped out of it. Parading her slender legs in front of him, she took the skirt in both hands and tore it in two. Before Roderick could ask what she was doing, she had climbed on to the bed. She took one hand and caressed his palm lovingly. Then she was tying half her skirt around his wrist. She bound him quickly, securing the remainder of the skirt to one of the bars on the bed's wrought-iron head.

'Bondage?' Roderick asked. There was no hint of refusal in his voice, just a note of pleasant surprise.

'How did you guess?' Judy said, tethering his other wrist to the bed. She could not stop herself from smiling at his eagerness for the game. She knew from personal experience that Roderick's father enjoyed a similar fetish. It had been nothing more than a calculated gamble to work out that father and son might share similar interests. Not that she would have told Roderick about her affair. There were only three people who had known about it, and Judy had already eliminated the only person who was likely to talk. If their brief relationship ever did become public knowledge, Judy was going to be the one to make it known.

Roderick laughed, unaware of Judy's thoughts. 'I've never known the appeal for this sort of thing. I mean, no one is ever properly tied to a bed, are they? There's always some way of getting out, isn't there?'

Judy grinned down at him. His father had said something similar and she had proved him wrong. She removed her blouse, revealing herself to him in just her bra and panties. Using the same quick skill she had displayed with the skirt, she tore the blouse in two and tied his ankles to the wrought-iron foot-board.

Glancing down at him, she admired her handiwork. He was tied spreadeagled on the bed and she doubted he would be able to move. 'Why don't you see how secure they are?'

Roderick tested the bindings. A doubtful frown crossed his brow as he realised he was well and truly bound. 'So what do you do to me now?'

She traced her hand down his chest, allowing her fingers to brush against the dark hairs around his cock. He was already hard and eager for her, his shaft pointing proudly upwards. She traced her fingers along it, tapping it gently with the tips. 'I do whatever I want to do now,' she told him. She cupped his balls and kneaded them gently in her palm.

Roderick sighed.

Judy rolled his testicles in her hand, squeezing them softly, then releasing them. His breathing deepened, and she squeezed them slightly harder. His cock twitched appreciatively. She licked the palm of her other hand and rolled the wetness over the swollen end of his erection.

Roderick groaned. He writhed on the bed, his arms and legs pulling strenuously at the restraints.

Rubbing her hand slowly up and down his anxious length, Judy grinned at him as he glanced awkwardly at her face. She continued squeezing his balls, using more pressure than she thought he was comfortable with. Each press of her fingers made his cock stand harder than the last.

'You like?' she enquired.

He swallowed. 'I like,' he agreed, not bothering to

find proper words for his enjoyment. His gaze alternated between her face and her hand as it continued to rub over the swollen end of his cock. It was obvious from the dull light of appreciation that glimmered in his eyes that his enjoyment went far beyond the simple 'like'. His breath turned to a shallow pant of excitement.

She continued to roll her wet hand over the end of his cock, constantly squeezing his sac with gradually increased pressure. She stopped when she felt his balls begin to throb. He was close to coming, she realised, and with two hours to kill she had no intention of letting him climax just yet. She dragged the pillow from beneath his head and shoved it underneath him. It held his arse away from the bed, thrusting his cock higher into the air. It also had the advantage of pushing his limbs harder against the restraints on his wrists and ankles.

With the pillow beneath him, Judy knew that Roderick had no chance of release until she untied him.

She pressed her mouth over his nipple and bit hard on the tiny nub.

Roderick gasped. 'Careful,' he warned her. 'That hurts.'

She laughed. 'It's meant to.' Her fingers found the eager pulse of his erection and she bit his other nipple while stroking his cock. His length shivered excitedly in her hand.

Roderick struggled uncomfortably beneath her, but Judy was not going to release him yet. Without allowing him to see it, she checked her wristwatch to gauge how much longer she had to keep him tied to the bed. It was only six-thirty, and she was not prepared to let him go until eight o'clock at the very earliest.

She teased his nipples with her tongue for a moment, then nibbled them mercilessly with the tips of her incisors. He moaned beneath her, grumbling half-heartedly about the discomfort, but hardening beneath her fingers all the time. Judy could sense his impending orgasm, and she stopped herself from biting before it went too far.

'Being tied up is only the beginning of proper bondage,' she said conversationally. 'Part of the excitement is being restrained and feeling vulnerable. There's another aspect to it that is even more fun.'

Roderick raised his eyebrows in a question. 'You sound like quite an authority.'

Judy grinned. 'I wouldn't have called myself an authority, just an enthusiastic amateur.' She placed a leg on either side of his body and stared down at him. Reaching behind herself, she released the clasp on her bra and allowed it to fall from her body. She rubbed her breasts gratuitously above him, making a show of stimulating her own nipples and massaging the orbs. 'Do you like looking at my tits?' she asked, aware of his approving smile.

Roderick nodded. 'I could look at them all day,' he replied eagerly.

Judy shook her head. 'You couldn't,' she explained. She reached for the bra and moved it over his face. 'This is part of the game,' she explained. 'If you don't see what's happening, you get more excited.' Placing one of the bra's cups over each of his eyes, she quickly tied the straps around the back of his head, securing the make-shift blindfold. She doubted it was the most effective blindfold in the world, but she considered it more than adequate for her purposes this morning.

'I can't see a thing,' Roderick complained.

'That's the whole point,' Judy told him patiently. She glanced out of the window and saw the street was still quiet. It was a reassuring sight and she took a measure of relief from it. Perhaps she was being over-cautious about Emily but Judy knew the woman was a bad penny with a knack for always turning up when she was least wanted. Judy had her own bitter experiences of this happening.

She reached for Roderick's nipple and squeezed it between her fingers.

He gasped excitedly; his cock twitched furiously.

Encouraged by his eager response, Judy dug the tips of her fingernails into the swollen nub on his chest and pressed hard. She could see the nails pressing deeply against the flesh, almost cutting into him. She knew the sensation must be exquisite, and she envied him the enjoyment she was giving.

'Please,' he begged. 'No. That's too much, I can't . . .'

He got no further.

She shifted position on the bed as he pleaded for her to stop and placed her crotch over his mouth. The gusset of her panties pushed against his chin and she rubbed herself slowly upwards. The heat of her cotton-clad sex covered his mouth.

Knowing exactly what was expected of him, Roderick began to lick. His tongue stroked against her warmth through the fabric.

Judy shivered, surprised by the unexpected thrill of arousal. She had intended tying him to the bed as a diversion. She had not anticipated getting much in the way of pleasure for herself. However, her body responded with a passionate arousal that longed to be satisfied.

Roderick's tongue traversed the gusset of her pants stimulating a plethora of exciting sensations. She could feel each fibre of the fabric pressing against the eager wet lips of her hole. He tried to manoeuvre his tongue around the pants and inside, but she wriggled out of his reach each time he attempted this. She allowed him to lap at her crotch until the pants were sodden with a combination of saliva and pussy juice. With the fabric soaked, his tongue slid more easily over her sex, intensifying her enjoyment.

Judy rubbed herself up and down his face, allowing him to tongue her from the tip of her clit to the

99

forbidden hole of her anus. The fabric was so sodden it clung to her skin, outlining the folds and crevices of her pussy. Delighted by his touch, Judy moaned loudly. She shifted position and began to remove her panties. She glanced out of the window as she was doing this and swallowed nervously.

Carrying a small case, Emily was walking towards the hotel.

'Fuck!' she gasped angrily.

Roderick made a questioning sound from the bed and she considered him impatiently. Without any hesitation, she took her panties off and rubbed them beneath his nose. 'Do you like the smell of these?' she asked him, her mouth close to his ear.

He groaned in response.

'Did you like the taste of these?' she insisted. 'Just now, when you were licking them, did you like the taste of my knickers?'

'Yes,' he gasped nervously.

She pushed them slowly between his lips, filling his mouth with the sodden knickers. His cock raged harder than ever before. Judy glanced at his twitching organ, surprised by the excitement he was receiving from being gagged. She had expected him to enjoy the game, but she had not thought he would like it this much. Moving her mouth close to his face, she whispered softly in his ear.

'I need one more tiny prop to satisfy you properly,' she told him. 'I'll be back in ten minutes. Don't go away.'

Bound, blindfolded and gagged, Roderick nodded.

Judy rushed around the room, grabbing clothes from her suitcase and snatching the car keys from Roderick's jean pockets as she dressed. She stepped into a pair of heels and checked her appearance before leaving. If she wanted things to work out her way, she had to get rid of Emily once and for all.

Snatching her bag from the bedside cabinet, she fled quickly from the room.

This time, there would be no mistakes.

'Emily!'

Surprised, Emily glanced up when she heard her name being called.

There were so few people on the morning streets that she had no difficulty seeing the woman who hailed her. Not that it would be difficult to miss Judy in a crowd, she thought wickedly. The peroxide blonde in her short skirt and low cut top would have been difficult to miss anywhere. Emily's gratitude cut through the ungracious thoughts. After being on board the *Amazon Maiden* for the last two days, she was even happy to see Judy.

'Judy? How did you get here?'

'I could ask you the same thing,' Judy replied, rushing over to her. 'Roderick's been worried sick. We both have. We've been searching everywhere for you.'

Emily shrugged and grinned inanely. This was even better than finding a telephone, she realised. She could finally start to put her ordeal of the last two days behind her. 'Well, now you've found me,' she said. 'Where's Roderick? Is he in that hotel?' She pointed at the doorway Judy had just left.

Judy shook her head. 'Roderick's still out searching for you,' she explained. 'You must be desperate for something to eat or drink though,' she said quickly. 'Let me get you something.'

Emily shook her head. 'I'm fine, Judy. Honestly,' she insisted.

Judy glanced at the bag she was carrying and raised a suspicious eyebrow. 'You haven't been stealing have you?'

With a broad grin, Emily shook her head. 'A friend gave it to me, when he discovered I was penniless and without a change of clothes.'

'A friend?' Judy sounded intrigued and she made it obvious with her question.

'Nothing like that.' She paused before continuing, aware that Judy's attention had been caught by someone else on the quiet street. Wondering if Roderick was there, Emily turned and followed the direction of Judy's gaze. She groaned inwardly when she saw Captain Wilde and Vincent walking slowly up the road towards them. Closing her eyes, she hoped he would ignore her.

'Who the hell is he?' Judy murmured. There was a definite note of approval in her voice.

Emily glared at the captain as he waved a hand in her direction. She ignored him pointedly. 'I have no idea who he might be,' she said quietly. 'And he doesn't look like the sort I'd be interested in anyway.' Noticing the captain cross the road and come closer to her, she said, 'I wouldn't say no to that coffee and a snack. Is there somewhere in your hotel?' Without waiting for Judy to reply, Emily was pushing the woman into the doorway.

There was a small café in the foyer, and Emily hurried them both into a discreet booth. She allowed Judy to order coffees and she asked for a packet of cigarettes to go with the order.

'Have one of mine,' Judy said, passing her the half-used packet.

Emily took one and accepted a light from Judy. A memory tickled the back of her mind and she could feel a question resting on her lips.

As though she had seen the thought surfacing, Judy spoke first. 'You seemed like you were in a hurry to get away from that guy,' Judy observed. She glanced at the small case Emily was carrying. 'Did he give you that?' she asked. 'Or did you have to work for it? Come on, tell me, what's been happening?'

Emily shook her head and took a long draw from her smoke. She watched the waitress place a pair of black coffees on the table, along with a new pack of cigarettes.

'I don't want to talk about it,' Emily told Judy. She glanced around the foyer, dryly admiring the plain, unimaginative decor. 'This is the hotel you're staying in?'

Judy nodded. 'It's not much, but it's the best one here.' She seemed intrigued by Emily's lack of communication and leant forward in her chair. Eager curiosity shaped her posture. She lit her own cigarette and said, 'Come on, Emily. What's been happening?'

Emily sipped her coffee. 'How long will Roddy be?'

Judy sighed. 'He shouldn't be long,' she said. 'A couple of hours at the most.' Casually, she raised the cup of coffee to her lips. She glanced at Emily as the woman stared disdainfully around the foyer. With a sly smile she tipped her coffee on to Emily's dress.

'Shit!' Emily stood up, exclaiming and brushing at the burning liquid.

Judy jumped from her seat, a concerned expression etched on her features. She dropped her empty coffee cup to the table where it landed with a clatter. 'Shit! Emily! I'm so sorry. It just slipped and I ...' She exercised an apologetic smile. 'Quick, go to the bathroom, just down there. I'll clean things up here and join you.'

Treating the woman to an exasperated frown, Emily started in the direction Judy had pointed. She paused at the restroom door and glanced back. 'Can you bring my case?' she asked. 'It's got a change of clothes in it.'

Judy smiled warmly. 'Sure I will,' she said kindly. 'And I'm really sorry about that.'

Emily waved her apology away. 'Forget it, Judy,' she said magnanimously. There was a small, reluctant smile on her lips. 'I'm back with you and Roddy now. Things are working out again.'

Judy watched the door close on Emily's back. Daggers of anger sparked from her eyes. As soon as she thought it was safe, Judy snatched the bag from under the table and headed quickly towards the exit. But before she could make it to the world outside, a thought stopped her. She paused and glanced warily at the door of the restroom. Walking back to the discreet booth they had shared, Judy picked up the unopened pack of cigarettes, then went out to Roderick's jeep.

Twenty minutes later, Emily wanted to scream. She stood in front of the hotel reception desk, arguing fiercely with the stern-looking manager. She still wore the short summer dress, but now it was thoroughly soaked. She had rinsed it in the restroom's sink, anticipating Judy joining her. Instead, the waitress had pulled her from the bathroom, shouting something unintelligible. From what Emily could glean of the woman's tirade, the bill for the two coffees and pack of cigarettes remained unpaid, and she was being held responsible.

Neither the manager, nor the waitress spoke any English, and they did not understand Emily's mangled attempts at their language.

She closed her eyes against the verbal battering of foreign abuse she was receiving. This was hell, she decided, and she had been sent here for some deplorable sin committed in a previous life. It was the only explanation that made any sense, and she clung to it like a drowning man reaching for a straw. There was no sense praying for salvation she realised. For her, salvation was not going to happen.

With her eyes closed she did not see the man appearing at her side. The first she was aware of him was the crisp growl of his voice, barking stern commands in an unfamiliar language.

She turned to see Captain Wilde and Vincent standing on either side of her. The manager was talking animatedly to the captain, gesturing disparagingly at Emily as he spoke.

Captain Wilde waited for him to finish and nodded

agreement. He grinned triumphantly at Emily. 'You really do have a knack for getting yourself into trouble, don't you?'

Emily glared miserably at him. 'I can't find my friend,' she said wearily. 'Can you tell this foreign idiot that she's staying here with my fiancé and that they will settle my account?'

He shrugged. 'I can tell him that much, I suppose,' he said good-naturedly. 'Do I tell him that you think he's an idiot?'

Emily glowered angrily and stopped herself from replying. She watched as Captain Wilde spoke quickly and fluently to the manager and was vaguely comforted by the fact that the man seemed to have regained control of his failing patience. He nodded understandingly as Captain Wilde spoke and then replied softly and carefully.

Captain Wilde nodded and frowned. He turned to Emily. 'You have my deepest apologies,' he said quietly.

She scowled at him. 'What did he say?'

'He said he thinks you are the idiot,' Captain Wilde began. 'He also said that the woman you were with was here with a man. They were driving a dull blue jeep.'

'That's them,' Emily said excitedly.

'It's gone,' Captain Wilde explained. 'I know that for a fact actually,' he added. 'The mad bitch who was driving it nearly ran Vincent and I over as she headed out of town.'

Emily stared at him, unwilling to believe what he said but not doubting him for a second. 'She's left me?'

He shook his head. 'They've left you,' he said, emphasising the first word. 'The manager was just saying that he's had a maid banging on your boyfriend's door. There's no reply.'

Emily rubbed her fingers through her hair. She glared sullenly at the reception desk. 'Can he get me a telephone?' she asked.

The captain translated the question for the manager.

He shook his head sadly. Emily understood the words 'no' and 'telephone' and she waved a silencing hand at Captain Wilde before he could translate.

'Does anyone have a loaded gun I can borrow?' she asked miserably.

Captain Wilde turned to the manager and barked another question at him. When the man replied, the captain nodded and placed a handful of notes on the counter. He turned and smiled at Emily. 'I really am a soft touch,' he told her in a self-deprecating voice. 'I've been sailing for the last twenty-five years, ever since I was eight, and I haven't bailed boats out as much as I've bailed you out. I've just settled your account.'

Emily was too tired to continue being angry. She glanced at the pile of notes he had left on the desk and turned to the captain. 'It was an expensive cup of coffee,' she told him dryly.

He smiled. 'You had a room to pay for as well. You're getting to be quite the expensive charity case.'

Emily did not bother rising to his bait. 'Why would they leave me?'

He shrugged. 'It's difficult to imagine anyone wanting to get away from you.'

'I could use slightly more practical suggestions,' Emily scowled.

The meaning behind his broad smile was so obvious she could not bear to look at him. She glared miserably around the hotel foyer trying to calculate her options. She had two choices: either stay in Port Maga and fend for herself, or ask Captain Wilde for help. It was difficult to decide which of the options was less appealing.

Staring around the seedy foyer, she realised that Port Maga was going to be as inhospitable as the rest of Amazon Basin had been. Knowing that she had no real choice if she ever wanted to get back home again, Emily

106

turned to Captain Wilde. 'Do I have to beg you to take me to Havalaña?' she asked.

He nodded. 'That was the condition,' he agreed. 'Would you care to start begging now?'

Emily could not stop a scowl from curling her lips.

The captain placed a protective arm on her shoulder and guided her towards the hotel door. 'Beg me on the way down to the dock,' he said. 'If you're real good, I may even let you aboard.' He nodded at Vincent, and the blond man rushed ahead of them to open the doorway.

'What will I be expected to do on your boat for the next week?' Emily asked.

He laughed as they walked. 'You'll be expected to do whatever I say,' he told her. 'Having seen the pleasure you got from being tied to the mast, I don't think it will be anything you won't really enjoy.'

'You have to keep bringing that up, don't you.'

'I do,' he agreed. 'It excited me quite a lot. I can see myself doing it a lot more in the next few days.'

Emily shivered, repulsed by the notion of giving in to him.

They walked in silence for a while, as though they were a group of friends enjoying a morning stroll. The streets were quiet and uncluttered, and Emily felt the tropical sun warming her body and drying out the sodden dress she wore. Her mind was hastily searching for a solution to her problem, but she could not think of anything. If the situation had not been so hopeless, she knew her desperation would have given way to panic. As it was, she could not even find the enthusiasm for that emotion.

'You'll have to forgive me,' the captain said. 'But none of this sounds like you begging me. You've been on board the boat for the last two days. You know what happens. You also know what you have to do if you want to get to Havalaña.' The anger in his voice was rising all the time. 'So, you can either leave my company now, or you can start begging.'

Emily glared at him. They had reached the riverside and she saw the majestic hull of the *Amazon Maiden* waiting patiently for them. It was still early and the lack of traffic on the river meant the port was deserted. The three of them were the only people in sight.

She felt miserable and alone.

'Go on board, Vincent,' Captain Wilde said quietly. 'Prepare to weigh anchor.' He turned to Emily. 'We'll be leaving in twenty minutes. Are you going to join the crew?'

Emily glared hatefully at him. 'Please may I come on board your boat, Captain Wilde?' she asked, spitting the question at him through gritted teeth.

His smile was ferocious. 'That does not sound like begging.'

'Oh! Please, great Captain,' she said sarcastically. 'I beseech you, oh great one. May I be permitted to –'

The palm of his hand struck her cheek hard enough to cut the sentence in two.

Emily stared at him, shocked and resentful.

'You obviously don't want the ride,' he said. 'Good-bye, Emily.' He turned his back on her and began to walk towards the jetty.

'Wait!' Emily cried. 'I'm sorry. I . . . I . . . I'm sorry, OK?' She reached a steadying hand out to stop him. Her fingers touched the warm sun-kissed flesh of his back.

He paused and turned to face her. Studying her expression, she saw he was trying to gauge her sincerity.

'I've never begged for anything before,' she explained quickly. 'It goes against my nature and I was just . . .'

'Either beg, or go,' he told her simply.

'I have money,' she told him. 'Back at home, in England. I have money and no matter how much you want, I can . . .' Her words tapered off as she saw the black plain of indifference that coloured his eyes. There was only one thing left for her to say. 'I beg you,' she whispered. His smile was so despicable she could not bare to look at it. Her gaze fell to his feet.

'Beg some more,' he told her.

'Please,' she said, swallowing thickly and almost choking on the words. 'I'll do whatever you want. I need to get to Havalaña, and I'll do whatever you demand of me.'

His grin was too broad for him to remain indifferent. 'Beg me on your knees,' he said. 'I always think that's more convincing.'

Emily dared not look at him, for fear that he might see the mixed expressions in the back of her eyes. A part of her was considering him with loathing so strong she knew he would not allow her back on board. Another part of her was warmed by the thrill of a secret sexual arousal. She stared sullenly down at the rotten wood of the jetty and lowered herself to her knees. 'I beg you,' she whispered.

'Kiss my feet,' he told her.

Emily closed her eyes. She tried to think of another option, but she knew there was none. Slowly, praying that fate would find a way of intervening, she moved her lips down and kissed his foot. He was wearing a pair of plain black deck shoes and she kissed the bridge, above the fabric. Tears of shame welled in her eyes. It did not matter that they were all alone at the riverside and no one else knew what she was doing. Emily hated herself for giving in to the captain. She was aware of the distant pulse between her legs throbbing sullenly. It was an echo of the arousal she had experienced whilst tied to the mast. The feeling sickened her, and her self-loathing intensified. To have to do this was bad enough, she thought. To get enjoyment from it was worse.

Ignoring the throb of excitement, she continued to place soft, tender kisses on his feet. 'Please let me come aboard,' she whispered.

Captain Wilde grinned down at her. 'Not bad,' he encouraged. 'I suppose I could use you aboard my boat,' he said after a moment's thought. 'You kiss feet very well.'

Emily could detect the threat of something more in his voice. She glanced up at him and saw that in spite of their open position, on the end of the jetty, he was pulling his shorts down. She should have expected this much, she thought, knowing what he was going to ask next.

'Kiss me here,' he told her flatly.

Emily paused for a moment, despising herself and the quickening tempo of desire that pulsed inside her. She moved her mouth towards him and prepared to kiss his cock.

He was as big as she had expected him to be, at least the same length as Vincent had been, but with a thick girth that made his cock twice the size of the blond man's. Judging by the way his shaft hung downwards, Emily guessed he was not fully erect and she shivered, wondering how much bigger it could get. She placed a gentle kiss on the end of his shaft.

'Kiss it more,' he told her sharply.

Emily did. She pressed her full, sensuous lips against the shaft of his cock, delivering soft pecks to the entire length. As she moved her mouth over him, she inhaled the subtle sweet fragrance of his arousal. His huge cock began to harden forcefully beneath her touch.

'Now suck it,' he told her sternly.

Emily groaned inside. She could feel her nipples pressing hard against the short summer dress she wore. Between her legs, the lips of her sex were moist with hateful excitement. Not daring to give the action any thought, she placed her mouth over the tip of his cock and sucked. Her tongue traced against the tip of his swollen purple end and she felt his length stiffening.

'That's good,' he murmured appreciatively. 'That's very good.'

Encouraged by his approval, Emily continued to work her mouth on his length. Slowly, she eased the cock in and out. Her lips pressed hungrily around his shaft, wetting the entire length. She moved slightly away and showered the tip of his cock with tiny, appreciative kisses. She continued to kiss the underside of his shaft, moving her mouth lower until her nose was nuzzling at his tight sac. After flicking the tip of her tongue softly against each of his balls, she opened her sensuous lips wider. Stroking his balls with her fingers, she moved her mouth back to the tip and began to taste him again.

The hateful wetness of her arousal was slowly building up between her legs. It was sickening to think she could get enjoyment from submitting to this man, but she could not deny the fact of her own mounting excitement.

The captain placed his hands on her head and pulled her fully on to his length. He was so large she had to stretch the lips of her mouth wide to accommodate him. He pressed his cock fully into her, the swollen end pressing against the back of her throat.

'Swallow,' he barked. His voice was a low guttural command, excitement colouring his gruff tone.

Emily did as she was asked, excitement building inside her. She pushed herself on to his length and allowed the tip of his cock to slide down the back of her throat. It was an act she had never performed before, and she was simultaneously repulsed and aroused. The pressure of his cock was enough to make her gag. She could feel an impending explosion welling in the thickening shaft of his cock, and her pussy muscles began to clench hungrily with anticipation.

Despite the submissive situation, or more likely because of it, she thought glumly, Emily realised her own orgasm was disturbingly close. As she knelt on the jetty, sucking the captain's cock, she forgot her loathing and hatred. It did not matter how much she despised him, or the position he had put her in. She was enjoying it. In the instant of her climax, that thought was all that mattered to Emily.

She felt his seed shoot inside her mouth.

His cock pulsed furiously as he climaxed, and he released a soft groan of delight. His hands held her head tightly, keeping her in position until he was fully spent.

'That's it,' he told her. 'I don't want you to spill a single drop.'

Emily swallowed his come greedily. The salty taste was cloying and overpowering, but as the waves of her own pleasure washed over her she did not care. She sucked him eagerly, determined to take every last drop of semen from his huge length.

'Enough,' he said, pushing her head away. 'Turn around and bend over.'

Emily did as he commanded, wiping the last trace of his seed from her lips. She had no idea what he wanted from her now and she did not care. She had already submitted herself to him. He could not make her feel any worse than she already felt.

With her back to him, she felt the captain raise the hem of her dress.

'Nice arse,' he murmured quietly.

She shivered.

His fingers went to the panties she wore and she felt him trace a line along the length of her labia. The lips responded eagerly to his touch and she trembled with a mixture of excitement and disgust. When he pulled the panties to one side, a cool morning breeze touched the heated flesh of her sex.

Emily sighed quietly.

She felt his finger touch the rim of her arsehole and almost squealed. She did not want to endure this sort of intimacy. This went beyond anything she had been prepared for when she consented to do his bidding. Poignantly aware of her situation, Emily dared not stop him. Unhappily, she braced herself for his finger's intrusion.

Determined to do whatever he wanted, she stayed still and allowed him to probe the tightly puckered hole.

He pushed two fingers rudely inside her. One slid easily between the lips of her labia, pushing effortlessly into the excited, sodden warmth of her pussy. The other entered the forbidden darkness of her anus.

Her inner muscles clamped greedily around his fingers, and she groaned with a fury of elation.

He held his fingers inside her for a moment longer, moving them gently against the dark, eager flesh within.

Emily felt another orgasm sweep through her. Electric explosions of delight racked her body. She held herself still, fearful of the captain's retribution if she dared to move. A low grateful cry fell from her lips and she heard herself sobbing words of gratitude to him.

'Stand up,' he barked, sliding his fingers out.

Emily did, allowing her dress to fall casually into place. She stared into his face, not surprised to see the lecherous grin on his lips. He was holding two fingers towards her and she knew instinctively that they were the ones he had used inside her.

'One last thing,' he told her. 'And then you may be my slave aboard the *Amazon Maiden*.'

Emily closed her eyes. 'Haven't I done enough?' she wanted to ask. She did not dare give voice to the question.

'Lick my fingers clean,' he said. 'Then you may board.'

Knowing she had no other choice, Emily moved her mouth over his extended fingers and began to lick her own juices from his hand. The taste of her pussy honey was florid and sweet, enough to inspire the memory of her earlier excitement. She licked every last drop of the juice from his hand, almost enjoying the submissiveness.

'And the other one,' he said crisply.

Emily stared at the finger, knowing where it had been and unwilling to have it against her lips. She dared to stare into his face, trying to gauge how serious he was with this request.

'Lick it clean, or I leave you here,' he said firmly.

Emily moved her mouth over the finger and began to lick the sour sweet taste of her arse from his finger. As before, when she had first pressed her mouth against his cock, she felt repulsed by the arousal that the taste inspired. Knowing that she had no other choice, and aware of what she had done to get this far, Emily licked his finger clean.

Her face burnt crimson with shame and she shivered, cold with self-loathing. The hateful throb of her arousal only seemed to intensify. She gave in to the pulse of her own desire as she traced her tongue along his hand. Even when she had finished licking the last remnants of her warmth from his hand, she continued to tongue his fingers, waiting for him to tell her to stop.

'Very good,' he said, removing his hand. His smile was broad and welcoming. 'Come on board,' he told her. 'You're one of the crew now.'

Emily shuddered and fell into step behind him. The enormity of what she was about to endure was so great she dared not even think about it. As she climbed aboard the *Amazon Maiden*, Emily shivered beneath the heat of the tropical sun.

Five

Judy stepped into the hotel room and closed the door softly behind her. She could hear Roderick thrashing on the bed before she saw him. Checking her watch, she realised he had been tied there for two hours. She smiled as she thought of his predicament, then chastised herself for being so wicked. After driving out of Port Maga she had waited for a while, studying the breathtaking beauty of the plains and smoking a couple of Emily's cigarettes. She knew there would be no need to wait for too long, and she had driven back to the port within half an hour.

The hotel manager had seemed surprised to see her, but she had fielded his questions easily. He sympathised with her plight when she explained about 'the mad woman, chasing her around the country', and assured Judy that the woman would not be allowed back in his hotel.

Glancing at Roderick, Judy saw he had lost his erection. He had managed to spit the knickers from his mouth and he was pulling furiously at the bindings on his arms. Her grin broadened. The blindfold was still in place and her entry had been so discreet he was oblivious to her presence.

She moved close to the bed and knelt down beside him.

'Who's that?' Roderick asked sharply.

She grinned and stayed silent. With the nails of one

hand, she drew her fingers along his chest. It was a harsh gesture and she saw red lines appear in the wake of her fingers as she scratched.

Roderick gasped with surprise. 'Judy? Is that you?'

Judy stayed silent. She took hold of his cock and squeezed it tightly between her fingers. It hardened eagerly beneath her touch. Tugging it softly to and fro, she teased his length to full erection.

'I haven't been enjoying this,' he told her. There was more than a note of firmness in his words. He sounded bloody angry. 'You can stop doing that now, because I'm not happy with you.'

Judy placed her mouth over his cock and sucked him gently.

Roderick drew in a breath of delighted air. It seemed as though his annoyance was instantly forgotten. He tried to sit up on the bed, but the bindings held him tight.

Judy stepped out of her clothes and joined him on the bed. She sat down with her arse above his face and pushed her pussy on to his mouth. Without a moments hesitation, he slid his tongue against her pussy lips. Judy forced her sex against him, encouraging Roderick to push further inside.

He forced the entire length of his tongue into her, almost drowning with the heady scent of her musk. The lips of her labia were already moist with excitement, and he licked her clean as she pushed against his face. The tender folds of her pussy's lips opened eagerly for him. Working lovingly on the flesh of her sex, he pushed the tip of his tongue hard against her clitoris. Roderick's arousal was so intense that his cock stood hard and proud.

Judy sensed his excitement and knew she was only part of the cause. A big part of his arousal was due to her silence. She knew he was savouring the erotic image of being fucked by a stranger. His father had confessed

116

to the same powerful fantasy after one of their lengthier bondage sessions, and Judy could see that Roderick was a lot like the old man. It was a ludicrous notion, she thought, but it was obviously exciting him tremendously.

Judy stifled a gasp of pleasure as she rubbed herself against his face. She had not expected Roderick to show such potential when it came to cunnilingus. His tongue licked softly against the wetness of her pussy lips. She felt the flesh of her sex being teased slowly to a state of delicious arousal. His saliva moistened and warmed her sensitive lips. If she had known he had so much talent, she would have tied him to a bed in the first village they arrived at and kept him there. Breathing deeply, she rode herself over his face, forcing him to lap at her lips, hole and clitoris, as and when she saw fit.

Beneath her, Roderick moaned.

Judy suppressed her own sighs of enjoyment, not wanting to give her identity away just yet. She knew he would be fantasising about someone else riding his face, and she did not want to spoil the illusion just yet.

His cock twitched eagerly against his belly and she grabbed it with both hands. Squeezing cruelly, she pushed the foreskin down and held his dick tightly at the base. With the swollen end of his penis exposed, she teased her wet tongue over the rounded end.

Roderick's cries of delight were muted by the pressure of her hot cleft on his mouth.

Judy smiled to herself, placing her lips over his erection. She allowed her tongue to trace the rim of his cock's head, teasing the hypersensitive tag of skin above his glans. His balls were tight and hard. He was so desperate to come she could almost see the throbbing, urgent pulse of his sac.

Judy pushed her pussy forcefully over his face. She felt his tongue slide inside her and she squealed with delight. Her orgasm was a liberating eruption of joy.

Tremors of delight shook her body and she bucked her hips furiously backwards and forwards. The sodden lips of her sex moved briskly over his nose and mouth, coating his face with the dewy wetness of her climax.

When Roderick began to gasp for breath, Judy finally relented. She moved her pussy away from his face and guided the wet lips of her labia over his cock. As she straddled him, she kept her hand at the base of his length, holding his foreskin tight. Sliding slowly up and down his shaft, she watched his lips contort into a grimace of pleasure. His face was still coated with the sweet dew of her pussy honey and she moved her mouth towards him. She had always enjoyed the taste of her own juice, and there was something exciting about licking it from Roderick's face. When she had cleaned the last remnants from his face, she kissed him, her tongue probing his mouth fully.

Between her legs, she felt his cock tremble and knew he was ready to ejaculate. How he had managed to stave off his climax for so long was a mystery to her. She squeezed her fingers harder into the base of his shaft, wondering if it was possible to delay his climax by not letting the semen shoot from his body. She took his cock from between her pussy lips and rolled the swollen end against the sticky wet lips of her labia.

Roderick's cry was a dark grunt of elation. His cock pulsed furiously in her hand; Judy felt globules of his seed spray against her lips and thighs. She cursed softly, tugging the last droplets of come from his body. She could feel the sticky fluid clinging to her flesh, and without looking, she knew her pussy lips would be streaked with smears of his thick, white semen. When he was finished, she moved slowly up the bed and lowered her come-spattered pussy over his mouth.

Staring down at him, Judy smiled and watched as Roderick's eager tongue began to lick her clean.

* * *

Emily stood naked in the captain's cabin, wondering exactly what was going to happen next. 'I can endure a week of whatever he's going to throw at me,' she told herself. 'I know I can,' she insisted. After all, it was only a week. But despite her strong will and determined resolution, Emily wondered if she was being overly optimistic.

'Until you're fully trained,' Captain Wilde told her, 'you can wear this.' He threw what looked like a sheet of rubber at her.

Emily snatched it from the air, fearful of the retribution she would incur if she dropped it. She puzzled over what the thing was for a moment before realising it had holes for her arms and legs, amongst other things.

'Dawn will help you into it,' Captain Wilde told her. 'And then you can report to the pilothouse for duties.' He considered her slowly, contempt apparent in his eyes. 'Unlike Dawn and Vincent, you seem completely useless. Therefore you'll be dealing with the majority of menial tasks on board the boat.'

They stood in silence for a moment. If Emily had not felt so drained and defeated she knew the air would have been hostile and combative.

'As a slave,' Captain Wilde said tersely, 'you are supposed to thank me for the garment and the instructions.'

Emily stared sullenly at him. 'Thank you, Captain Wilde,' she said quietly.

He was still staring at her, his anger rising, and Emily wished she knew what he wanted from her. 'You're dismissed,' he said tiredly. 'I'll see you in the pilothouse in thirty minutes.'

Emily nodded and left the room. Thirty minutes seemed like a long time, she thought. All she had to do was put on the stupid rubber outfit he had given her and then report to the pilothouse. Normally, she was used to changing entire outfits in less than ten minutes, and that included having a shower as well. It occurred to her that the life of a slave on board the *Amazon Maiden* might not be as bad as she had been anticipating. When she entered the cabin used by Dawn and Vincent, Emily realised how mistaken she had been about the garment.

'The orgasm suit!' Dawn moaned when Emily showed it to her.

Emily shrugged. 'It's not what I would have called it,' she said.

Dawn tossed her a bottle of baby oil and told Emily to rub her body with it.

'What on earth for?'

Dawn grinned sourly. 'You'll see,' she said, bitter experience making her words heavy. 'You'll see.'

Emily did see. Even with Dawn's help, it took a good ten minutes of struggling, grunting and groaning to get the outfit on. The rubber was designed to cling as tight as her real flesh. In spite of its natural elasticity, it was so small it was almost impossible to get on. She pushed her head through the neck-piece and then had to struggle to get her arms through the holes where the sleeves should have been. She managed it, but it took a lot of hard work and half the bottle of baby oil.

Emily arranged her breasts inside the top, aware that her nipples were meant to jut through the holes on the front. She pushed them out, surprised to see that they were standing erect.

'Now what?' Emily asked.

Dawn was behind her, and she helped Emily to finish dressing. Hanging from the back of the body suit was a flat black triangle of rubber, edged with a belt and decorated by two metal-ringed holes. When Dawn pulled it between Emily's legs, the brunette saw this was the completed outfit. The belt tied snugly around her waist and the metal rings sat uncomfortably over her pussy and her anus. She glanced in Dawn's mirror and could not stop herself smiling at the reflection. The outfit accentuated the perfect contours of her body. The full swell of her breast was confined tightly inside the black, clinging outfit. Her slenderness was more evident than ever before, and the high cut of the leg-line emphasised the natural athletic beauty of her long, powerful legs. Stepping into a pair of black heels, she studied her mirror image again and grinned at it.

'It never looked that good on me,' Dawn said, sounding mildly upset.

Emily grunted laughter. 'It doesn't look that good on me,' she replied. 'I look like an inner tube.' Pressing her fingers against the protruding nipples, she amended herself. 'Actually, I look like a burst inner tube. I thought rubber was meant to be shiny?'

Dawn sighed heavily. 'Again, that's where I come in,' she said. She reached for the bottle of baby oil and poured it over the shoulders of Emily's rubber suit. Using a cloth, she began to massage the liquid into the clinging fabric.

Emily tried to remain indifferent beneath Dawn's touch, but it was difficult. The woman continually brushed her cloth over the rubber, stimulating the flesh beneath with such a casual air that Emily found the sensation debilitating. It would not have been so bad, Emily thought, if her nipples had not been exposed. As Dawn worked up a shine on the rubber, her cloth repeatedly caught the tender nubs. Emily could feel them tingling with anticipation before Dawn moved to her back. Even then, the constant rubbing and polishing was like an erotic massage.

Afterwards, she had to concede that all Dawn's efforts were worth it. She had admired the look of the rubber suit before. Now that it was polished, her body glistened with its shiny new black skin. Ripples of light caught her breasts and hips, shining silver in the bright light of the cabin.

'Not bad,' Emily said reflectively. She turned around and saw that the cheeks of her arse were partially covered by rubber. Her black coated buttocks glistened as provocatively as the rest of her body.

'And with time to spare,' she said, noting there were still two minutes before she was due in the pilothouse.

Dawn studied her critically. 'You'll do,' she said eventually. She smiled when she saw the frown on Emily's face. 'Actually, you look stunning,' she said. 'But if I haven't done my part properly, Captain Wilde will punish me.'

Emily nodded. She moved towards Dawn and placed a soft kiss on her cheek. Her fingers fell naturally to the swell of Dawn's breast and she rubbed her thumb over the urgent thrust of the woman's nipple. Pressing hard against the thin fabric of her top, the hard nub of flesh stiffened to her touch.

Dawn pulled away, a shocked expression straining her features. 'No,' she hissed quietly. She almost slapped Emily's hand from her breast. 'No!'

Emily stared at her, hurt and confused. 'What's wrong?' she asked. 'The other night, I thought we . . .' Her voice tailed off.

Dawn was shaking her head, a look of abject refusal on her face. 'You're a slave now,' she reminded Emily. 'You're one of us; and slaves are not allowed to fraternise with other slaves. Not unless the captain or Laura expressly commands it.'

'I'm sorry,' Emily said, embarrassed and feeling a little ashamed of herself. She had not intended to fraternise with Dawn. She had only wanted to say thank you for the help the woman had given. 'I didn't mean to compromise you,' she explained.

Not trusting herself to say anything else, Emily rushed from the cabin and went quickly to the pilothouse.

'Here she is,' Captain Wilde proclaimed as Emily climbed the stairs. 'Our newest slave, honey, and she's all yours.'

Laura turned a scathing eye on her husband. 'Fed up with her already, Captain?'

He laughed indulgently.

Emily blinked against the brilliant daylight, unaware that it had been so dark below deck. Captain Wilde and Laura stood together at the pilothouse's main console. They had their arms draped lovingly around one another. He was adorned in his familiar uniform of black shorts and matching deck shoes. Laura was wearing a silk kimono and Emily suspected that beneath it she was naked. The pair were smiling at her with blatant longing.

Because she felt uncomfortable with their scrutiny, Emily looked away.

She saw Vincent standing at the wheel, guiding the ship through the clear waters ahead of them. His gaze flicked over her rubber-clad body and an appreciative smile twisted his lips. But he was as well trained as Dawn. Without needing to be told, he fixed his concentration back on the boat's controls.

'Say hello to your new mistress,' Captain Wilde instructed Emily.

She stared at Laura, not daring to allow any expression on her face. 'Hello, Mistress,' she said flatly. She had not known she was to become Laura's property for the week, but she accepted the news with a note of gratitude. At least she would not have to submit herself to Captain Wilde again, she thought, enjoying a moment's mental relief. The optimistic notion was quelled by the realisation that Laura could command such a thing whenever she chose.

Laura smiled. 'You are good at breaking them,' she observed.

Captain Wilde grinned. 'I haven't broken this one,' he told his wife. 'She'd happily tie me to the mast and whip the skin from my arse given half the chance. She's just acting broken for as long as it suits her needs.' He stared at Emily, daring her to refute his words.

'Is that true?' Laura asked.

'I don't know,' Emily replied quietly. 'When I've pictured the captain tied to the mast, he hasn't had his back to me.'

There was a deathly silence in the pilothouse. The couple stared solemnly at her, taking in the full meaning of her words.

Captain Wilde broke the silence with a huge, hearty guffaw. 'That's rich, that is,' he chuckled.

Laura joined him, but the laughter on her lips and in her voice never reached her eyes. She stared warily at Emily. 'I see you're wearing the orgasm suit,' she observed. 'Unfasten the belt.'

It was a command, not a request or suggestion, and Emily complied at once. She allowed the front flap to fall down, exposing her thatch of dark pubic hair.

Laura nodded her approval. 'Now turn around and bend over. Your outfit is missing a couple of accessories.'

Staring directly ahead of herself, Emily had no idea what the woman meant. She considered herself to be beyond caring. Her interest only returned when she felt the cool tip of a vibrator nuzzling at the lips of her pussy. The tip was slick with lubricating jelly, and it slid easily inside her. Emily believed it would have entered quickly anyway. Having Dawn massage a shine into the rubber suit had been stimulating enough to inspire hot wet arousal between her legs.

'Good,' Laura complimented her. 'And now for this one.'

Before Emily could raise a word of protest, she felt a second vibrator press against her arsehole. Like the first one, this too was coated with a cool, slick lubricant. Emily felt it slide easily inside her. The sensation of fullness between her legs was overwhelming. She suppressed a tremor of excitement that threatened to reveal her arousal.

Laura reached between Emily's legs and quickly pulled up the base panel of the orgasm suit. She fastened the waistband and then knelt down to inspect the gusset. Without having to see for herself, Emily knew that the speed controls for the two vibrators were protruding through the metal-ringed holes at her crotch. She stood motionless as Laura twisted first one, then the other.

Emily felt both vibrators begin to buzz merrily. A tingle of excitement began to well deep within her. She swallowed nervously, amazed by the powerful stimulation that screamed between her legs. Her breath was a ragged pant and her chest was heaving furiously in the tight confines of the rubber body.

'Enjoying that?' Laura asked.

Not trusting herself to speak, Emily nodded dully. She could feel herself close to climax and the intensity was so strong she dared not move for fear of bursting with pleasure.

'Hold your chest out,' Laura commanded. She reached on to the console and picked up two small items that Emily recognised instantly. Holding them by the fine-linked chain, Laura moved closer to Emily and dangled the nipple clamps in front of her face. 'Do you know what these are?'

Emily nodded, still not daring to speak. She pushed her chest forward and watched as Laura placed them first on her left nipple, then her right.

The pain was exquisite, a stark contrast to the tingling merriment that exploded in the depths of her hot wet channels. The cruel bite of the clamps coloured her pleasure with a delicious, dark urgency. Her breath had been short before. Now her lungs convulsed in short, erratic spasms. She tried valiantly to appear nonchalant and unperturbed by the stimulation, but her acting was not fooling anyone.

Laura smiled and turned to her husband. 'And you say that she's all mine?'

He nodded grandly. 'To do with as you wish.'

Laura grinned and reached back to the console again. Instructing Emily to go on to the deck, she followed her closely. There was a dark malevolence in her smile that Emily had not noticed during her first days on the *Amazon Maiden*. It was an unsettling sight.

For Emily, every step was a revelation of new kinds of pleasure. The vibrators continued to whirr, jostling slightly with each movement of her legs. Orgasm after orgasm swept through her body. The wealth of pleasure that coursed through her was so severe she began to shake.

'Down on all fours,' Laura instructed coldly.

On the deck, Emily went down on to her hands and knees. The explosion of joy inside her body was not enough to stop her from feeling stupid and conspicuous. She felt even more ridiculous when Laura fastened the strap of leather around her neck. It was an oversized dog's collar, loose fitting and decorated with long metal spikes. Emily felt foolish wearing it. Her cheeks burnt bright red with shame when the woman attached a leash to it. Instead of thinking about her situation, Emily tried to concentrate on doing exactly as Laura told her. It was easier that way.

'Captain,' Laura called. 'Could you bring me the chains?'

Emily saw the man come swiftly when the woman spoke. She shivered with anger, unhappy that he had to be a part of this humiliation. Hadn't she already endured enough shame and embarrassment at his hands?

Without needing to be instructed, the captain fastened manacles to her wrists and ankles, securing them tightly. Her wrists were joined by a sturdy length of heavy link chain. When she glanced between her legs, she saw that her ankles were fastened in the same way. She guessed there was about a foot of chain between the manacles and not much more between her feet. Movement, she realised, was going to be virtually impossible.

Laura thanked her husband and Emily watched the man walk away. Before she had a chance to enjoy the relief of his leaving, Laura tugged the leash sharply. She had started to move along the deck and was pulling Emily along with her. 'Come along,' she said. 'It's time for a little walkies.'

Feeling more absurd than ever, Emily followed the woman artlessly around the deck. It would have been awkward enough without the vibrators droning purposefully inside her. The delightful thrills they were producing were now so constant she had almost forgotten them.

The tilt and roll of the boat was more noticeable on the main deck. Each pitch and sway seemed to take the deck from beneath her hands and feet. Unable to move properly because of the chains, Emily struggled to maintain her balance as she tried to keep up with Laura's brisk pace. She honestly believed she could have managed it without incident, but with Laura tugging at the leash she repeatedly lost her footing and twice fell heavily to the deck.

Laura remained indifferent, tugging harder at the collar whenever Emily tripped.

By the time they got back to the pilothouse, Emily was feeling bruised, breathless and resentful. She glared sullenly at Laura's knees, the only part of the woman's body she could see without straining her neck.

'That was pathetic,' Laura said sternly. She snapped her fingers towards the captain and Emily saw his feet come into view. 'Thank you, Captain,' Laura said softly.

Emily did not see what was happening, but she knew Laura had taken something from the man. She felt the urge to spit on his shoes and stopped herself, knowing she was in no position to show defiance. Her hatred was more intense than the pleasure thrilling her body, and she welcomed the black emotions.

A welt of pain exploded against her buttocks. She raised her head and moaned loudly. The movement caused the chain on her nipple clamps to sway and she was treated to a second bolt of punishment, emanating from her breasts. Her moan tapered off before it could become a scream.

Laura raised the cat-o'-nine-tails high in the air, then brought it down sharply against Emily's arse again. The many tips of the cruel leather whip bit hard against the taut flesh of her backside.

'That was the slowest, most pitiful trip I've ever taken around the boat,' Laura spat. She brought the whip down a third time.

Emily stayed rigid beneath the blow, unwilling to suffer the pain of having the nipple clamps move again. If her cheeks had been burning before she realised that they now must have been aflame. The depth of her humiliation was greater than anything she could have imagined. In Port Maga, while she was licking the captain's fingers clean, she had thought things could not get worse. Standing on all fours, chained, dressed in rubber and having her arse whipped, Emily could have looked back on the moment fondly.

'You are going to walk around the deck with me for the next hour until you get it right,' Laura told her crisply. She lashed the whip across Emily's arse indiscriminately, reddening the bare cheeks with the cat's tails.

Emily swallowed, almost choking on the words. 'Yes, Laura,' she whispered.

Laura delivered one last stinging blow to the cleft between Emily's legs. The tips of the whip pushed hard against the buzzing vibrators. Unable to stop herself, Emily flinched away from the impact and felt her nipples stinging painfully as the chain on the clamps began to swing again.

'Come on,' Laura said crisply. She was pulling the

dog leash again, leading Emily on another tour of the deck. 'When we get back to the pilothouse, I'll let you suck the heel of my shoes,' she said generously.

Trying fervently not to stumble, Emily followed in silence. She did not trust herself to answer Laura at the moment. All the words that came to her were the sort that would incur punishment.

'That's the way,' Laura encouraged blithely. 'You'll be fully trained before we reach Enoba.' She giggled and added, 'Either that, or you'll be black and blue.'

Emily glowered at the woman's ankles as she hurried along behind her. She did not know where Enoba was, and she did not really care. She had to endure this punishment for another seven days. After that she would find a way of turning the tables and making both Laura and the captain pay. The thought of vengeance was a small consolation, but she clung to it desperately.

As she moved, the pleasure between her legs became a maelstrom. Even her clamped nipples began to emit a dull pulse of delightful sensations. Lost in her own black world of bitter retributions, Emily barely noticed the pleasure. Roderick and Judy had deserted her, twice, she realised angrily. The captain and Laura were already abusing her more than she could tolerate. All that she had left was the hope of revenge.

Judy stared down at her prisoner, admiring the sight. Roderick's chin and lower jaw were glistening with a wet coating of her pussy juice and his own come. His tongue continued to work at the slick heat of her moist interior; she shivered, thrilled by the pleasure he was delivering to her pussy. She pushed herself harder on to him, forcing him to lick every last droplet of sex cream from the lips of her labia.

Happily, Roderick complied.

The man was so malleable Judy could have enjoyed another orgasm thinking about how her future with him

129

could unfold. He would willingly do everything she said, obey her every command. It was the way a man should be, she thought, grinning.

Roderick made a small appreciative sound as he stroked his tongue along her pussy lips.

Now is the time for the master stroke, Judy thought carefully. She slipped her sodden cleft away from him, sliding from the bed, and placing her mouth next to his ear. She could smell the scent of her own juices on his breath and found the aroma invigorating. Her fingers reached down towards his cock and she teased it idly with her fingers.

'Are you happy, Roddy,' she asked quietly.

He groaned. The broad smile on his lips should have been a sufficient response, but she wanted to hear him say it. 'I'm happy,' he told her; there was a blissful contentment tainting his words. 'Very happy,' he assured her.

She rolled his cock between her fingers, watching it stiffen slowly and assuredly. He was still blindfold and unable to see the disparaging smile that graced her lips.

'How happy?'

He seemed to consider this for a moment.

'I'm happier since we lost Emily,' Judy explained as she waited for his response. 'Things have been better since she disappeared, haven't they?' She began to use more force on his erection, pulling it hard with her wet fingers.

Roderick moaned happily beneath her. 'I'd still like to find her,' he said carefully.

'Of course,' Judy agreed quickly. 'It would be barbaric to leave her to fend for herself. But even if we did find her, things are different now, aren't they?'

He chuckled in agreement, content to lay there as she wanked his cock and whispered softly in his ear. 'Of course things are different,' he assured her. 'After all, she was the one who told me to fuck off. The relationship between Emily and I ended when she did that.'

130

Judy smiled at his face. She could feel his climax building, and she wondered how desperately he wanted to come. Tugging faster at his cock, she asked, 'Why don't you and I get married?' After she'd asked the question, she stopped her fingers working on his length.

Roderick stayed still for a moment.

Judy wondered if he was considering the question or waiting for her to continue wanking him. She knew that he would realise the two things were inextricably linked. She kept her hand still against the base of his cock, waiting for his response.

'You want us to marry?' Roderick sounded bewildered. 'But we're practically brother and sister,' he reminded her. 'We couldn't seriously think of marriage.'

She laughed and moved her mouth over the end of his cock. After tonguing the tip of his shaft, she said, 'We're not so much like brother and sister that you'll stop me from doing this.' She moved her mouth away from his cock, waiting for the urgency of his arousal to answer her question. She did not doubt it would work in her favour. 'I thought you were serious about us, Roderick,' she whispered.

'I am,' he insisted.

She made a small, scornful sound. 'Serious, but without commitment,' she observed. 'How delightfully nineties.'

Tied to the bed, unable to see and with limited movement available to him, Roderick struggled to protest. 'I am serious,' he assured her. 'I was just saying, what will people think?'

'Don't you love me, Roderick?' Her voice may have sounded frail and vulnerable, but there was nothing humble about the rest of her demeanour. 'Is that what's wrong? Don't you love me?'

'Of course I love you,' Roderick said quickly.

As he lay beneath her scornful expression, Judy doubted he had even considered the issue until this moment. 'Then why don't you want to marry me?' she demanded.

'We can marry,' Roderick said quickly. 'If you want us to get married, then we can marry, OK?'

Judy began to play with his cock again, easing the rock hard flesh forcefully between her fingers. 'OK darling,' she agreed simply. 'But only if it's what you want.'

Roderick allowed her to play with his cock. 'It's what I want,' he assured her. 'Really, it's just what I want.'

As she wanked him, Judy grinned triumphantly.

Bound hand and foot, her body tingling with the constant whirr of the vibrators, Emily completed her tour of the main deck without stumbling. Her hands ached from being used like feet. Her feet ached from the awkward position they had been forced into. The only sensation she could feel springing from her nipples was the distant feeling of despair they emitted between flaming bolts of delight. Panting like a dog, she glanced shyly up at Laura, wondering if the woman approved of the way she had walked.

Laura collapsed on to a heavily padded sunlounger. She snapped her fingers and Emily manoeuvred herself quickly to the woman's side. 'You did that well,' Laura said, holding Emily's chin with her hand. 'It took some time, but I think you're finally learning.'

Emily nodded, no longer troubling herself with thoughts of defiance. She watched as Laura spread her legs on the sunlounger, revealing her naked body beneath the silk kimono. Her large breasts rose and fell slightly with the rhythm of her breathing.

Emily glanced hesitantly at the woman's nipples. They were large and erect, slightly darker than the rose-tinted flesh of her broad areolae. Her gaze swept downwards and she found herself staring at the fluffy bush of blonde pubic curls that covered Laura's sex. She

132

was sitting so that the lips of her labia could not be seen, but Emily suspected they were already moist with arousal.

Laura pulled her chin sharply, forcing Emily to stare into her eyes.

'Look at me while I'm speaking to you,' she commanded. 'Not my body.'

Emily nodded, lowering her eyelids by way of apology.

Laura's smile was predatory. 'You liked what you saw?' Without waiting for a reply she said, 'That's good. You'll enjoy it all the more.' Laura lay back on the sunlounger and pulled Emily's face towards her. Guiding Emily's mouth towards her breasts, she whispered softly, 'Please me, Emily. Please me.'

Emily pressed her tongue over Laura's nipple and tongued it gently. She worked the tip over the huge nub, aware that the woman was murmuring soft words of approval. She traced her mouth over the pale pink flesh of Laura's areolae, stimulating the skin effortlessly.

Laura sighed with delight and reached between Emily's breasts. With an almost casual flick of her fingers, she unfastened the nipple clamps, dropping them to the floor.

Emily groaned with gratitude. The clamps had been giving her a wealth of pleasure, but they had also been damned uncomfortable. A wave of relief washed over her, as strong and powerful as any of the orgasms she had experienced. Feeling indebted towards the woman, Emily sucked harder on her breasts.

'Vincent,' Laura called calmly.

Emily sighed. She wondered if Laura was going to get the man to release her wrists and ankles. They were still held tightly by the chains and manacles making every movement a chore. She knew that to be released from the manacles would be as great a relief as having the nipple clamps removed.

'I'd like a drink, Vincent,' Laura said quietly.

Emily felt her hopes of release dashed. She stopped herself from thinking badly of the woman, determined instead to please her as she had demanded. She moved her head and began to suck at Laura's other breast.

'No,' Laura said firmly. She placed her hand on Emily's forehead and grabbed a handful of her hair. With a surprising show of strength, she pushed Emily's mouth between her legs.

Emily inhaled the musky scent of Laura's sex. She saw the woman shift position, raising her pussy lips so that Emily could tongue them. Hesitating, not sure what was expected of her, she slowly lowered her mouth on to the woman's sex. Her nose moved softly through the pale hairs of her blonde pubic bush. Carefully, she guided her lower lip towards the wet lips of Laura's pussy. As she had suspected, the woman was sodden with arousal. Her lips glistened with pussy honey.

Cautiously, Emily flicked her tongue against the wetness. Her mouth was enjoying the sweet juice of the woman's desire, and she took a grim morsel of satisfaction from the taste. Emily knew that she had caused that arousal. The pussy honey she was gently licking had been inspired by her. With this thought paramount in her mind, she nuzzled against Laura's sex and began to run her tongue greedily over the lips.

Laura moaned gently. She kept her hand on Emily's head, reminding her of the inferior position she was relegated to. While Emily licked at the sweet, succulent cleft, Laura took her drink from Vincent and sipped it languidly.

'You look divine there, honey.' Captain Wilde called the words from his position behind the wheel.

Emily tried not stiffen at the sound of his voice, fearful there would be a penalty to pay. She continued to probe her tongue against the yielding flesh of Laura's sex. Her cheeks and nostrils were coated with the heady

134

scent of love juice, and she found it easy to forget everything else in the world except for the beautiful demanding mistress beneath her. The vibrators were still buzzing, held tightly inside by the rubber bodysuit. She found that just by thinking about them, she could enjoy the tingling delight of their movement. Not thinking about them, the pleasure was a distant joy, like the half-heard melody of a whispered refrain.

'I feel divine,' Laura called back to him. 'Care to join us?'

As she heard the heavy fall of his footsteps on the deck, Emily realised the captain had not needed much in the way of encouragement. She heard him bark an instruction at Vincent, telling him to take over the wheel. Then she could feel his loathsome presence, nearer than she wanted him to be.

'You're far too soft with your slaves,' he told his wife, a note of censure colouring his words. 'You shouldn't let them have the joy of tasting you,' he said sternly. 'They don't appreciate the pleasure you're allowing them.'

Emily stole a glance at her mistress.

Laura nodded agreement. 'I can't help myself,' she said honestly. 'I suppose I'm just one of those people who's too generous for their own good.' She smiled wryly at her husband, nodding casually down at the woman between her legs. 'Mr Masters is going to love this one,' she told him.

The captain smiled in reply. 'I don't just think John will like her,' he said. 'She could even tempt Al from his usual predilections.'

Laura grinned her agreement. 'Just so long as they're not too besotted to sign the contract.'

The captain kissed his wife passionately on the lips. His hand went to her breast and he stroked the orb lovingly. Moving his fingers gradually around the pale flesh, he ignored the nipple and areola, concentrating on the neglected expanse of sensitive skin.

135

Laura groaned excitedly and shivered. 'How long is it since we enjoyed one another?' she asked him.

Captain Wilde laughed. 'It's the best part of a day I'd wager,' he told her. 'Do you think we should start making amends?'

Laura giggled. 'I think we're long overdue,' she told him. She moved position and pulled Emily so that she was lying beneath her. Placing a leg on either side of Emily's head, Laura rocked her buttocks provocatively in front of the captain, encouraging him to enter her. 'Carry on tonguing me, Emily,' Laura instructed coolly.

As the captain plunged his cock into the woman, Emily did as she was told.

She pushed her tongue against the wet lips of Laura's pussy, relishing the flavour of her arousal. As the captain plunged his stiff dick into his wife's wet hole Emily could see his cock spreading the woman's lips apart. Their bonding was only millimetres from her face and Emily shivered with excitement as she watched the scene. The captain used his wife roughly. His cock pounded hard inside her and he uttered low, guttural commands of approval as she forced her hips back against him.

Emily continued to lick, wetting the lips of Laura's sex. The flat of her tongue occasionally brushed over the insistent force of his erection. Beneath the pair, as they fucked, Emily knew she was nothing more than a peripheral pleasure in the union, but even this thought excited her. She was bound like a slave, wearing the most ridiculous, uncomfortable costume ever designed, and her sole purpose was nothing more than a cursory titillation for the lovers above her. These were surely the lowest depths she could ever have sunk to, she thought. But as well as disgusting her, Emily felt excited by the depravity of the situation.

She kept her eyes wide open as the pair screwed. The sight of Captain Wilde's cock was exciting enough, she

136

realised. Watching it slide into the depths of a pussy only inches from her face was a pleasure she would never have imagined. Emily shivered and pressed her tongue firmly against him.

Captain Wilde groaned.

With her tongue on his cock, Emily could feel the orgasm welling inside him. She flicked her tongue gently across the stubble of hairs that covered his balls. It was a subtle stimulation and she did not mean to hasten his orgasm. Nevertheless, Emily could feel the explosion of his seed building in the tight sac.

'Lick me, Emily. Lick me!'

Laura's voice was a furious command and Emily dared not disobey her. She moved her mouth away from the captain and began to concentrate on the nub of pleasure that was Laura's clitoris. She tapped the tip of her tongue against the hardened pearl of pleasure, determined to please the woman as much as she was able.

Laura groaned, a wealth of sensations building up inside her.

Emily continued to lick at Laura's clitoris, her tongue occasionally catching the shaft of the captain's mammoth girth. Both tastes were exciting and stimulating, thrilling her more than she would ever have admitted. The intimacy of sharing their sex was a pleasure Emily found intoxicating. Coupled with the servility of her position, it was a devastating combination.

When Captain Wilde finally came, Emily felt his cock pulse against Laura's lips. Because she was stroking her tongue against those lips when it happened, she savoured the feeling of his climax, so close to her mouth and, at the same time, so far away. She shivered excitedly, relishing her own unexpected orgasm.

Delighted by the response, even if she did not approve of the subjugation, Emily pressed her tongue hard against Laura's cleft. Her tongue brushed the lips of the woman's sex, teasing folds of skin stretched tight to accommodate the captain's impressive girth. Her efforts were rewarded by a squeal of delight from the woman above her.

Laura came noisily and copiously, making her pleasure known to everyone on board the *Amazon Maiden*. Screams of jubilant triumph wailed from her body. Her back arched and she shifted herself slightly away from Emily, before pressing the wanton lips of her sex back down against the slave.

Captain Wilde held her hips against his cock, determined to spend every last remaining drop of his seed deep inside his wife. Emily felt his cock pulse and twitch against her mouth. Her nostrils were filled with the sweet, salty fragrance of his climax.

Purposefully, she continued to lick at Laura's pussy, aware that the woman had not told her to stop.

'Enough,' Laura gasped eventually, pushing Emily away. She moved forward and allowed the captain's flaccid member to fall from the lips of her sex.

Emily felt his cock brush against her chin and saw him smiling darkly down at her. His attention did not bother her. She had already reached the depths of humiliation. She knew there was nothing else he could hold over her that would be worse than what she had endured since this morning.

'Come along,' Laura whispered, tugging Emily's leash as she spoke. She kissed her husband indulgently on the lips and thanked him for making love to her. Speaking to Emily, she said, 'You'd better follow me; I'm going to have a shower and I'll need you to clean me up.'

Reluctantly, Emily followed.

'Enoba?' Roderick asked. 'Where the hell is that?'

Judy groaned.

She knew it had been a mistake to take one last trip to the riverside, but Roderick had insisted. Because she felt confident she had seen the last of Emily, Judy had relented. She had left him tied up for two hours and then tormented him cruelly for her own satisfaction. If she wanted him to keep his promise of marriage, it was only right to let him have his own way occasionally, she told herself.

Besides, she thought practically, even if Emily had been left behind, she probably wouldn't be waiting around the riverside to see if anyone came along to help her. A long time had elapsed since the boat's departure. Glancing at her watch she realised it was close to a full two hours.

All her rationalisations and hopes vanished when they reached the docking clerk's office. The clerk was no longer the pleasant grinning local she had spoken with earlier. He had been replaced by a rugged looking American youth who answered Roderick's questions easily.

Judy could have slapped him.

'Eighty miles down the river,' the clerk explained. 'It's about three quarters of the way between here and Havalaña,' he added. 'You know, the big city for these parts.'

'We know where Havalaña is,' Judy told him through gritted teeth.

'Did you see a young woman on board?' Roderick asked. 'Dark hair, long legs and . . .' He stopped, aware that the American was shaking his head.

'I didn't even see the boat.'

Roderick turned to Judy. 'We have to go to Enoba,' he said firmly.

'It's pointless,' Judy sighed. 'We don't even know if she was on board that bloody boat.'

Roderick turned to the American. 'We lost a friend of ours a couple of days ago,' he explained. 'We think she's on board the *Amazon Maiden*.'

The American shrugged. 'You'd better hope she is,'

he drawled calmly. 'The natives around here aren't known for their hospitality.'

Roderick sighed.

Judy tried to suppress a smile of triumph.

'Are there any authorities, or someone else, who could help us?' Roderick asked.

The American shook his head again. 'None worth troubling,' he said solemnly. 'Your best bet is to get down to Enoba and hope she's on board that boat.'

Judy glared angrily at him. She did not let Roderick see the expression. Nor did she let him see her frown of disapproval when he next spoke.

'That's us decided,' he said sharply. 'Next stop, Enoba.'

Emily stared around the captain's cabin, wondering where to begin. She caught sight of her reflection in a mirror and grinned in spite of herself. The tight fitting rubber suit displayed the contours of her figure to the utmost advantage. Despite the arduous day she had endured, the woman in the mirror looked ready for anything.

It was getting close to midnight now, and Emily felt exhausted. She had suffered a long and miserable day, and though the idea of sleep appealed to her she knew that it would prove elusive when she eventually got to bed. There were too many unpleasant thoughts turning over in her mind. She still wanted to know why Judy had betrayed her and left her alone in Port Maga. She was also wondering what had happened to Roderick. He must have left the port with Judy, she thought. Either that, or Judy had ditched him somewhere. She tried to close the thoughts off, more uncomfortable with the memories than with the other events of the day.

After sex on the deck, Laura had wanted Emily to lick her in the shower. Emily had obeyed, kneeling in front of the woman and tonguing her pussy as the water

140

cascaded over her. She had nuzzled and lapped at Laura's clitoris, pushing the woman beyond the brink of orgasm time after time. Afterwards, Laura had demanded a massage, and Emily had happily obeyed. Then the vibrators had both been removed. Strangely, as Laura was taking them out, Emily had experienced mixed sensations of sorrow and gratitude.

Before, she had not believed it would be possible to enjoy too many orgasms. After having the vibrators burn furiously in the depths of her hot wet channels, Emily had modified that opinion. She now knew there was only so much a body could take. Even so, feeling the slow, buzzing egress of each of the vibrators, she had felt a tinge of remorse, certain that she could have enjoyed their delightful punishment for just a little while longer.

After taking them out, Laura had forced Emily to lick both implements clean before she used them on herself. She had then used the two dildos with furious abandon, forcing herself to reach one climax after another. Her final climax had been so intense she had screamed happily before collapsing on the bed in a quivering heap.

Now Laura was sleeping, and Emily had been instructed to clean the captain's cabin.

She glared sullenly around the room, wondering where she should begin. A pile of cluttered papers covered the desk in one corner. To Emily's casual eye it looked like the only untidy area in the cabin. The bunk was made, and the surfaces were relatively dust free. Emily could think of nothing else that might need doing in the room, so she moved towards the desk and began to tidy the scattered papers.

In her other life, before the nightmare of this holiday had begun, Emily had been a corporate finance manager. She considered herself good at her job, for what that was worth now. Seeing the papers on Captain

Wilde's desk, Emily enjoyed a handful of fond memories about her past life. She recognised the format and the layout of the contracts and knew she was staring at the outline for a substantial corporate finance package. As she scanned the wording of the contracts, Emily amended her first thought. This was not a substantial corporate finance package; it was a very substantial corporate finance package – a major one.

She rummaged through the papers on the desk, dimly noting the names of the companies involved. Masters and Thomas were major names and she raised her eyebrows in mild surprise when she read them. Her eyebrows continued to rise as she saw the basis of the deal being offered. Unable to believe it, she re-read the documents a second time, sure she must have missed something.

The contract was not the deal Emily would have expected. As she poured over the documents, Emily realised that Captain Wilde and Laura were not offering a standard corporate deal. They were proposing a personally managed contract, but it seemed heavily weighted in their favour. The profits that the couple would be reaping went beyond anything she had ever seen on such a deal. Remembering what the captain had said about not discussing business at his business meeting, Emily nodded to herself. A slow smile of understanding began to spread across her lips. It seemed obvious that Laura and he hoped a night of passion would be distracting enough to make the negotiators overlook such details as rates of return and glib references to contract management.

If she had been negotiating the contract, Emily knew she could have made Masters and Thomas a far better offer. At the same time she would have still been earning herself a very lucrative commission from the deal.

An idea was forming in her mind when she felt the hand fall heavily on her shoulder.

'Enjoying a little light reading?'

Emily turned around and found herself face to face with Captain Wilde. The angry frown on his face was enough to make her feel cold inside. He was glaring passionately at her, and she knew that she had transcended another one of the unwritten rules of her slavery.

Staring at the page of the contract she held in her hand, he raised a speculative eyebrow. 'Enjoying a little light reading?' he asked again.

Emily glanced at the paper in her hand and struggled quickly to find a suitable explanation. 'I was just tidying these things away, and –'

'Come with me,' Captain Wilde said. He dragged her from the room, his face as dark as thunder. 'I think you need a little more discipline.'

Groaning inside, Emily followed. She could feel the terror welling inside her like a bubble. Whatever she had experienced before would be nothing compared to the punishment she knew she was about to receive.

Six

'In there,' Captain Wilde roared. He held Emily by the hair as he made the command and hurled her into the cabin.

Emily squealed, stumbling awkwardly into the room and trying to maintain her balance. Her top half lurched forward and her legs struggled to keep up with it. Crashing into the cabin's wall, she managed to stay on her feet. She held herself stiffly, glaring furiously at the man.

'What is it? What's going on?' Dawn sat up in her bunk, bewildered. She glanced at Emily, then at the captain and an air of calm appeared on her face.

Watching her, Emily realised the woman knew exactly what was going on. There was a light of experienced acceptance in Dawn's eyes that chilled Emily. She could sense that the woman knew what was about to happen and was reluctantly prepared to go along with it. She wished Dawn could have shared the information with her. Enduring the captain's wrath and having to put up with his violent temper was more than Emily was prepared to deal with. If the man had not been barring the cabin door with his broad body, she would have jumped overboard and taken her chances with the crocodiles.

He had caught her reading through the contract and she understood his unhappiness. The document was so obviously loaded in his favour that he must have known she had spotted the blatant discrepancies. Now, she guessed, he was going to make sure she did not pass her knowledge on to anyone else. The thought left her feeling cold and terrified. 'What have I done?' Emily demanded. 'Why are you treating me like this?'

'I'll treat you any damned way I want to treat you,' Captain Wilde snarled. 'Do I have to keep reminding you? I'm the captain of this damned boat.' He reached for the bedspread that covered Dawn's naked body and pulled it angrily. Dawn gasped, as though the sheet had been attached to her. She sat up on the bed, modestly trying to cover her bare body.

Not that there was much to cover, Emily thought disparagingly. She glanced slyly at Dawn's flat chest and her delightful pierced nipples. Her gaze fell lower and she grinned unconsciously as she saw the woman place a protective hand over the pierced lips of her labia.

Even though she had just been asleep, Dawn was still a striking beauty. Her long dark hair fell over her shoulders, framing her petite face. Her shrewd blue eyes glanced from Emily to the captain with wary excitement.

Emily trembled when she saw the captain glowering at her. She knew he was going to punish her. He had caught her reading the contract and that was obviously an unforgivable sin. When he had burst into the room she had been thinking about re-negotiating it. Her thoughts had strayed idly from her imprisonment aboard the *Amazon Maiden* and she had wondered if it would be possible to tempt Masters and Thomas with her own proposal. It was a ludicrous notion. She knew the chance would never reveal itself to her.

But she wondered if the captain had read her mind. That in itself was a fanciful notion, but fear pushed the thought to the forefront of her mind. If he had known, or even suspected such an idea, she dared not think of the punishment he would inflict on her by way of retribution.

'I'm going to ask you this question once more,' he said. His words were ragged, his barely controlled temper spitting the sounds from between clenched teeth. He glanced at Emily. 'What were you doing in my cabin?'

Emily momentarily closed her eyes and swallowed. Her heart was beating so fast she wondered if it was likely to explode. 'Laura told me to clean it,' she whispered. 'I was obeying her order.' She watched his face, hoping fervently that he would accept what she said. Her words did brush at the truth. Laura had told her to clean the captain's cabin. Emily was just neglecting to tell him about the reading material she had found.

He glared at Dawn. 'Why weren't you cleaning my cabin?' he demanded. 'That's your job, isn't it?'

'Yes, Captain,' Dawn whispered. She began to apologise.

He cut her words off with a slap across the cheek. Striding purposefully towards Emily, he said, 'What the hell did you think you were doing looking through my papers?'

Emily shivered beneath his furious glare. 'I was trying to tidy them,' she told him meekly. She hated the undercurrent of servility that coloured her words, but she knew it would be the only thing likely to save her. 'They were all over the place. I was just trying to sort them out for you.'

'Why were you reading them?' he asked forcefully.

Emily felt the words like a slap. 'I was trying to get the pages in order,' she told him, forcing as much sincerity as she could into the improvised explanation. 'You punish me enough on board this boat when I do the right thing. If I'd jumbled the papers up, I thought I'd get a lot worse than I've already had.' She stared at him nervously, praying that he believed her.

His dark mood seemed to mellow and he graced her with an approving grin. 'You're right,' he said, nodding.

Turning to Dawn, he pulled her roughly from the bed. 'But that still doesn't tell me why you weren't tidying my room.'

Dawn cowered away from him, obviously terrified by the ferocity of his anger. 'Please, Captain Wilde,' she begged. 'I didn't know Emily was going to do that.'

Emily stared at the pair, a heady wave of relief washing over her.

He was not suspicious of her, she realised. His anger and rage had been transferred to Dawn; Emily experienced a pang of guilt. If he had known of her trespass, the captain would not have missed the opportunity to punish her. As it was, Emily saw she had inspired his outrage and knew he was about to vent his spleen on Dawn.

Her relief was so strong, Emily felt her knees begin to tremble. She watched the pair through a comfortable haze of gratitude. Dawn should have been tidying his cabin and he wanted to know why she had reneged on her duties. His anger was now directed at Dawn. And, while Emily knew she would be unlikely to escape his temper, she knew that he would not be punishing her as severely as she had initially feared.

Captain Wilde turned back to Emily. 'So, now you're doing the job of my slave?'

Emily stared at him uncertainly. 'I'm sorry,' she began.

He did not allow her to go any further. 'Sorry isn't good enough,' he spat. He turned on Dawn. 'And you've risen above your status as a slave, have you?'

Dawn began to refute the allegation, but he spoke over her protests.

'Lying asleep while someone else does your job. Is that how a slave behaves?' he demanded.

Dawn shook her head, unable to meet the fury of his gaze.

'Here,' he said angrily. 'Take this, Dawn,' he insisted. He pushed his cane into her hand.

Dawn accepted it reluctantly.

Emily glanced from Dawn to the captain, wondering what she could expect from the man now. This was a turn of events she had not anticipated. She had never expected him to relinquish his cane. The damned thing had seemed to be glued to his hand.

'You think you've risen above slave status,' Captain Wilde observed. 'Show me how you treat your subordinate.' With one long, wicked finger, he pointed at Emily.

Emily caught her breath, unnerved by the way events were progressing. She wanted to say something in her own defence but she knew such an intrusion would be treated harshly. Staring at Dawn, she willed the woman to refuse the order she had been given. Emily knew it was a vain hope, but it was the only one she had left.

Dawn stared uneasily at the cane in her hand. 'But I . . .'

'Show me now,' he hissed. 'Or, God help you, I'll show you how it's done like you've never felt it before.' His finger was still pointing at Emily. 'Punish your slave, while I watch; or I'll have her punish you. The choice is yours, Dawn.'

Dawn needed no further prompting. She walked slowly over to Emily and kissed her softly on the cheek. With her lips inches from Emily's ear, she whispered, 'Sorry.'

It was one softly spoken word, but it was enough for Emily to realise she was in trouble. She considered Dawn uneasily, not knowing what to expect from the woman. She doubted Dawn could be as ruthless or cruel as either Captain Wilde or Laura, but she did not discount the possibility.

'What do you want me to do?' Emily asked.

Dawn turned to Captain Wilde.

He smiled indulgently at her. 'Undress your slave,' he commanded. 'She looks good naked.'

Dawn turned back to Emily and nodded. 'Take your suit off,' she said crisply.

Surprised by the coolness in her voice, Emily stared at Dawn. A wicked glint lit the corner of her eye, and Emily realised there was an untapped streak of devilment lurking beneath Dawn's servile façade. The prospect was darkly unsettling.

Glancing down at the rubber suit she was wearing, Emily began to obey. Her fingers fumbled with the strap of the belt and she mumbled an apology. She had been wearing the suit all day. A slick coating of sweat covered her body beneath the black flesh of the garment. It was going to be difficult enough to take it off, she thought, without her fingers being paralysed by fear.

'Faster,' Dawn said sharply. She flicked the tip of the cane against Emily's thigh, striking hard and quick.

Emily felt as though she had been bitten and she flinched from the implement. Hurrying to undress, she released the belt and allowed the front panel to fall free. There was no sense of embarrassment at revealing herself to the pair in such a way. She had already realised that aboard the *Amazon Maiden* she was beyond shame.

Aware the captain was avariciously studying her thick swatch of pubic hair, Emily began to try and ease the suit from the rest of her body. It was an ardent struggle. Her body's sweat helped her a little, but the rubber still bit and pulled at her flesh, making the experience more painful than she had expected. When she eventually removed it and threw it down on the floor, she stood in front of the pair defiantly naked.

'What now, Captain?' Dawn asked.

He grinned at her. 'She's your slave, Dawn,' he reminded her. 'Do what you want with her. I'm just here as an observer.'

Dawn nodded and took a step closer to Emily. She traced a finger against the sweat-drenched flesh of her breast, smiling as she did it. 'Lick it, bitch,' she commanded, raising the finger to Emily's mouth.

Emily pushed her tongue out and drew it along the wet finger. She could taste the bitter saltiness of her own sweat and she tried not to savour it. Again, she felt the hateful pulse of excitement throb between her legs. She was being used and humiliated by the pair. The rational part of her mind told her she should be resisting them, but her libido craved the experience.

'Your body's soaking,' Dawn noted. She seemed to study Emily's face. Her sharp blue eyes looked hard now, as though they had been carved from flint. Emily realised she was seeing a different Dawn from the one she had come to know over the past few days. This was a side of Dawn that could enjoy wielding the cane.

Emily swallowed nervously.

'Do you like being wet?' Dawn asked, malicious intent prevalent in her tone.

The captain chuckled darkly.

Emily wondered what he found so amusing. She suspected that there was some clue in Dawn's words, but her *naïveté* concerning the boat's customs and the crew's games left her in the dark. 'I don't mind being wet,' Emily replied. She did not dare say yes or no to the woman in front of her, feeling sure that either response would incur some sort of penalty.

'Kneel down then,' Dawn commanded. 'Kneel in front of me and lick my hole, bitch.'

Doing as she was instructed, Emily knelt down in front of Dawn and began to push her tongue against the pierced lips of Dawn's labia. It was an uncomfortable position. Her neck ached with the strain of reaching upwards, but she managed to inspire a soft moan of pleasure from Dawn as she flicked her tongue against the woman's clitoris.

'That's good,' Dawn whispered, placing a hand on Emily's head and holding her hair tightly.

Emily made a small gasp of protest then relented. After all that she had endured so far, she was prepared

150

to tolerate having her hair pulled a little. The sweet succulent taste of pussy juice evoked the stirrings of arousal inside her. She traced her tongue against the eager wetness of Dawn's cleft. She was aware that Dawn and the captain were exchanging a smile, but she had no idea why.

'So, you don't mind being wet,' Dawn repeated. Her words were soft with pleasure. 'That's fortunate.'

Emily moved her mouth away from the woman's sex and stared up at her doubtfully. 'Fortunate? How?'

She barely had a chance to finish the sentence before she realised exactly what Dawn had been intimating. A golden shower of piss sprayed from between Dawn's legs, washing over Emily's face, neck and shoulders.

Emily tried to pull away, shocked by the tepid flow that ran over her. Dawn still held her hair and pulled Emily's face tight against her sex. 'Lick me, you fucking bitch,' she insisted. 'Lick me, while I piss in your mouth.'

Emily gasped and gagged, determined not to submit to this request. She tried pulling her head away but Dawn held her firm. The idea was so darkly exciting she wanted to submit, but at the same time she hesitated. She yearned to wallow beneath Dawn's legs, lapping at the golden spray and feeling it warm then chill her bare body.

At the same time, she longed to be away from them all. Giving in to Dawn now would be an admission of servility. This act went beyond anything else she had done so far. This was the ultimate in submission. If she gave in now, she doubted she would ever recover enough self-esteem to return to her previous life. The thoughts tumbled through her head in a chaotic whirl-wind.

'Drink it,' the captain commanded darkly. 'Or, so help me, I'll cane your arse from now until morning.'

The words were enough to make Emily open her

mouth. She felt the liquid spray against her lips and her tongue. Then her mouth was filling with the warm florid-scented water. Pushing her tongue against the source of the spray, Emily felt Dawn's amber flow coat her face, soaking her cheeks and splashing down over her breasts and her stomach.

Dawn giggled happily as Emily tongued her. Her relentless flow continued to douse the woman before her. Her giggles turned into moans of pleasure, and before she had stopped pissing she cried out happily with satisfaction.

Beneath the golden shower, Emily felt herself nearing her own orgasm. She did not know if it was spurred on by the warmth of Dawn's piss or the totality of her humiliation. She gave herself over to the euphoric eruption of pleasure that welled inside. Every muscle in her body seemed to throb with delight as the orgasm swept over her. Her skin turned to gooseflesh beneath the warm waters and she shivered happily. Her tongue continued to lap at the shaved flesh of Dawn's sopping hole, savouring every last drop of the wetness.

'Quite a show,' Captain Wilde said quietly.

Emily glanced uncertainly at him. She had been so lost in the pleasure of enjoying Dawn that she had almost forgotten the man was watching them.

'You looked like you got quite a lot out of that,' Captain Wilde said nonchalantly.

Before she realised what she was doing, Emily nodded agreement. A small smile of gratitude appeared on her wet lips. 'It was exhilarating,' she told him honestly. 'I'd never . . . Before I mean . . . I'd never . . .'

'But you weren't supposed to be enjoying it, were you,' he said darkly, speaking over her words.

'I . . .' Emily hesitated, not knowing what to say for the best. She stared at the cruel smile twisting his lips and knew he had more in store for her. This time, she doubted it would be as pleasant as the experience she had just enjoyed.

'Come with me,' he snapped sharply. Not waiting for her to move, he grabbed Emily's arm and wrenched her from the floor.

Naked, still dripping with the remnants of Dawn's golden shower, Emily stumbled quickly after him. He dragged her into his cabin, then threw her on to the bed.

'Dawn!' he bellowed. 'My cane!'

It was in his hand before the echo of the words had died down. Emily buried her face in the pillow of his bunk and braced herself for the sting of his cane striking her backside.

'Lie next to her,' Captain Wilde roared.

Emily knew he was talking to Dawn and she was not surprised when she felt the woman fall on to the bed beside her. Her fear was so great that she could not even register mild excitement at the nearness of the woman's naked flesh. Captain Wilde was determined that they should both be punished. He would make sure that there was little pleasure to be gained from this episode.

The cane sliced swiftly through the air, whistling on its downward arc. Both women braced themselves for the explosion of impact. They gasped in unison as he brought it simultaneously across both pairs of raised buttocks.

Emily glanced up from the pillow and stared at the untidy desk in the corner of the room. She could see the scattered papers of the contract and felt her resolve hardening. Perhaps he did have the upper hand at the moment, she conceded. He was the one wielding the cane; he was the one in control. She stared at the contract wondering if he knew how tenuous his command was.

The cane bit her arse a second time, inflicting an exquisite flash of pain. Feeling Dawn flinch beside her, Emily knew he had caught them both again.

She had already experienced one orgasm within the last five minutes and she did not think her body was

153

prepared for another so soon. Nevertheless, she stole a hand under her body and rubbed the sodden swell of her cleft. As the captain's cane stroked repeatedly across her arse, she moved her fingers slowly up and down over the hardening nub of her clitoris. Her fingers gently circling the rigid ball, then pressing forcibly as each stroke of the implement bit into her buttocks. Her arousal was not caused by the blow of his cane, although she knew that was helping. The true source of her excitement came from the thought of outwitting the captain.

Delight coursed through her body and she moaned loudly. The cane hit her arse three times in swift succession. Because she could feel Dawn lying still beside her, Emily knew that these blows had been specially targeted on her. She gritted her teeth and pressed her fingers more ardently on to the heated swell of her sex.

As the waves of pleasure washed over her, Emily held on to one last thought. Whatever else happened between here and Havalaña, she was going to make sure she got into the captain's cabin again. She was going to study his contract with a meticulous eye for detail and learn everything about the deal that was being offered. If she ever got the chance to make the information work for her, she was going to use it. That, she thought contentedly, would be cause for celebration. That would be the perfect revenge.

The captain pulled her from the bed. 'There really is no punishing you, is there?'

Emily shrugged, trying to look as though she did not understand what he meant.

He stroked his hand over her breast harshly, rubbing the nipple between his finger and thumb. 'I've broken harder slaves than you before,' he said quietly. The unmasked menace of his threat chilled her. 'I don't think you're beyond my capabilities.'

Emily stayed silent, knowing any response she made

154

could be interpreted as a challenge. She stared at his chest, not daring to meet the wrath of his eyes.

'Go and clean up Dawn's cabin,' he snapped, twisting her nipple angrily as he spoke. 'You can sleep in there tonight once you've finished.' Turning to Dawn, he slapped the palm of his hand across her bare arse and rolled her over. 'While you, you little slut, are going to stay in here for a while.'

As Emily watched, the captain stepped out of his shorts and brandished his huge length over Dawn. The brunette smiled adoringly up at the man and moved her face eagerly towards him.

Shivering, Emily turned away and left them. She knew that if the captain saw her hesitancy he would find some other depraved act for her to perform. Already exhausted by his demands, Emily walked briskly from the room. Whatever it took, she was determined she would avoid enduring another of the captain's punishments this evening. Knowing there was only so much she could take, Emily truly believed she had reached her limits.

She mopped the floor of Dawn's room before collapsing wearily on to the bunk.

Every square inch of her body ached profusely. Her inner muscles throbbed accusingly, as though they blamed her for the relentless pleasure they had been forced to endure. As soon as her head hit the pillow, Emily was asleep. She did not even notice two hours later when Dawn slipped into bed next to her. Emily's exhaustion was so total she could have slept throughout the whole of the next day.

When she was woken at five o'clock the following morning, Emily realised this was one pleasure she would not be experiencing.

'Enoba off the port bow, Captain.'

Emily glanced up when she heard Vincent's words,

unable to believe what she was hearing. The last four days had passed in a ceaseless blur of sex, work and humiliation. She had spent each day dressed in the rubber outfit, doing exactly as Captain Wilde and Laura commanded. By the end of each day, she had been so exhausted she had collapsed into bed, only to be woken the following morning for the whole thing to start again.

And now they were less than an hour away from Enoba, the last stop before Havalaña. She shook her head, bewildered by the fleeting passage of time.

'It's a step up from Port Maga,' Captain Wilde observed. He had rushed to the pulpit with his binoculars and he was studying the approaching port on the horizon. 'Not a big step up,' he called. 'But I'd guess the lice are smaller than the dogs in this one.'

Laura, draped on her sunlounger, smiled to herself. She was laying naked beneath the morning sun's rays. Her body was beginning to colour to the pale golden hue of an Aztec goddess. 'You're a xenophobe, Captain,' she told him lightly. 'If they don't have a church spire and a village green for cricket, you dismiss the place as a Third World hovel.'

He laughed. 'I think you're exaggerating slightly, honey. But I'll take it as a compliment.' He was still peering through the binoculars, adjusting the lenses. 'I don't fucking believe it,' he exclaimed suddenly. 'I don't fucking believe it!'

'What's wrong?' Laura was climbing from her bed, moving towards him. In an act of uncharacteristic modesty, she began to wrap a kimono around herself.

Emily glanced towards the captain, concerned by his tone of voice.

'Son of a bitch,' he murmured. 'Emily, get over here.'

She was running along the deck before she realised how quickly she was obeying his command. Normally she would have chastised herself for being so servile, but her curiosity was piqued and she needed to know what had surprised him. 'What's wrong? What's the matter?'

He held the binoculars out to her as she neared him. 'Look at the port,' he said. 'There's a dirty blue jeep there. Do you recognise it?'

Emily snatched the glasses from his hand and trained them towards Enoba. But the roll of the boat and a lack of familiarity with binoculars made it difficult, and she could not find the vehicle he meant. 'Where?' she demanded.

'What are you talking about, darling?' Laura wanted to know. 'I thought all jeeps were a dirty blue colour. Why is this one so special?'

Emily finally focused the lenses on the jeep. 'It's Roderick's,' she gasped softly. 'He's in Enoba.'

'I'm right, aren't I?' Captain Wilde said triumphantly. 'I thought I recognised the damned thing.'

'What are you two talking about?' Laura demanded.

'That's the hired jeep my fiancé was driving,' Emily explained.

'The one that nearly ran me over in Port Maga,' Captain Wilde added. 'I told you. It was being driven by a mad bitch.' He shook his head, amazed that the vehicle was there.

'I wonder why they're in Enoba?' Emily whispered.

'I just hope that woman's had some driving lessons on the way down here,' Captain Wilde grumbled. 'We may be sailing through the middle of nowhere, but even here they take a dim view of lunatics who mow down innocent pedestrians.'

Laura stroked her husband's arm affectionately. 'Darling,' she whispered. 'You are neither innocent, nor pedestrian.'

He smiled fondly at her and placed a gentle kiss on the corner of her mouth. 'Excitement over,' he decided. 'Back to your chores, Emily.'

Emily stayed where she was. She stared at him meekly and said, 'May I go ashore at Enoba?' She glanced down at his feet as soon as she had made the request, knowing that he would be angry with her.

157

'Shore leave?' he demanded.

'Do you want to leave us?' Laura asked quietly.

Emily shook her head. 'I don't want to leave you. I just want a couple of hours to try and find my friends and see what's wrong.' It was easier to talk to Laura, she thought. The woman had a kinder disposition and, even though she could be just as demanding as Captain Wilde, Emily considered her to be more approachable. 'I still don't know why Judy deserted me in Port Maga,' she explained. 'I'd like to find out at least that much.'

Captain Wilde made a disgusted sound in the back of his throat. 'It'd be the last we ever saw of you.'

Emily shook her head. 'No. I promise. I'll come back. You have my word. I'm travelling with you all the way to Havalaña.' She stared earnestly into his face, hoping he could see how honest she was being.

'We should let her go,' Laura said quietly. 'It's her decision as to whether or not she comes back.'

'I will come back,' Emily said quickly. 'I just need to find out what's happening with Roderick and Judy.'

Captain Wilde stared from one woman to the other, not bothering to mask his contempt. The smile that surfaced on his lips was like the hungry leer of a shark. If she had not been so determined to get his permission, Emily would have shied away from the expression.

'I have an idea,' Captain Wilde said suddenly.

Emily held her tongue, knowing better than to answer back to the man.

'Laura wants to let you have time ashore; I don't. It's fairly simple. I think this calls for a challenge.'

Emily stifled a groan of resentment. Over the past four days she had come to know the captain's challenges too well. She remembered Dawn being tied to the wheel while the captain and Laura challenged one another to try and beat her off course.

Whilst she cringed from the memory, Emily recalled that she had been subjected to one of the captain's challenges the previous evening. He had maintained that Dawn could fit more wine up her vagina than Emily. Laura had said Emily would be able to hold more. The two women had been forced to lay on their backs with their legs in the air while Laura and the captain poured chilled Chianti into them.

As a forfeit, the losing slave had to drink all of the wine that the winner had held. Emily's head still throbbed with the remnants of a mild hangover.

Every day had been made special by one of the captain's challenges, and Emily shrank from the prospect of enduring another. Determined to get ashore, she put her doubts aside and stared levelly at him.

'What's the challenge?'

He grinned. 'As I said, it's fairly simple. You want to go ashore. I say no, Laura says yes. Laura and I will take you below deck now. You have to make us come. If Laura comes first, you get your shore leave. If I come first, you have to stay, agreed?'

Laura smiled at her husband. 'You really do have the wickedest imagination.'

Emily stared at the pair of them, simultaneously repulsed and excited. Whatever it took, she had to get off the boat and on to the shore when they reached Enoba. It was not simply a matter of finding Roderick and Judy. A plan was forming at the back of her mind that was so perfect she dared not concentrate too heavily on it. If either the captain or Laura had suspected the nature of her thoughts, Emily knew they would never allow her to leave the *Amazon Maiden*. There was no chance that she would have refused the captain's offer of a challenge. 'If I please Laura first, I can go ashore?' she asked.

Laura exchanged a glance with the captain. 'The girl's eager,' she said. 'I think I'm in for a lot of pleasuring.'

Captain Wilde seemed quietly confident. 'Let's go to your cabin, honey,' he told his wife.

She nodded her enthusiastic assent and he led the way. Emily and Laura followed quickly in his wake.

In the cabin, the captain and Laura quickly undressed.

Seeing them naked, Emily had to concede that they were an impressive pair. The captain's body was broad and muscular, coated with a dark tan that suited his swarthy complexion. The dark thatch of pubic curls around his rigid member looked disturbingly inviting, and she desperately wanted to trace her fingers through the hair.

Laura inspired Emily's arousal just as much. Her large breasts heaved softly with mounting excitement. Emily glanced at the pale patch of fluffy blonde curls between her legs, tempted by the sight. She stared from one to the other, not sure what she should be doing.

'You'd better take that rubber suit off,' Laura said practically.

'She'll only be putting it back on once I've climaxed,' Captain Wilde said dourly.

Laura helped her out of the rubber suit in spite of her husband's words. Deliberately, her fingers stroked at Emily's naked body as she removed the garment. She paused over Emily's breasts, her fingers caressing the sensitive flesh before she tugged the rubber over them. As she helped, Laura stepped closer, pressing the cool flesh of her naked body against Emily's.

Emily shivered excitedly. Free of the rubber suit, her hands began to eagerly explore Laura's body. She cupped the huge mounds of her orbs and kneaded them tenderly with her splayed fingers.

Laura sighed softly, already excited by the soft caress of Emily's hands.

'Not fair!' Captain Wilde declared loudly. 'Get on the bed, honey,' he commanded. 'If this is to be a proper challenge, it needs to be done fairly.'

'Of course, darling,' Laura replied, a sly smile twisting

her lips. She jumped lithely on to the bunk and sat at the head. Her legs were wide apart and Emily could see the pouting lips of her sex. They were already glistening with moisture and she found herself hungering to taste the woman's wetness. Without waiting to be asked or commanded, she climbed on to the bunk and pushed her tongue against the delicious folds of Laura's sex.

Laura moaned excitedly.

Spurred on by her enjoyment, Emily stroked her tongue slowly against the labia before pushing her tongue deep into the sweet tasting cleft.

'That's it,' Laura encouraged. 'Keep doing that and I'll be coming ashore with you.'

Emily giggled, pleased by the way things were progressing.

Her mirth stopped when she felt Captain Wilde's hands on her backside. She was kneeling on the bed, her face buried in Laura's pussy. Her arse was high in the air so that the captain could do with it as he pleased. The puckered ring of her arsehole and the moist pout of her sex were both available to him. Emily realised distantly she was not just displaying them to him, she was offering herself willingly. The sense of humiliation this thought inspired was enough to make her nipples stand hard with excitement.

He caressed the cheeks of her arse with a fondness that bordered on delicacy. Emily was surprised by how subtle his touch could be. The flats of his palms tenderly stroked the silky flesh of her backside. His thumbs intruded gently on the hyper-sensitive flesh of her inner thighs, but there was no urgency to take or dominate her.

Responding to the subtlety of his touch, Emily shivered. Excitement was building inside her and she marvelled at the easy way the man was arousing her. He was a skilled lover, and she had to admit that he had surprised her with his knowledge of her body over the past few days. Even though she did not particularly like

161

him, she could not have wished for a more adept partner in bed.

The captain's thumbs edged ever closer to the heat of her sex while his hands caressed her arse.

With her tongue stroking and licking at Laura's pussy, Emily felt a thrill of pleasure wash over her. She did not know if she could make Laura climax before the captain, but she felt certain that neither of them would orgasm before she did. Remembering her resolution to get off the boat, Emily tried to ignore the man behind her and his deft, intrusive fingers. She concentrated her efforts on Laura's pussy and stroked the tip of her tongue against the woman's clitoris.

Laura shivered and groaned simultaneously.

Emily moved her mouth away from Laura's sodden hole and lifted her head to the woman's face. She was graced by Laura's smile and she kissed it, softly at first.

Laura returned the kiss passionately. Her tongue worked its way into Emily's mouth and the two women enjoyed a furious, heated embrace. Emily moved her hand between Laura's legs and began to tease the wet folds of flesh with the tips of her fingers. She tried to make the movement casual and unhurried, but her eagerness betrayed her. Before she could stop herself, she was sliding her index finger into Laura's hot wet channel and using her thumb to rub hard against the woman's clitoris.

Laura moved her mouth away from Emily's and tilted her head back with pleasure. 'Oh God! Yes!' she whispered excitedly. Her hands caressed Emily's breasts, brushing softly over the hardened buds of her nipples.

Behind her, the captain was not idle. His hands had continued to trace soft circles against the silky smooth flesh of her arse cheeks. Each orbit of his palms had brought his thumbs closer to the heat of her sex. Though she was trying fervently to ignore the pleasure he gave her, Emily could not lock it from her mind completely.

His fingers were a whisper away from the lips of her pussy, teasing the dark, wiry hairs with each passing movement.

There was a formidable strength in his hands. She had been held by him before and knew that his grip could prove inescapable. But there was also a gentleness to his touch that she found breathtakingly exciting. It was the duality of an iron fist in a velvet glove, she thought. He was inflexible, cold and ruthless, but in moments like this he seemed capable of infinite tenderness.

His fingers brushed firmly against the swell of her sex.

Emily shivered. Unconsciously, she raised her arse higher for him, eager to feel the touch of his fingers on a more intimate level. She moved her mouth away from Laura's and lowered it to one eager breast. The nipple jutted forward for her and she wrapped her lips around it, sucking gently on the tip.

Laura groaned as Emily pushed her fingers deeper into her heated wetness. Her thumb continued to draw impatient circles over the hard ball of Laura's clitoris. She groaned delightedly as Emily teased her tits with her tongue, lost in a world of glorious gratification.

'You sound close,' Captain Wilde observed.

Laura smiled at him. 'I am,' she told him breathlessly.

'You look beautiful that way, honey,' he said. Without another word he placed his hands on Emily's hips and held her tight.

Emily braced herself for the thrust of his entry. She could feel the swollen head of his prick pressing against the moist lips of her sex and she knew he was about to plunge his cock into her. He was well-built, and in this position Emily felt certain his cock would not just fill her, it would stretch her to the limit.

She tried to wriggle her hips away from him, but his grip was resolute. He held her tight and then pulled her slowly on to his length.

As the huge cock filled her aching pussy, Emily

muttered a small groan of elation. She could feel the throbbing pulse of her arousal scream with delight. Her pussy was incensed by the dull friction of his cock riding in and out. A bubble of pleasure rose within her so quickly she felt lost for breath.

Valiantly, she tried to continue sucking Laura's nipples. He was pulling her away from the woman and Emily wanted to protest. However, the euphoria he created between her legs was a pleasure she did not want to forsake. She tried to keep her fingers inside Laura's pussy, aware that she was bringing her close to an inevitable climax.

Captain Wilde continued pulling her back towards him.

As her hand slipped away from Laura's heated wetness, Emily realised she was on the verge of climax. She saw that the captain was stopping her from pleasing his wife but for the moment that did not seem to matter. The only thing that was important to her was the pleasure Captain Wilde was delivering to her hot, aching pussy.

'Kiss me, Emily,' Laura insisted. There was a petulant undercurrent to her words that Emily barely noticed from the plateau of joy she had reached. She stared at the woman through heavy-lidded eyes. As Emily watched, Laura parted her labia and rubbed an encouraging finger over the nub of her clit. 'Kiss me here, Emily,' Laura pleaded. 'You know you want to.'

Emily realised Laura was right. The need to taste her succulent juices was so overwhelming it was impossible to ignore. Trying not think of the divine joy she was receiving from the captain's cock, she lowered her head to Laura's pussy and began to lick it. The woman was drenched with excitement and Emily was intoxicated by the heady fragrance of her musk. She licked and teased the blonde's sex into a frenzy, drinking greedily from the incessant flow of Laura's juices. All the time, Captain

164

Wilde's cock pounded between her legs, filling her to the limit, then pulling out so that she felt drained and empty.

She moved her hands to Laura's erect nipples and teased them between her fingers.

Laura gasped and placed her hand on Emily's head, pressing her mouth hard against her sex.

Behind her, Captain Wilde reached forward and grabbed Emily's hair, pulling her back. For a moment, Emily felt as though she were the rope in a game of tug-of-war. She resisted the captain, feeling sure that if she tilted her head back and pushed herself on to him he would climax. His cock was riding her furiously hard and she knew that his climax was imminent. Each time he pushed into her, she could feel the tension mounting in his balls. His thick cock twitched in anticipation, and Emily knew he was on the verge of coming.

She pushed her head down, unmindful of the scream of pain that erupted from her pulled hair. Forcing her mouth on to Laura, she pressed her tongue flat against the thrust of her clitoris.

Laura bucked her hips forward and rubbed the mound of her pelvis against Emily's mouth. As she did this, she screamed euphorically. Her eyes rolled back and she bucked her hips unconsciously. A small golden spray of delight spurted from between the lips of her sex.

Emily felt the spray splash her nose and face and smiled triumphantly. Licking greedily at Laura's satisfied pussy, she pushed herself on to the captain's cock and felt him shoot deep and hard inside her. The thrill of his orgasm was enough to trigger her own and she yelled happily as the waves of pleasure coursed through her. He continued to shoot his seed into her; each twitch of his cock excited another wave of joy. His hands held her tightly as he climaxed and Emily realised he was pulling her further on to his length. It felt as though he were trying to skewer her with his mammoth cock.

Eagerly she pushed herself on to him, happy to accommodate as much of his divine length as her body would allow. She had closed her eyes, savouring each moment of pleasure in the delightful world of darkness that was always behind her eyelids. When she eventually opened them, she found Laura was staring at her, a smile of obvious appreciation twisting her lips. Her fingers were in her lap, and she was toying idly with the tender lips of her sex as she spoke.

'You've certainly earnt your shore leave,' she said, her words soft and breathless.

Emily smiled gratefully, squeezing her inner muscles tightly around Captain Wilde's shaft as he withdrew.

'Will you be returning?' Laura asked quietly.

Emily smiled and reassured her with a nod. 'I've promised I'll return,' she said. 'And I always keep my promises.' Besides, she thought darkly. I still have unfinished business aboard the *Amazon Maiden*.

Laura nodded and moved her hand from the cleft between her legs. 'Take whatever you want from my wardrobe,' she said. 'We'll leave you to get cleaned up and prepared for Enoba.'

Laura summoned her husband, and the pair then left Emily alone.

She showered quickly and towelled herself dry with even greater haste. Time had lost all meaning while the three of them had been enjoying one another, but Emily knew they must be close to the port. While she did not doubt that she would be allowed two hours shore leave, Emily did not want to waste a moment of it. The plan she had been forming over the past four days was starting to fall into place, and she was praying that she could make things work in her favour from now on.

She selected a smart bottle-green suit from Laura's wardrobe, attracted by the notion of power-dressing. Glancing idly through the drawers of the cabinet, she came across a length of chain and a padlock. There was a loop of metal attached to the chain and a key sitting in the hole of the padlock. Staring at it, Emily realised this was a contraption just like the one Vincent wore. She had no idea why Laura might possess a second one and not enough time to even contemplate it. Shaking her head, Emily closed the drawer and dismissed the device from her thoughts.

She checked her appearance in the mirror before leaving the room and was surprised to see the confident, striking woman who smiled back at her. Snatching a pair of sunglasses from Laura's bedside cabinet, she checked her reflection wearing shades. The effect was far more imposing and austere; she grinned broadly. This was the image she needed. She stepped happily from the room.

'You look sensational, darling,' Laura said, admiring Emily as she stepped through the main hatch.

Emily grinned. 'It does look good; thanks for lending it to me.'

'Not at all,' Laura said. 'And here.' She pushed a wad of crisp notes into Emily's hand. 'Don't refuse them and embarrass me,' Laura told her, seeing the hesitancy on Emily's face. 'You'll need some money while you're on shore. What you don't spend, you can give me back when you return.'

Emily nodded, touched by the woman's thoughtfulness.

'We're still five minutes away,' Captain Wilde said gruffly. 'Do you want to take a look at the jeep again now we're closer?' He held out the binoculars for Emily, not expecting her to refuse.

'You're both being very kind to me,' Emily said, touched by their unexpected gallantry. 'I'm sure I don't deserve so much kindness.'

'So am I,' Captain Wilde said sourly. 'But, please, look anyway.'

Emily grinned at his good-natured rudeness and took

167

the glasses from his hand. The port was so close now she could make out figures on the dock. The jeep was still visible, and after a moment's fumbling with the controls on the binoculars she could make out the characters on the registration plate.

It confirmed what she and the captain had both thought. This was Roderick's car. She was reading the letters of the number plate slowly to herself when her vision was interrupted by a couple moving in front of the bonnet. 'Shift,' she muttered rudely. A thought occurred to her and she moved the lenses up a fraction so that she could see the faces of the people blocking her view.

With his familiar ponytail and open, honest features, Roderick was an easy person to recognise, even at this distance. Emily felt a heavy weight lift off her chest, and her lips broke into a broad, eager smile. Her fiancé was there, waiting for her at the dock. The thought was liberating and she bit back the urge to cry out his name and wave excitedly to him. He was still far away and she doubted he would be able to notice her aboard the *Amazon Maiden*.

She kept the binoculars trained on Roderick's face long enough to see a woman's hand slide around his shoulder.

A snake of doubt uncurled itself in the pit of her stomach. Her fears intensified when she saw Roderick turn, his lips pouting into a soft kiss.

Emily put the binoculars down, her heart suddenly feeling heavier than ever before. She did not need to train her binoculars on the couple to know Roderick was kissing Judy. She had seen enough to realise that the pair were not just enjoying a platonic kiss either. The intimacy in their embrace had transcended anything platonic. Although Emily did not want to believe what she was seeing, she knew the couple were now lovers.

'Is everything all right?' Laura asked, concerned by the frown on Emily's lips.

Emily nodded, grateful for the dark glasses which were now concealing the tears welling up in her eyes. 'Everything's fine,' she said, careful to make the words sound normal. She released a ragged breath of fury and glared angrily over the side of the boat.

It was time to amend her plans, she thought. Whatever else she had been intending to do, that would have to take second place. There was something more important to take care of first, she realised. Before she dealt with her other plans, she had to sort out the pair who had left her to the mercy of Captain Wilde.

Seven

'It won't be the same boat,' Judy told Roderick wearily.

He was straining his eyes as the boat neared. The sun was high and bright, making him squint awkwardly. 'I think I can make out the name on the hull,' he said, ignoring Judy's doubts. 'I'm sure it's the Amazon something.'

Judy sighed and glared spitefully at Roderick's back. She wanted to get him away from the port and into Enoba. Though he had agreed to marry to her, there was nothing official yet. She wanted him to take her to a jewellery shop and get her an engagement ring. That would be a start. That would put some authenticity into their relationship. She had given the town's few shops a cursory glance when they arrived and she doubted any of the jewellers would even stock diamonds. She was certain there would be nothing that contained the number of carats she wanted.

'It's hot here, isn't it?' Judy said quietly, trying another tactic. 'Why don't we wait in the shade at the café over there?' She pointed towards one of the small, tatty buildings that enjoyed a view of the riverside.

Roderick shook his head. 'You go and wait there,' he said. 'I'll join you as soon as I've spoken to the people on board this boat.'

Judy sighed and stood beside him. If Emily was on board the boat, she needed to be with Roderick when he spoke to her. After Port Maga, Judy doubted the woman would be too happy with her, and she would need to defend herself from whatever version of the truth Emily came out with. Standing on the port, watching the boat come nearer, she dismissed the threat of impending problems and considered Roderick instead. They made a splendid couple, she thought. As they had walked this morning, she had caught sight of their reflection in a handful of shop windows and thought how suitably matched they were. He was still wearing jeans and a sweat shirt. It seemed like all he had packed in his wardrobe. She was dressed in a mini-skirt with stockings, high-heels and a tight silk blouse that accentuated her petite breasts. She knew it was not the ideal clothing for an equatorial region, but it made her feel good to dress with that little more finesse than the rest of crowd.

The fact that they made such a fine-looking couple only enhanced her plans. The idea of being married to Roderick was exciting in its own way, but she intended to use it to full advantage. Simply hinting at marrying him could be enough to make her a wealthy woman when she got home. She savoured the notion warmly and turned her mind back to the current situation. Though this was only a small part of her plan, it was crucial she dealt with it properly.

The majestic prow of the boat slowed as it neared the jetty and Roderick caught the mooring warp that was thrown to him. He tied it quickly and glanced up at the deck. 'Ahoy!' he called.

'Ahoy yourself,' the dark-haired man called down. 'Can I help you, son?'

Roderick swallowed. 'I'm looking for my . . .' He paused and started again. 'I'm looking for a woman.'

'Then you shouldn't be hanging around a dock. You'll only meet sailors around here, and not everything they say about sailors is true.' The man laughed darkly at his own humour. His mirth increased when he saw the long-haired youth on the jetty blush profusely; the bellow of his laughter rang louder.

'We were all on holiday together,' Roderick explained. 'She went missing about three hundred miles down the river. I wondered if you'd given her a lift.'

'Are you talking about Emily?' the captain asked sharply.

'You know her?'

Judy closed her eyes. Had she been Catholic, she would have genuflected.

'You're right. I did give her a lift, but I dropped her off in Port Maga.' He stared poignantly at Judy. 'Didn't I see you while I was there?'

Judy glanced up at him, remembering the features of the arrogant dark-haired man who had been sauntering across the road when she was trying to speed out of town. 'You might have seen me,' she said nonchalantly. 'We were there for a while.' She could feel her heart beating fast with relief. She was delighted that Emily was not aboard the boat. Perhaps they would have to go back to Port Maga now, but the chances of finding Roderick's former fiancée were becoming more and more negligible.

'Come on, sweetheart,' she said, circling her arm around Roderick's waist. 'Why don't you thank the nice sailor and we'll get back to the hotel?'

'How long ago was this?' Roderick demanded.

Captain Wilde shrugged. 'It would be about four days ago,' he said. 'But you'll have to excuse me now. I have docking procedures to follow.'

Roderick nodded. 'Thank you for your time,' he said quietly. He allowed Judy to lead him down the jetty away from the *Amazon Maiden*.

'The bitch was calling him darling,' Emily said. She slammed her curled fist against the deck. 'I'm going to ring her fucking neck.'

172

'Get to the back of the queue,' Captain Wilde growled. 'If anyone is ringing that bitch's neck, I get first shot at it.' He rolled his eyes in disgust. 'How dare she call me a sailor? It makes me sound like fucking Popeye.'

'She called him darling,' Emily said, bewildered by the way things had changed. Tears of frustration and anger welled behind the dark lenses of her sunglasses.

'What's happening, Emily?' Laura asked. 'Why the charade? Why did you have us pretend we dropped you back at Port Maga?'

Emily shook her head. 'I'll explain it all to you some other time,' she said, working hard to keep her voice free from tears. 'I just didn't want them to see me getting off the boat.' Smiling reassuringly at Laura, Emily added, 'I'm fine now.'

Captain Wilde grunted dark laughter. 'I think you're more than fine.' Studying her face, a wry smile surfaced on his lips. 'I think those two have just made a dangerous enemy when they crossed you. Are you going to let them find out how big a mistake they've made.'

'Why, Captain Wilde,' Emily replied primly, 'I'm sure I don't know what you mean.' She placed her hands on his broad chest and pecked him gently on the cheek. An idea occurred to her and she smiled thoughtfully to herself. Turning to Laura she said, 'Before I leave, there's something I need to borrow.'

'Take whatever you want,' Laura smiled.

'What are you doing?' Judy demanded sharply.

They were back in their hotel room, at her suggestion, and she had thought they were going to spend the afternoon in bed together. It would not have been a bad way to spend the day, she reflected. Roderick had developed quite an appetite for bondage games, and she could have happily tied him up and played with him for hours on end.

Instead of undressing, he had thrown his suitcase on

to the bed and was hurling his clothes angrily into it. 'What does it look like I'm doing?' Roderick replied sharply. 'I'm packing. We have to get back to Port Maga.'

'Why don't we just find some local authorities and ask them to help?' Judy asked petulantly. She felt safe in suggesting this now. Wherever Emily was, Judy knew she was out of the way. There was no chance of her making her way back into Roderick's life before the end of the holiday. By the time they got back to England, it would be too late for her. 'The authorities will be better equipped to deal with a search,' Judy explained. 'And there are more English speaking people here in Enoba.'

He shook his head. 'That's too much like giving up,' he said. 'I'd never forgive myself if anything happened to her.'

Judy moved towards him and placed her hands on his shoulders. 'Which is why we should get in touch with the authorities. They can organise a search. They can sort things out for her. They can stop something from happening before it actually does happen.' She placed her head against his chest as she spoke. Her fingers began to slowly ease his shirt buttons open as she talked to him.

'I suppose you're right,' Roderick conceded eventually. 'They should be the ones looking for her.'

Judy nodded, reaching the waistband of his trousers with her cool fingers. 'We'll go and see the local police this afternoon,' she said. Whispering into his ear, she added, 'As soon as we've finished.'

'Finished what?' he asked, puzzled.

Judy reached behind him and pulled the suitcase from the bed. It fell to the floor with a heavy thud. Before the echo of the noise had disappeared, she was pushing him backwards so that he fell on to the soft mattress. His shirt was open and the sight of his lean, naked chest excited her.

'As soon as we've finished this,' Judy said, standing on the bed and towering over him. She grinned down at him, aware that he was trying to glance up her skirt as she stood above him. 'Are you trying to look at me?' she asked coyly. 'You're a dirty little bastard, aren't you?'

Lying on the bed, beaming up at her, Roderick shrugged. 'Perhaps I am,' he conceded. 'I didn't think you'd complain.'

She raised the hem of her skirt, revealing the dark edge of her stockings and a glimpse of milky white thigh. 'Is this what you were trying to see? Were you trying to see the tops of my stockings?'

He grinned. 'I might have been. Stockings excite me.'

Judy laughed at his openness. 'Really?' She sounded surprised. 'How much do they excite you?'

He swallowed eagerly, the bulge in his pants was growing noticeably. Judy knew that he had not particularly cared for her when his mother had first introduced them. She had seen the same disparaging look on his face that a lot of men gave her. He had considered her to be obvious, brash and uninteresting. Now, after less than a week of sharing intimacy, he was prepared to marry her. She congratulated herself on manipulating him so well.

'Do you want to kiss the tops of my stockings?' Judy asked. Her voice was a sultry whisper. 'Do you want to kiss the tops of my stockings while I'm wearing them?'

He nodded, not trusting himself to speak.

Slowly Judy raised her short skirt so that she had more room to manoeuvre. Her legs were on full display, as was the black gusset of her knickers. Aware that Roderick was smiling appreciatively up at her, Judy lowered herself on to his face. Roderick's hands caressed her silk covered legs and massaged the muscles of her calves, then her thighs. As she neared his mouth with her inner thighs, he delivered a series of small kisses to her through the sheer hosiery. They were each making soft, guttural sounds of approval, losing themselves in the glorious joy of their shared intimacy.

Judy allowed him to kiss her a while longer, enjoying his adulation as she towered over him. 'That's good,' she said quietly. 'You can do that a lot longer.'

He grinned up at her. 'When we make love,' he began slowly. 'Would you leave the stockings on?'

Judy smiled down at him as she shook her head. 'I can't do that,' she whispered. 'If I left them on, what would I use to tie you up?'

Groaning excitedly, Roderick began to kiss her thighs even more ardently.

Emily had rushed from the *Amazon Maiden*, determined to follow the pair. They had not returned to the jeep, and so she assumed they were staying in a hotel near to the port. She caught sight of them and stifled a feeling of outraged fury when she saw they were walking with their arms draped around one another. Glowering furiously behind the black lenses of her dark glasses, she strolled purposefully behind them and watched as they walked into a nearby hotel.

The pair were so involved with each other she knew she could have stood next to them as they got their key from the concierge. However, favouring a more subtle approach, Emily maintained a discreet distance in her pursuit. She could not see the number on the room key and she did not trust her luck to hold out if she followed the pair up the hotel stairs towards the bedrooms. It was sufficient for her to see that they only took one key.

As soon as the pair had left the lobby, Emily rushed towards the desk.

'Which room are they staying in?' she asked the receptionist, pointing towards the retreating couple. 'What number room?'

'*Scusé*?' the woman asked.

Emily groaned inside. 'English,' she began slowly.

'The English couple who you just passed a key to. What number are they staying in?' She struggled to repeat the question in a bastardised version of Italian, Spanish and French, but the woman was nodding understanding before she had finished.

'They are in room 312,' she said, speaking slowly. 'You want I call them?' She was reaching for a phone on the reception desk as she asked the question.

Emily placed a steadying hand on the woman's, stopping her before she could warn Roderick and Judy. 'Don't bother,' she said quietly, staring at the phone. Another idea occurred to her and she grinned broadly. 'Your telephones,' she began excitedly. 'Are they capable of international calls?'

The woman paused for a moment, her bottom lip jutting out uncertainly as she tried to make sense of Emily's question. 'Yes,' she said eventually. 'We have telephones. International calls are made from here.'

Emily could have kissed her. 'Do you have a fax?'

'Fax?' The receptionist frowned.

Emily held her breath, wondering if she had been hoping for too much.

'Yes. We have fax,' the receptionist said after a moment. 'But is only for the use of hotel guests. You understand? You want I call your friends?'

Emily placed her hand firmly on the telephone, stopping the woman from using it. 'I want one of the rooms next door to them,' she said slowly. 'Would one of them be free?' Again, she held her breath, hoping that the woman would say yes. If one of the rooms was vacant, she could start work on her plans straight away. The idea was so appealing she dared not dwell on it, knowing that success rested on the receptionist's answer.

'No,' the receptionist said with a frown. 'Neither of those rooms is free.'

Emily groaned in despair and glared angrily at the polished top of the desk.

'Each room costs forty-eight *Real*s a night,' the receptionist explained. 'You want room 311 or 313?'

Grinning broadly, Emily reached into her pocket and began to leaf through the money Laura had given her.

Roderick lay naked on the bed. Above him, Judy was still fully clothed. The crotch of her panties was soaked with a mixture of saliva and pussy juices as she writhed eagerly against his face. A groan of elation swept over her as she pushed the heat of her sex against his manly chin.

'Undress,' Roderick gasped. 'Please, undress.'

Judy giggled. She reached her arms across herself and tugged the blouse from her body. She wore a black bra that matched the rest of her lingerie. It contrasted with her wan flesh and Roderick growled his appreciation. 'Do you want me to take my skirt off?' Judy asked coyly.

Roderick nodded.

'Kiss me some more, and I might,' Judy told him.

Needing no further prompting, Roderick pushed his tongue against the sodden crotch of her panties. He stroked the tip against the fabric, tracing the outline of her lips with a gentle wet pressure. Her stockings rubbed softly against his cheeks with a subtle frisson that heightened his arousal. His cock was a solid pole of desire, eager for her touch.

Judy released her breasts from the bra she wearing. Playfully, she teased the flesh with her fingers while Roderick watched. Her nipples were already stiff but they hardened forcibly as her fingertips brushed against them. Reluctantly, she pulled herself away from Roderick and climbed from the bed.

He watched as she slid the skirt from her narrow hips. She stood before him in just her stockings and panties, aware of the profound effect she was having. Roderick's cock twitched eagerly between his legs and he reached out for her.

178

Judy pushed him back on to the bed with one stocking-covered toe. 'Wait for permission,' she said, a broad grin creasing her lips. She reached down and slowly began to unroll one of her stockings. Trailing the flimsy garment between finger and thumb, she dragged it slowly over his chest and neck, before moving it down towards his hardness.

Roderick shivered.

She drew the stocking around his cock and balls, watching him twist and writhe. His movements were so stilted and rigid, she thought he looked as though he had been tied to the bed already.

'Perhaps I should just tie your dick up?' Judy suggested, watching his excitement with an expression of delight. 'You'd love to feel one of my stockings tight around your dick, wouldn't you?'

Roderick's sigh of elation was enough of a response for her.

Judy rubbed a finger against the swell of her sex, surprised by the mounting excitement inside. Stroking her fingers along the length of his shaft, she was aware Roderick was eager to play. She smiled down at him and began to unroll the second stocking. 'Perhaps I just might tie you up like that,' she said thoughtfully. 'Perhaps I just might.'

Roderick released a heartfelt moan of excitement.

She teased the second stocking along his chest and saw his erection rage furiously. Judy grinned down at him, excited by his urgent need for her. She rubbed the sodden seat of her pants idly, enjoying the slow build up of her arousal. Staring down at his naked body, an idea occurred to her and she slowly stepped out of her pants.

Roderick grinned approvingly, enjoying the sight of her nudity.

She took off her knickers and quickly pulled them over his ankles. Before he could make a word of protest, she had pulled them over his hips. She thought he made a marvellous spectacle: lying beneath her, wearing her panties. The head of his long cock pushed above the waistband and his balls sat awkwardly against the crotch.

Roderick grinned down at himself, thrilled by the cool wetness of the gusset against his sac. He held his breath as Judy tugged the stocking free from the base of his shaft.

The sensation of the silk pulling slowly against him had to be an exciting threat, Judy thought. If she pulled too quickly or too sharply she could hurt him. Instead, her slow deliberate tugging on the stocking hardened his erection and triggered a dull, desperate pulse in his balls.

Judy climbed back on to the bed and circled the stocking around his wrist. With a frown of annoyance, she realised there was no suitable place on the bed-head to tie him. Thinking quickly, she tied the remainder of the stocking to his other wrist, securing his hands together.

Roderick smiled up at her. The retroussé nipple of her right breast hung just above his face. He flicked his tongue over the end and grinned as she shivered. 'This is different,' he said, glancing above his head at his secured wrists. 'Nice,' he added quickly, for fear she should misunderstand him. 'Very nice. But different.'

Judy nodded. 'No bed-head,' she explained. She turned around on the bed and shoved her pussy in his face as she tied his ankles with the other stocking.

Roderick licked greedily at the slick wet lips of her sex. He forced his tongue into her, and then pulled it out slowly. Tracing the length of her sodden labia, he teased her clitoris, then moved his mouth in the opposite direction. His tongue nestled above the ring of her arsehole and he pushed softly against it.

Judy moaned with soft delight. 'Keep doing that,' she whispered. 'Please keep doing that.'

He laughed, and pushed his tongue further inside her.

She squirmed lithely against him. His thick tongue filled her tightly puckered hole, stretching the sphincter so wide it was almost unbearable.

Remembering that she needed to concentrate on his pleasure, Judy leant forward. Using a single stocking, she tied his ankles so that his feet were pressed firmly together. She was unhappy that he was not secured to the bed. Bondage was always more fun when the victim was held in one place. She wriggled her arse cheeks against Roderick's face and considered the problem for a moment. Feeling the twitch of his erection against her stomach, she decided on the best way to hold him in one position. With a sigh of contentment, she moved her arse from Roderick's face and tugged her knickers away from his hips. She pulled them quickly down his legs until they reached his tied ankles. Rolling him over, Judy tugged the panties upwards, behind his back. The crotch of the panties held his ankles and this was what she wanted. She pulled the pants high, towards his tied hands, moving his arms down so that they met.

'What are you doing?' Roderick asked. His words were mumbled into the pillow, but Judy heard him clearly enough.

'I'm making sure that you're secure,' she told him firmly. She pushed the pants through his tied wrists, then pulled the legs of her knickers back over each of his hands. Smiling down at her handiwork, she realised that Roderick was now well and truly bound. His hands were held behind him, and unless he could see how he was trussed Judy knew he would not be able to release himself. She rolled him on to his back, aware that he must be uncomfortable with his arms and legs behind him.

The thought brought a cruel smile to her lips. 'Now for the blindfold,' she said, retrieving her bra from the floor.

'Do you have to do that this time?' Roderick asked plaintively. 'I love to see you. You really excite me.'

Judy grinned broadly. 'Yes,' she told him. 'It's part of the game, I don't want you to see what I'm doing.' She secured the bra over his face, fixing the straps tight at the back of his head.

'At least you won't be able to gag me this time,' Roderick said quietly.

'Won't I?' Judy replied, surprised by his belief. She climbed on to the bed and pressed the lips of pussy over his mouth. 'There you go,' she said quietly. 'You can use this as a gag for the moment. Just make sure you use it well.'

Emily moved her glass away from the wall. She had heard enough from the adjacent bedroom, and she knew that it was nearing the time to act. She reached for the pack of cigarettes she had bought at the reception desk and lit one thoughtfully. The actions she needed to take were painfully clear, and she had no intention of shying away from them. If she was being honest with herself, she was actually looking forward to step one of her plan. It was going to be fun to be the one wielding the cane this time.

She checked her pockets to make sure she had everything she needed and was satisfied with the bulge in her jacket.

She stubbed the cigarette out in the ashtray and nervously lit a second. As soon as I've finished this one, she told herself, I'll make my move. A nervous tremor of excitement sparkled inside her stomach.

There were five raps on the door in short, sharp succession.

'Who the fuck is that?' Judy snapped.

Beneath her, Roderick growled with frustration. 'Ignore it,' he whispered. 'If it's important, they'll call back when we've finished.'

Judy nodded and continued to slide the lips of her sex

over his face. She felt close to orgasm already. Judging by the way his cock was pulsing eagerly, she guessed that Roderick was also on the brink. He was right, she agreed. Whoever was out there could call back later if it was that important.

The knock at the door came again. Five raps, hard and quick. This time they were followed by the mumbled words 'room service'.

'Shit!' Judy exclaimed angrily.

'Have you ordered something?' Roderick asked curiously.

'No,' Judy snapped, stamping towards the door. 'They're probably wanting to change the sheets or something. If I don't answer them, they'll use a key to get in.'

'You'd better tell them to come back later,' he said from behind his blindfold.

'I wasn't going to invite them in to have a look at you,' Judy snapped sharply. She glanced around the room for an item of clothing she could cover herself with, to protect her modesty. Her discarded jacket was a short one and her skirt was too skimpy to cover her properly. She hesitated for a second, wondering what would be the best thing to wear.

The five raps came again, and she realised she did not have the time to get anything. She intended to hide behind the door and tell the woman from room service to fuck off. Aware that she had to move quickly if she wanted to save Roderick the embarrassment of being discovered bound and blindfold, Judy rushed to the door. She threw it open and began to babble an abrupt rebuke in Portuguese, telling the woman that she was busy.

Emily's hand pushed through the half-open doorway and grabbed a length of Judy's blonde hair. Her other hand followed it and clamped over Judy's mouth, effectively silencing her.

'Hello, Judy,' Emily whispered quietly. 'We're all right to talk now, aren't we?' She glanced disdainfully at the woman's naked body. 'I see you've got nothing on.'

Judy's eyes were wide with terror. She struggled to escape from Emily's grip, but panic and terror made her attempts ineffectual. Emily was holding her with cold, calm, ruthless determination.

'Come with me,' Emily said quietly. 'We need to talk. Alone.' Without waiting for a response, she pulled Judy from the room, dragging her naked into the main corridor. She released her hand from Judy's mouth and snatched the key from the inside lock of the door.

'I'm naked,' Judy hissed, placing her hands over her breasts and bare vagina. 'Someone might see me.'

Emily slammed the door closed and tightened her grip on Judy's hair. 'Most of England has seen you naked,' Emily said scornfully. 'I doubt it will matter if a handful of South American's get a glimpse of you.' Without another word, she tugged Judy along the corridor to her adjacent room. Judy stayed silent until she heard Emily slam the door behind them.

'What's the meaning of this?' she demanded. 'What the hell do you think you're doing to me?'

Emily slapped her across the face. Her blow was hard and flat. It cut Judy's words off abruptly. Still wearing the dark glasses, she looked imposing and unapproachable. Her lips were thinned with anger and she appeared to be in absolute control. 'It's pay-back time, Judy,' Emily said calmly. Again, her flat gaze took in Judy's naked body. This time, a wry smile twisted her thin lips. 'To be honest, you look like you're dressed to pay-back.'

'Where did you disappear to?' Judy asked quickly. 'In Port Maga, we were having coffee. You said you were going to the bathroom, then you just vanished. Where did you disappear to?'

Emily slapped her across the face again. 'No more lies,' she said. 'You ditched me in Port Maga. You even stole my luggage for a second time. I think it's time we were honest with one another. Don't you?'

Holding her bruised cheek, Judy nodded. She sat down on the bed and stifled a sob. She seemed to have forgotten her nudity. Fear and anxiety had taken over.

'Get a cigarette,' Emily said, nodding at the bedside cabinet. She watched as Judy lit herself a smoke, then sat down beside her. 'That was what gave you away,' Emily said quietly.

Judy stared sullenly at her.

'In Port Maga, you lit my cigarette with my cigarette lighter. I would never have suspected anything, but in the last few days I've given that a lot of thought. I remember putting my lighter back in my bag after I last used it. The only person who could have gotten hold of it was the person who stole that bag.'

'Prove it.' Judy glared at her. 'I'll say I borrowed it from you before you lost your bag. It's your word against mine.'

Emily reached a hand towards Judy's bare body. The woman shrank from her touch, fearful of more punishment. Instead, Emily caressed the soft small orb of her breast. Her fingertips traced the areola softly. Without warning, she pressed a finger on either side of the nipple and squeezed it hard.

Judy gasped, shocked by the sensation.

'No more lies,' Emily said quietly. 'You've just had my last friendly warning. I promise you, if I have to caution you again, you'll regret it.' She released the nipple slowly, aware that the nub had hardened beneath her touch. 'You liked that, didn't you?' Emily observed.

Judy looked away, her cheeks blushing furiously. 'What do you want? she asked angrily. She drew nervously on her smoke as she spoke. 'Why have you come back?'

Emily reached over and took the cigarette from Judy's shaking fingers. She ignored the blonde's nudity and the chill of gooseflesh that covered her naked body. 'I've come back for three reasons,' she began slowly. 'Revenge, revenge and revenge.'

Judy shivered next to her. 'What are you going to do to me?'

Emily shrugged. 'I haven't decided yet,' she said honestly. 'Although, if we're being honest, you can get yourself into enough trouble without my causing more for you. Does Roderick know you've been sleeping with his father?'

Judy reached for a second cigarette from the pack and lit it. There was a thoughtful frown creasing her forehead. 'I thought you knew about that,' she said honestly. 'That was one of the reasons why I had to get rid of you and become attached to Roderick. Before we went away, people might have believed you if you'd said things about Roderick's daddy and me. If we'd gone back home engaged and without you, it would have just sounded like sour grapes.'

Emily nodded. 'I suspected as much,' she said. 'The ironic thing is, though I suspected, I would never have told anyone, even if I'd known the truth.'

Judy shook her head. 'You say that now, but I know what people are like. If the chance ever arose when you could have used the information for your own benefit, you would have done.'

Emily stared at her levelly. 'I didn't used to be like that,' she said quietly. 'I've only changed over this last week.'

Judy glared at her but said nothing. She studied the end of her cigarette before glancing awkwardly at Emily. 'So how are you going to get your revenge on me?'

Emily smiled. 'I have to think about that yet,' she said softly. 'You're fairly low down on the list.'

'You want revenge on Roderick,' Judy asked, puzzled.

Emily's grin revealed nothing. 'He's lower on the list than you are. For now, I need the pair of you to help me.' She began to unbutton the jacket she wore. Beneath it she was naked.

'What do you want me to do?' Judy asked nervously. She stubbed her cigarette in the ashtray and stared into the impenetrable lenses of Emily's sunglasses.

Emily was grinning. She slipped the top from her shoulders, revealing her naked breasts. 'I'm glad you asked me that,' she quietly. 'I was wondering how to get around to it.' She teased the flesh of her own naked breasts and pushed one towards Judy. 'Suck my nipple,' she commanded softly.

Judy glared angrily at her. 'What if I refuse?'

Emily laughed. 'You're in no position to refuse,' she said cheerfully. 'You'll do everything I tell you, and we both know that.'

Judy graced her with a frown of the blackest hatred before moving her mouth slowly towards Emily's nipple. Her mouth stopped a moment as she was about to touch the other woman. 'If I do this properly, are you going to forgive me.'

Emily dropped her cigarette to the floor and stamped on it casually. Her grin widened as she stared into Judy's upturned face. 'My forgiveness won't come that easily,' she said. 'But I suppose it's something for you to hope for.'

Judy studied her hesitantly, then moved her mouth over Emily's nipple.

Emily gasped, excited by the touch of the woman's lips and tongue. She did not know if this was something Judy had done before, but her skill left Emily wondering. Judy gently suckled the breast, not concentrating on the nipple, but instead teasing the sensitive flesh of her dark brown areolae. She delivered gentle kisses to the orb before pressing her lips and tongue on to the eager hard nub of Emily's nipple.

Emily moaned. She buried her fingers in the hair at the base of Judy's neck and held her head tight against her breast. When she felt as though she had extracted enough pleasure from that breast, Emily pushed the woman's head roughly towards the other one.

Judy made a small sound of annoyance, but it was a half-hearted noise and Emily was not interested in her protestations. She held the woman against her, forcing her to lick and suck at the excited bud of pleasure. She was enjoying this a lot more than she had anticipated. Her intention had not been to have Judy do this to her. She had simply wanted to exert control over the woman before putting her real plans into action. However, the sight of Judy's naked body had inspired a thrill of excitement in her. All of this coupled with Emily's natural sense of adventure and her experiences of the past week had made the command inevitable.

This is what holding the cane feels like, she thought, enjoying the wealth of pleasure emanating from her breasts. It felt like the first time in days that her breasts had been tongued properly. On board the *Amazon Maiden* she had been pleased like this, but each morsel of joy was paid for with a greater degree of pain. The whippings, beatings and time with nipple clamps had all taken their toll on her. Now, Emily wanted to be pampered, and she was determined that Judy would do the job for her.

Relishing her position in the seat of power, Emily pushed Judy's head away and removed the suit's trousers. She pulled her panties off quickly and lay down on the bed.

'Go on,' she said flatly. 'Please me. You might just do it well enough for me to forgive you.' Seeing Judy hesitate, she grabbed a fistful of her hair and pulled the woman's face toward her pussy. 'You've run out of options, Judy,' she said quietly. 'Just do it.'

Judy obeyed. She buried her tongue in Emily's hole

and pressed her mouth against the lips. There was no delicacy or skill employed as she licked. Her tongue simply pressed flat against the heat of Emily's sex, occasionally prodding between the cleft.

Emily grinned tightly, surprised by the woman's lack of skill.

'Dear me, Judy,' she said, with a frown. 'You really are going to have to improve if you want to earn my forgiveness. You just can't lick pussy, can you?'

Between her legs, Judy probed her tongue deep inside Emily's lips. She pushed her hands on Emily's inner thighs and tried valiantly to tilt her head at a more comfortable angle. More by accident than by skill, the tip of her tongue caught Emily's clitoris. Emily barely noticed the enjoyable sensation that the touch inspired. She was extracting far more pleasure from dominating and humiliating the woman.

'Try licking my arsehole,' Emily suggested. 'Perhaps that's where your forte lies.' She raised her backside from the bed, pushing it towards Judy's face.

Judy paused unwilling to succumb to Emily's command. Reluctantly she flicked her tongue quickly against the woman's arse.

Emily shivered, her grin widening. 'That felt like a good start,' she told her encouragingly. 'Now do it properly.' She tightened her grip on Judy's hair and pushed her head down between her legs.

Judy rolled the tip of her tongue tentatively around the slick wet ring of her arsehole.

Emily groaned happily. Now the pleasure was beginning to feel as exciting as the thrill of being in control.

Judy moved her hands, spreading the cheeks of Emily's arse wide. She traced her tongue around the puckered rim a second time. The air was redolent with the heavy charge of excitement, and Emily could feel a change coming over Judy. The woman was obviously excited by the dark sensation of submission. As she plunged her tongue deep into the forbidden depths, Emily realised she had actually submitted to her.

Emily squealed delightedly. She could feel Judy's nose pressing against the cleft of her sex as her tongue pushed deeper in the taboo orifice. Revelling in the pleasure of her power, Emily felt the rush of orgasm sweep through her. She groaned delightedly, pushing Judy's face harder against her sex.

'Very good,' Emily said. She lifted Judy's head and smiled at her.

Judy was blushing furiously. Her cheeks were burning crimson and her eyes were cast downwards.

'I thought we'd find your forte,' Emily said. 'You did that better than I thought you would.'

'You made me do it,' Judy said, her words dull with emotion. 'Just don't make me talk about it.'

Emily moved her fingers to Judy's chin and lifted her head. As soon as they made eye contact, Emily kissed her. Their lips pressed together and Emily explored Judy's mouth with her tongue. She kissed the blonde with a ferocious passion. Her hand reached for Judy's breast and she squeezed cruelly hard. The tips of her fingers found the woman's nipple and she pressed the nub roughly.

Judy groaned softly. Her hand reached instinctively for Emily's body.

Emily stopped her fingers before they could connect. 'You're wrong, Judy,' she said quietly. 'I can make you talk about it if I want to. From now on, you're mine, and do you know what I find most exciting about that prospect?'

Judy glared at her sullenly and shook her head. 'No. What?'

Emily continued to tease the woman's breasts as she spoke. 'I like the idea that you want me to dominate you.'

Judy stared uncertainly into Emily's eyes. 'That's not true,' she said, her voice faltering. 'I . . .'

Emily applied a gentle pressure on the end of her nipple and Judy's words faded to a groan of delight. 'It is true, isn't it?' Emily whispered softly.

With her head against the other woman's shoulder, Judy nodded miserably.

'Good,' Emily said quietly. 'We understand one another. Now you can come with me.' She climbed off the bed and started to pull her clothes back on.

'Where are we going?' Judy asked.

'To see Roderick,' Emily explained. She fastened two buttons on her jacket and started towards the door.

'Wait!' Judy exclaimed. 'What about me? I have no clothes. What if someone sees me?'

Staring levelly into her eyes, she said, 'If a man sees you, I'll let him fuck you while I watch.'

Judy stared at her, uncertain as to whether Emily was serious or not. She could read nothing from the impenetrable depths of the sunglasses the woman wore but Emily knew the thin, cruel smirk on her lips left little doubt about her sincerity. Meekly, she followed Emily along the corridor and into the room she had shared with Roderick.

Emily could see a wave of dull relief wash over Judy when the door closed behind them, and she smiled. She knew the blonde's relief was tinged with a hint of disappointment. The idea of being humiliated had a dark allure that Emily herself had already learnt. When their eyes met, she realised Judy was staring at her with a newly acquired respect. It was a gratifying sight, and she took some pleasure from it.

Reminding herself that she had other things to do, Emily turned her attention to the bed. Roderick lay there, bound and blindfold. His arms and legs were tied behind his back, beneath him. His narrow chest looked broader in this position and his cock stood hard and proud.

'Judy? Is that you?' he asked. 'Who was at the door? Why did you take so long?'

Emily turned to Judy and put her finger to her lips.

Judy nodded and stayed silent. On Emily's instruction she walked over to the bed and stood next to Roderick. From the bedside, Judy clearly could not stop herself from watching Emily undress.

Dropping her jacket and trousers to the floor, Emily stood proud and naked and made her way over to the bed. She kept the dark glasses on, unwilling to let her eyes reveal her emotions to either of the pair. Admittedly, Roderick was blindfolded, but Emily did not intend to keep him that way for ever. She nodded at Judy and pointed at Roderick's stiff cock.

Aware of what was expected of her, Judy placed her hand on Roderick's length and squeezed it hard.

Roderick moaned with appreciation. His cock hardened in her hand and he shivered beneath her touch. 'Judy, that feels fantastic,' he gasped. 'I knew it was you.'

Emily's lips curled into a sneer of contempt. She was aware that Judy was watching her and she stared back indifferently. Gesturing silently, she encouraged the blonde to use both hands on Roderick.

Judy did as she was asked, working Roderick's stiff length between her fingers, rubbing both hands up and down his erection.

'That's it,' Roderick encouraged her. 'Yes, yes. That's it!'

Emily knelt down beside him and ran a finger over Roderick's chest. His excitement was so intense that he did not seem to notice there were three hands playing with his body. When Emily placed her fingers around his nipple and gently squeezed the soft bud of flesh, he did not seem to notice the fourth hand.

'God yes!' he exclaimed. 'That's it.'

Emily pressed her mouth to his breast and bit hard.

Every muscles in Roderick's body seemed to contract simultaneously with the explosion of exquisite pain. His cock twitched furiously in Judy's hands and he shook his head from side to side, lost in his own world of captive pleasure. Emily moved her mouth away from his chest and stared sullenly down at his bound body.

'Why didn't I meet you years ago,' he murmured softly.

Emily tugged the blindfold from his eyes. 'Because you met me first,' she said flatly. 'That's why.'

Roderick stared helplessly at her. His gaze took in her nudity and a lascivious smile twisted his lips before he could stop it. 'Emily? What the hell are you doing here? Where have you been?'

With a sneer of disdain, Emily pushed the bra in Roderick's mouth. 'Be quiet,' she said absently. 'I'm not in the mood to talk with you.' She snapped her fingers at Judy and gestured for her to move away. Reaching for her jacket, she removed the chain and padlock she had borrowed from Laura's cabin and started fastening them around Roderick's balls. The contraption was easier to manipulate than she had imagined, and within a minute Emily had secured his testicles. She fastened the padlock tight against him, then dropped the key back into her jacket pocket.

'What is that?' Judy asked.

Emily smiled. 'It keeps him hard, until I want him to stop being hard. It's going to be his first taste of servility.'

Roderick's eyes widened in protest. He struggled against the bindings at his wrist and ankles but Judy had tied him securely.

Staring at the bright light of panic that glinted in his eyes, Emily knew that he was worried. The thought warmed her. She looked down on him without disguising her disgust. Her fingers casually stroked the end of his cock, then she held it tight.

Roderick swallowed nervously and stared up at her. The bra was still stuffed in his mouth, making speech impossible. Like many men, Emily knew he would have sold his soul to have two naked women in the bedroom with him, especially herself and Judy. She realised they were both attractive with divine, desirable bodies. Judy had discovered his one personal fetish when she first tied him to the bed. She supposed that if he had thought about it before, the idea of having her and Judy fuck him whilst he was bound and gagged would have been his ultimate fantasy. She watched as he shook his head from side to side, as though he was trying to wish the fantasy away.

The pulse between his legs beat hard, restricted by the tight chain that Emily had fastened around him. She continued to hold his cock as she climbed on to the bed, guiding it against the cleft of her sex.

Judy watched Emily with a salacious smile on her lips. She stared into her face as she sat on Roderick's cock.

With deliberate slowness, Emily began to ride up and down Roderick's length.

She stared down at him, allowing his cock to fill her, then tugging it to the brink of her pussy lips. Repeatedly, she pushed herself down on him, watching his face contort with panicked pleasure.

'Take that bra from his mouth and let him lick you,' Emily told Judy.

Judy moved quickly. She heard Roderick begin to mumble a protest, but she silenced him by pressing the lips of her sex over his mouth. Smiling broadly, she faced Emily as Roderick pushed his tongue deep inside her.

As Emily rode up and down Roderick's cock, she played thoughtfully with Judy's breasts. Her fingers squeezed and stroked the woman's orbs, concentrating on her hard, urgent nipples. Glancing sternly into Judy's face, she leant forward and kissed the woman.

Judy gasped, surprised. The tips of her nipples hardened with the depth of her arousal. She smiled uncertainly into the dark shades over Emily's eyes.

194

Emily's face was inscrutable. Moving her mouth to Judy's ear, she kissed the tender flesh beneath the lobe and ran her tongue against the soft invisible hairs above her jaw-line. 'Remember, Judy,' she whispered softly. 'You're mine now. I can do with you as I please.'

In spite of her words being whispered, there was a note of iron in her voice that Judy could not miss. She stared unhappily at Emily and nodded her acquiescence. After a moment, an impulse spurred her to kiss Emily's mouth.

Riding Roderick's cock, Emily allowed the kiss to happen. She slid herself from him and snapped her fingers for Judy's attention. 'Suck him,' she said sternly. 'I want to talk to him.'

Judy obeyed without question. She raised her pussy away from Roderick and went to the bottom of the bed so she could get his organ close to her mouth. She tongued his length clean of Emily's wetness, savouring the mixture of tastes and enjoying a feeling of lurid arousal. When she had removed the last trace of Emily's pussy juice, she began to suck the swollen end of his erection. At the same time, she teased his tethered balls with her fingers.

Emily straddled Roderick's mouth and stared down at him. Only the top half of his face was visible, his mouth was buried deep within the heat of her cleft. His eyes were open wide and he was studying her warily as he licked the slickness from the lips of her sex.

'You do realise that I'm very angry with you, Roderick, don't you?'

He nodded. His tongue continued to tease her, but his eyes stayed fixed on her face.

Emily smiled to herself, aroused by his touch. 'Are you enjoying what Judy's doing to your cock?' Emily asked softly.

Roderick paused and Emily could read his thoughts in his open expression.

He was clearly worried to say yes considering her mood. He knew from past experience that she could be unpredictable and he would have never seen her in a darker mood than this. There was a volatile explosion welling within her and she did not doubt he could sense it.

He nodded slowly in response to her question. His nose pressed against the swell of her clitoris when he moved his head, exciting her even more.

'I'm glad you're enjoying it,' she said. 'And I'm surprised you haven't come yet. Judy seems to be making an awful lot of noise down there.'

Roderick frowned, aware that he should have climaxed by this point.

Emily grinned at his discomfort. Judy sounded to be doing an excellent job of fellating him, slurping noisily on his erection. The tense atmosphere of electric sexual excitement was so strong it was almost tangible. She knew from experience that he was not a great lover, and she could sense his bewilderment. He was in the control of two gorgeous naked women, one of them sucking his cock for all she could manage, and still he had not climaxed.

She smiled darkly into his puzzled frown. 'Perhaps I shouldn't be surprised,' Emily explained. 'After all, I was the one who tied your balls with the chain, wasn't I? Did I explain what that does?'

He moved his mouth away from her sex. 'You said it would keep my cock hard,' he told her.

Emily nodded and shifted her hips so that her sex was over his mouth again. She waited until he was drawing his tongue over the lips of her sex before she began to speak to him. 'That's right, it will keep your cock hard until I unfasten it.' She smiled coldly down at him, excited by the rising panic she could see in his eyes. 'If I put the padlock on the next link tighter, you'll remain hard no matter what I do to you. If I loosen it by one link, you'd be able to climax, and with a bit of effort you'd be able to piss.'

Roderick swallowed nervously. He looked as though he was about to protest; so she shifted her sex down on his mouth.

'I can be as cruel or as kind as you make me,' Emily told him. 'I just want your assurance that you'll be doing as I say from now on.' She moved the lips of her sex slightly away from him, allowing him the chance to respond.

'What have I done to make you treat me like this?' he demanded breathlessly.

'Do you really need to ask?' Emily replied sourly. She thrust her backside back over his mouth, so that he couldn't interrupt her as she spoke. 'You leave me alone, stranded and penniless in the middle of a foreign country. Then, instead of looking for me, you spend your time tied to hotel beds whilst you fuck the brains out of your step-sister. Don't make me think about the things you've done to me with your behaviour,' she told him sharply. 'If I start to think about this last week, I'm just going to get angrier and angrier.' She paused and forced herself to calm a little. Smiling harshly down at him, she added, 'You wouldn't want me to get angry right now, would you? You might discover a cruel person beneath this frail feminine exterior.'

Roderick studied her with an apprehension that bordered on terror. His tongue continued to run over the lips of her sex, teasing the delicate folds of her musky lips. His nostrils were filled with the sweet scent of her arousal and his lips and cheeks were spattered with the sticky remnants of spilt pussy juice.

Emily could feel his heart beating furiously inside his chest, spurred on by a combination of excitement, arousal and fear.

'What do you want from me, Emily?' he asked carefully.

Emily smiled down at him. 'I want your servility,' she replied. 'I want your submission. I want your assurance that you'll do whatever I say, whenever I say it. After what you've put me through, I don't think that's too much to ask.'

Roderick stared up at her doubtfully.

Emily reached behind herself and placed her fingers around Roderick's length. She could feel Judy's mouth dancing up and down on the end of his cock and she squeezed his rigid his shaft hard between her fingers.

Roderick moaned.

'Tell me you're not enjoying it, Roderick,' Emily urged him. She pushed herself on to his mouth and rubbed the tip of her clit furiously against his lips. 'Tell me you're not enjoying this punishment, and I'll release you now and let you fuck off back to your precious England. Once you're there, I won't screw over your life by telling everyone how you dumped me in the middle of a rain forest so you could fuck your step-sister.' She glanced over her shoulder and studied Judy angrily. 'I won't even mention Judy and your father,' she told him. 'That will be a secret between the three of us. All you have to do is tell me that you're not enjoying it.'

As Judy trailed her tongue against the sensitive flesh of Roderick's glans, Emily continued to wank him and forced him to lick her sex.

'But I think you are enjoying it,' she said quietly.

Roderick stared miserably at her.

'I think you're enjoying it a lot more than you dare admit, even to yourself. If that's the case, I think you should admit it now. It will help get our new relationship off on the right footing.'

Roderick nodded. 'I am enjoying it,' he whispered.

Emily stopped her grin from becoming too wide. 'That's good,' she said encouragingly. 'And you agree to submit to me?'

He nodded again.

Emily held her breath, waiting for him to say the words. She was holding the base of his cock hard in her hand, as though she was trying to squeeze a response from him. The seconds ticked slowly by and she realised Judy too had stopped sucking Roderick's cock as she waited for his reply.

Roderick stared at her. Emily had made it obvious that if he wanted to enjoy this sort of sex again he only had one option. She knew she had left him without choices, a fact confirmed by the triumphant smile on her face. 'I agree,' he said quietly. 'I agree to submit to you.'

Emily released his cock from her fingers and climbed off the bed. She slapped his cheek playfully and went to her jacket. Retrieving the key from the pocket, she went back to Roderick's cock and released the padlock from his balls.

Roderick sighed heavily with gratitude. The pulse in his cock was a furious drumbeat and he could feel himself nearing climax with the sensation of relief alone.

Emily pushed Judy's head away from the tip of Roderick's cock and straddled his length. She pushed herself heavily on to his shaft and groaned happily with pleasure. It only took a few moments of riding him before she felt the familiar waves of pleasure sweeping over her. The rush of orgasm came as a climactic flood of joy. A scream of triumph broke her lips and she writhed and bucked her hips against him.

Emily's pleasure was too great for Roderick to contend with. Her inner muscles clamped against him so ferociously he could not hold off his own climax any longer. The seed shot from the base of his balls in a white hot explosion of delight.

Emily continued to ride him until she felt sure he was completely spent. The aftermath of her orgasm was a soft ebb of exhilarating pleasure; she could have enjoyed it for the rest of the day. If she had not made more important plans, she would have been tempted to try

199

and enjoy it anyway. She slid herself from Roderick's failing member and began to fasten the chain around his balls again.

'What are you doing?' he murmured. 'You said ...' His voice trailed off when he saw the questioning frown on her brow. He did not need reminding that she had not mentioned releasing him.

Emily replaced her frown with a tight smile. She secured the padlock around the base of his balls and sat on the corner of the bed. Turning to Judy, she said, 'Lick my pussy clean. As soon as you've finished, I want to talk to the pair of you.'

Kneeling obligingly in front of her, Judy began to lick Roderick's come from the lips of Emily's sex.

Later, after Emily had dressed and Roderick had been released from his bondage, she explained what she wanted from them. 'I want you to check into the best hotel in Havalaña,' she explained. 'You both have your instructions and you know what to do. There's a fax machine downstairs in the lobby. You can make a start from there.'

'You won't be travelling to Havalaña with us?' Judy asked, puzzled.

Emily shook her head. 'I still have a few details to sort out before our meeting. Just make sure you contact those people I've said, understand.' She started towards the door, a confident spring in her step.

When she had left the *Amazon Maiden* it had been her intention to punish them far more harshly than she did. While she was in the hotel room she had forced herself to calm down her punishment. Roderick and Judy deserved a lot worse than Emily could give them in two short hours, and Emily was going to make sure they got it. In giving precedence to her plans for the captain and his contract, she had gone easy on the couple.

'What if you get to Havalaña and find we're not

there?' Roderick asked quietly. He was staring at her levelly and she knew he was searching for a note of weakness.

Emily smiled, intrigued by his defiance. She stepped back towards the bed where he sat and placed her hand on his length. His cock hardened to her touch and she teased his foreskin slowly backwards and forwards. 'You'll be there, Roderick,' she said calmly. 'And not just because you know I can fuck over your life back in England if you defy me.'

He tried to maintain his charade of insolent defiance but it was a difficult mask to keep up beneath Emily's austere frown. 'Why else?' he asked calmly. 'Why else do you think I'll be there?'

Emily grinned and held up the key to the padlock. 'You need to get to Havalaña so I can unfasten you,' she explained. 'I can't see you explaining your way through customs with that fastened to your balls,' she told him, glancing meaningfully at the padlock. 'And I don't think you'd trust yourself with a wire cutter.' She moved her hand away from his cock and slapped his face hard.

'Now remember, Roderick, I'm in charge. No more defiance. I only want your submission.' She graced the pair of them with a smile and made her way quickly to the door of the hotel room. Waving cheerfully, she paused on her way out and said, 'I'll see you both tomorrow, in Havalaña.' A dark frown crossed her brow and she added, 'Fuck up my instructions, and you'll both be in trouble.' The expression disappeared before it could be properly seen. She grinned again and stepped through the door into the hotel corridor. 'Have a nice journey down there,' she told them.

Eight

Emily stepped over the rails and steadied her feet on the deck of the *Amazon Maiden*. She smiled, proud of herself at the easy way she had climbed on board, having found it a difficult and awkward task the last two times. This time it had felt like the most natural thing in the world.

'Son of a bitch,' Captain Wilde muttered sourly.

Laura grinned. 'Another victory to me, I believe,' she chirruped jubilantly. 'I told you she'd come back.'

Captain Wilde stormed over to Emily. 'I thought we'd seen the last of you.'

Emily returned his hard gaze defiantly. 'Our arrangement was for you to take me to Havalaña, wasn't it?'

He glared ferociously at her. 'It wasn't an arrangement,' he said tersely. 'And I never said I'd "take you" there.' He rolled his eyes and turned to his wife for sympathy. 'She makes it sound like a fucking pleasure cruise!'

Laura pushed her husband out of the way and linked arms with Emily, leading her towards the main hatch. 'Ignore my husband,' she said cheerfully. 'He's just a bad loser. Although, after the practice he's had since you arrived, I thought he might have improved.'

'Don't exhaust her, honey,' Captain Wilde called after them. 'I'm still the captain of this boat, and I do have rights.'

Waving nonchalantly at him, Laura led Emily below

deck towards her quarters. As they walked, Emily stared longingly at the door to the captain's cabin. She desperately wanted to get another glance at the contract before tomorrow's business meeting. Her mind was still unclear on one or two points she had read concerning the management of the account. Determined to put one over on the captain, Emily wanted to make sure she knew exactly what she was contending against. Sadly, she realised that Laura had other plans. Knowing that the contract would have to wait until later, Emily followed the captain's wife into her cabin.

'How did your time ashore go?' Laura asked. 'Did you find your friends?'

Carefully, Emily nodded. Her plans for revenge were so close to the forefront of her mind Laura's words made her suspicious of being discovered. She knew she was just being paranoid, but because she had never been involved in intrigue like this before she could not help herself. 'Everything went quite well,' she said cautiously.

'Yet you're back on board the *Amazon Maiden*?' Laura noted.

Emily nodded. 'I told them to meet me in Havalaña,' she explained. 'They're going to contact the British Consul and sort out my missing paperwork themselves. I should be able to turn up at the last minute and simply sign the appropriate documents.' She trailed slowly behind as she walked, forcing herself to remember that she was meant to be submissive and servile. After the two hours she had spent in Enoba, Emily felt anything but servile.

She was still riding high on the wave of euphoria that had come from dominating Roderick and Judy. However, because she did not want Laura or the captain to suspect any of her plans, Emily knew she had to act like a submissive again.

'And was there another reason why you came back aboard the boat?' Laura asked as she entered her cabin.

203

Emily swallowed. Her heart was already pounding furiously in her chest. Laura's question seemed to point directly at a clear knowledge of what she intended. 'Another reason?' Emily asked nervously. 'I'm not sure I understand what you mean.' She closed the cabin door then turned around. She was not surprised to see Laura standing naked in front of her. The robe she had been wearing was pooled around her ankles. Her ample breasts, slender waist and pale pubic bush were being displayed to perfection. In spite of her nervousness, Emily grinned.

'I think you did have another reason for coming back,' Laura said quietly. She took a step towards Emily, a salacious smile spreading her lips. 'And I think I know what it is.'

Emily tried to suppress the rising wave of panic that built in her chest. She watched Laura reach for the jacket she was wearing.

The woman's fingers deftly began to tease the buttons open. 'There's no need to hide it any longer,' Laura assured her. 'Your motives aren't that obvious. It's just that, I can always tell with this sort of thing.'

Emily felt her jacket fall to the floor. Her breasts were bared and she realised dully that the nipples were hard and aching. She tried to ignore the sensation, concentrating on Laura and the disconcerting revelations she hinted at. 'Is it that obvious?' she asked carefully.

Laura nodded and smiled reassuringly. 'Yes, it is to me.' She unfastened the button at Emily's waist and lowered the zipper, allowing her trousers to fall to the floor.

Dressed only in her panties, Emily stood inches away from the naked woman. Her heart beat so furiously in her chest she was sure it would explode.

'I just know people,' Laura went on. 'From the moment I first saw you, I thought you fitted into one of two categories. You were either truly submissive, or really dominant. Sometimes those sorts of people are so similar, it's hard to tell the difference.' She laughed and added, 'Sometimes, they don't even know it themselves until they've experienced one or the other.'

'And which am I?' Emily asked. She felt Laura's hand caress the sensitive flesh of her neck, her fingers quickly trailing down to the swell of her breast. 'Which category do I fall into?'

'I think that's obvious, isn't it?' Laura whispered softly. 'We both know why you came back.' Her finger had reached the thatch of dark curly hairs nestling above Emily's sex. The intimacy of her touch was infuriatingly exciting. Her fingertips seemed to emit an electric pulse of arousal.

Emily closed her eyes, not daring to breathe. 'Why did I come back?'

Laura placed a soft, tender kiss on Emily's shoulder. 'I think –' she began, moving her fingers through the swatch of pubic hair. 'I think you're truly submissive and you wanted to come back to enjoy the last leg of our journey to Havalaña.'

Emily opened her eyes wide with surprised relief.

'Am I right?' Laura asked softly.

She had been holding her breath so carefully, Emily gasped for air before replying. She fought to suppress a triumphant grin, delighted that her true motivations remained a secret. 'I hadn't really thought about it,' she replied tactfully. 'I suppose you could be right.'

Laura's fingers reached the lips of her pussy and Emily felt the tingle of her arousal swell into a euphoric roar. Using her index and ring finger she gently spread the lips of Emily's sex. Slowly, she drew her middle finger against the hot wet opening between Emily's legs.

Emily gasped and closed her eyes. Her relief quickly gave way to sexual excitement. She wanted to embrace and caress the woman in front of her. Laura's lips were a kiss away from her own, and she wanted to thank the woman properly for the pleasure she was provoking. Reminding herself that she was supposed to act like a submissive aboard the boat, Emily stood still as Laura fondled her. It took a stupendous effort of will-power not to reach out and touch her, but Emily managed it. Her concentration was so rapt, Emily did not even notice when Laura stepped away. The first thing she realised was when Laura spoke to her from the other side of the cabin.

'Help me into this,' she commanded briskly. 'There's something I want to ask you.' She was holding a strap-on dildo in her hand, the black straps dangling limply from one end.

Emily took the device and glanced curiously at it. She had used a vibrator before she came aboard the *Amazon Maiden*, and since being on the boat she had used a wide variety of dildos. But none of them compared to the huge weapon she held in her hands. The ones she had used before had either been ivory coloured rocket ships or pale imitations of erections moulded in a vile pink colour. This was a huge length of ebony latex. Her fingers squeezed the middle, finding a good deal of pliancy in spite of its solid hardness. The dildo felt as much like a cock as the real thing with one exception. Emily could never imagine a cock of such gigantic proportions. The strap-on was enormous. She hurried herself into action, aware that Laura was waiting patiently for her. As she fastened the device between the woman's legs and around her waist, Emily whispered, 'What did you want to ask me?'

Laura smiled down at her. 'What are you going to do when you return to England?'

It was a surprising question and Emily considered it carefully before replying. 'I hadn't thought,' she replied honestly. 'Since I found myself stranded, I saw home as a goal. I hoped everything would go back to normal when I got there.' She smiled sadly, realising how fanciful this idea was. 'I suppose I should give that part of my plan a bit of a re-think,' she went on. 'I've begun to forget what "normal" is like.' She smiled into Laura's face, the expression tinged with genuine sadness.

Laura's question made Emily realise how little thought she had given the matter. Regardless of how the business meeting went in Havalaña, she would be going home the following day, if the British Consul could work that quickly. Whether her plans for revenge were successful or not, she knew that when she returned home things would have changed.

She had gone on holiday with her fiancé and his step-sister. She would be returning to England with two submissive lovers and a new found knowledge of sex that she could never have contemplated before. Her hopes of life returning to normal vanished as she realised she had forgotten what normality was.

She stepped away from the fastened strap-on and briefly admired her handiwork. Laura looked stunning with the prosthetic cock attached. Its enormous size and girth stood proudly before her, emphasising her slenderness and perversely accentuating her femininity.

'Lay down,' Laura instructed Emily. 'I want to make love to you.'

Emily climbed on to the bed and lay on her back. She opened her arms to welcome Laura as she joined her.

Hazy midday sunlight filled the cabin with a cheerful bright light, reflecting Emily's mood of fun and adventure. With the strap-on dildo, Laura seemed like the perfect lover. The combination of her feminine curves and desirable beauty, coupled with the enormous cock she was sporting made for a dynamic blend.

They kissed passionately.

Emily could taste the woman's excitement as Laura plunged her tongue into her mouth. Her hands went instinctively to Laura's hips and she traced her slenderness with the heels of her hands. Between her legs, she could feel the strap-on dildo pushing urgently against the heat of her sex.

As Laura kissed her, her hands caressed Emily's body. She bucked her hips forward, pressing the tip of the dildo against the wetness of Emily's labia. With one languid thrust, she entered her.

Emily gasped, shocked and excited by the stimulation.

Laura continued to kiss her, pushing her tongue eagerly into Emily's mouth. Her hands and fingers caressed and stroked the wanton curves of Emily's body. Slowly, she forced the strap-on deeper into the velvety depths of Emily's sex.

Emily groaned with pleasure. The strap-on seemed to fill her and carry on filling her. Its enormous girth stretched the lips of her pussy wide as it plunged inside. The inner walls of her vagina struggled to accommodate the mammoth size. Tentatively, she squeezed herself against it and was thrilled by the waves of delight that screamed through her. When the dildo reached the neck of her womb, Emily released a low guttural cry of joy.

The feeling of excitement welling quickly inside her made Emily realise her orgasm was just a whisper away. As Laura began to withdraw the dildo from the warm confines of her hole, Emily pushed her hips forward, trying to keep the length within her.

Laura eased herself back until the tip had almost fallen from the lips of Emily's pussy. Still moving slowly, she began to push it back inside again. The rhythm was so measured and deliberate that Emily was soon lost in a world of delightful, strange stimulation. She kissed Laura's mouth hungrily, her fingers stroking and teasing the blonde's hips, waist and breasts. She teased Laura's nipples, aware that the hard buds of her arousal were pressing furiously against her own.

Throughout their love-making, Emily felt debilitated by a wealth of pleasure. This was how making love should be done properly, she thought. No dominance, no submission; just two people, indulging in the art of mutual pleasure. The act was not normal, she realised that much. Laura was sporting an artificial penis and they were both women, but that did not matter. All that mattered was that they were two equals, loving one another as equals. After all the pain, humiliation and cruelty of the last week, Emily felt liberated by the experience.

Emily bucked her hips furiously back and forth. Her pussy eager to savour the sweet pleasure of the strap-on's massive girth. With her hands on Laura's arse she cupped and caressed the rounded cheeks. As Laura began to pull away, Emily tried to hold herself against the dildo.

Smiling, Laura withdrew the dildo slowly, then plunged it back inside.

Emily groaned as the huge length widened her pussy again.

Her cries intensified as Laura quickened her tempo. The dildo was lubricated with Emily's pussy juice and slid into her easily. The strap-on glided in and out of her wet hole, moving faster and faster as Laura hastened her pace.

She pushed the device as deep as it would go, extracting a cry of ecstasy from Emily with each full forward thrust. By the time Emily climaxed, her groans of delight had turned to shouted words of encouragement. The sounds were ringing around the inside of the cabin and carrying all the way up to the deck.

'Yes!' she urged Laura emphatically. 'Yes! Fill me!'

She opened her eyes wide at the moment of climax and saw the woman was staring directly at her. The expression in her eyes conveyed her absolute understanding of the joy that Emily was receiving. A smile split her lips and she stared down on Emily with rapt fascination.

As the waves of delight rushed over her, Emily screamed with gratitude. Bolts of pleasure rushed through her body, warming and chilling her instantaneously. For a second she was boiling hot, her temperature soaring to fever pitch. Then she was freezing cold, chilled by the light dousing of sweat that covered her body. Her screams ebbed off to a sob of bliss-filled delight.

Unable to accept any more delightful punishment from the strap-on, Emily pulled away and lay limp on the bed, her breathing ragged.

Laura lay next to her, embracing her naked body. The strap-on pushed rudely between them, but the shared intimacy was enough to make them unmindful of it. Laura kissed Emily's face and neck softly. Her tongue traced droplets of sweat from her chest and she moved lower, licking the salty sweet fluid from Emily's breasts.

Groaning with the aftermath of her orgasm, Emily carefully guided the woman's head away. The strength of her climax had been intense and gratifying, but it had taken its toll on her. Each muscle in her body still tingled with delight and throbbed dully when she moved. The idea of enjoying any more pleasure right now, no matter how appetising the prospect seemed, was frightening. She noticed that Laura was grinning at her and she returned the smile.

'Why don't you come back to England and stay with the captain and I for a while?' Laura suggested softly. 'You've enjoyed yourself on the boat, haven't you?'

Emily grinned broadly. 'I don't think you need me to answer that, do you?' She replied. She placed a tentative finger against her own nipple and moved it away quickly, aware that even the mildest stimulation was still uncomfortable.

'I'm not saying the holiday can go on for ever,' Laura went on. 'But what I am saying is that it can feel like that. You've discovered a new side of yourself. If you spend some time with us, perhaps you can discover even more.'

Emily frowned uncertainly. The memory of their love-making was rekindled by the painful flare of every movement she made. If Laura had been inviting her to enjoy that experience again, Emily would not have hesitated to answer. The unique joy that had come from being made love to by a like-minded spirit was so intense, Emily could not find words to describe the joy. However, she knew that the invitation was not being made for her own pleasure. She realised that Laura had a dominant streak that was tinged with cruelty. She also knew that the captain would be continually in attendance with all his menacing demands and tyrannical commands. Considering the pair of them, Emily doubted she would have much chance for pleasure unless she submitted herself to them wholly.

And she had already decided that she no longer wanted to play the part of a submissive.

Sexual power was an intoxicating aphrodisiac, and she found the prospect of controlling it far more exciting than submitting to it. Her time on board the *Amazon Maiden* had been a sexual revelation, and she was happy to embrace every aspect of her newly acquired knowledge. She relished the idea of being able to live a purely hedonistic existence and was thrilled by the prospect of being treated as a sexual plaything. If Laura had been making the suggestion that they live together alone, she would have said yes without a second thought. Under those circumstances, she would have been willing to submit herself, be servile to the woman's dominant demands.

It was the thought of Captain Wilde that stopped her.

She was still trying to exact her revenge on the man, and she could not allow herself to think beyond tomorrow's business meeting. Perhaps she could submit to the man again. Anything was possible she supposed; it was

211

not as though the experience had been unpleasant. It had simply been humiliating. She smiled tactfully at Laura, knowing she was in no position to make a decision just yet.

'Can I think about it?'

'I wouldn't expect any less,' Laura replied, kissing her softly on the lips. 'Think about it all you want, you'll always be welcome.'

Emily's smile saddened. She wondered how true that would be after she had submitted her competitive contract to the two negotiators.

An hour later, Laura was back on board the deck of the *Amazon Maiden*, talking animatedly with her husband. From her position in the pilothouse, Emily could not hear what they were discussing and at that point she did not care. The pair were distracted enough for her to sneak a final glance at the contract. She made her way quickly down the companionway and started through the saloon towards the captain's cabin. The air was cool below deck and she relished the drop in temperature. She was dressed only in a loose silk blouse, showing off more of her long legs than modesty would normally have allowed under other circumstances. It was not the way she would have chosen to dress, but the hot weather made it close to a necessity.

Surreptitiously glancing over her shoulder, she paused outside the captain's cabin. Her hand fell on the knob and she tested it carefully, not sure if it might be locked. That would spoil her plans, she thought dourly.

The door opened easily for her. Nervous, she held it ajar, building up the courage to enter the room.

'That's the captain's cabin.'

The voice stopped her in her tracks. Her stomach performed a nervous somersault. Glancing at Vincent as he came nearer, she wondered how she had missed seeing such a big man in such a confined area. 'Excuse me?' she said, trying fervently to look innocent and barely managing it.

'That's the captain's cabin,' Vincent repeated. 'Yours is two doors along.'

Emily shook her head and smiled, feigning stupidity. 'All these doors look alike,' she said simply.

Vincent nodded agreement. 'For such a small vessel, it's easy to get lost.' He smiled easily at her. 'I was pleased to see you'd come back.'

Emily returned his grin. She closed the door of the captain's cabin, wishing she had been given the opportunity to sneak in there. Realising that Vincent wanted to speak to her, she tried to take her mind off her plans and concentrate on what he had to say. It was a difficult task; her thoughts were filled with the contract in the captain's cabin. The importance of reading it one last time was paramount.

'How are things going?' Emily asked him, walking slowly towards her own cabin. She was barely conscious of the way she was dressed and the effect it might be having on the man. So much of her legs were on display that little was left to Vincent's imagination.

He shrugged. 'It's been the best trip Dawn and I have ever enjoyed,' he said flatly. 'Laura and the captain are excellent hosts.'

Emily studied him carefully, wondering if he was being sarcastic. 'Excellent hosts?' she repeated dumbly. 'I'm sorry. Is there another captain and another Laura on board this boat. I don't think I understand.'

He grinned at her and followed her into her cabin. 'I'm sure you understand perfectly,' he said quietly. 'You came back didn't you?'

'Yes,' Emily began. 'But I –' She stopped herself before she could say anymore. Vincent was a sexual submissive, she reminded herself. His pleasures and motivations differed from her own, but because of the charade she was currently adopting Emily knew she had

213

to account for that when talking to him. His thoughts were the same as Laura's. He assumed that Emily had come back on board to endure more pain and humiliation. She did not dare to disillusion him for fear that he might betray her to the captain.

'How do you and Dawn know them?' Emily asked, intrigued as to how the four had become acquainted.

Vincent grinned. 'We've worked for them for the past four years,' he explained. 'I suppose you could say that our relationships began as affairs, but the captain and Laura have such an open marriage I don't think it's the word they would have chosen.'

Emily returned his grin. 'I'd noticed,' she said dryly.

'They both have fairly dominant natures,' Vincent explained. 'So I guess they were each looking for someone with a submissive personality. Laura found me. The captain found Dawn. It's an unusual relationship, but I think we're all quite happy with it.'

Emily was fascinated. 'And don't you miss your normal life?'

Vincent looked puzzled. 'How do you mean?'

'Work, the office, your home, your family . . .' Her voice trailed off beneath his patronising smile.

'Of course I don't miss those things,' he told her. 'I still enjoy them. So does Dawn. We spend our days in the office. We visit family and friends whenever we feel the need to and when Laura and the captain invite us to their house we attend for whatever reasons they have in mind.' He laughed heartily. 'We're just sexually submissive,' he explained. 'We're not aliens from another world.'

Emily returned his grin. 'I suppose I was being a bit stupid, wasn't I?'

Vincent laughed at her openness, not bothering to contradict her.

'Did you want to say something earlier, Vincent?' Emily asked suddenly.

He shook his head. 'I've already said it,' he told her. 'I wanted to say welcome back on board.'

Her grin was tinged with a hint of sadness. 'I'm only staying until tomorrow. When we reach Havalaña I'm leaving.'

Vincent graced her with a knowing smile. 'Do you really think it will be that easy?'

She laughed. 'This isn't more of Captain Wilde's bullshit, is it?' she asked. 'Remember? Like the last time when he sent you down here to convince me I couldn't get off at Port Maga?'

Vincent shook his head. He had the good grace to blush. 'I'm not feeding you a line this time,' he assured her. 'I meant it as a serious question. Now that you've discovered this way of life, do you really think you'll be able to give it up when you return to England? I know Laura's given you an open invitation to the house.'

'I don't intend to give it up,' she assured him. Her thoughts turned to Roderick and Judy and she suppressed the knowing smile that threatened to breach her lips. 'I just think I'll be playing it by my rules.'

His frown showed his lack of understanding, but Emily did not bother to explain. 'Who's at the helm?' she asked quietly.

'Dawn's covering for me while I'm down here,' Vincent explained. He leant forward and placed a chaste kiss on her lips. 'Good luck with your future. It's been a pleasure knowing you.' He frowned as though a thought had suddenly occurred to him. 'Why not reconsider Laura's invitation? It would be good to see you at one of Laura's parties.'

Emily was genuinely touched by his friendly intimacy and she felt a twang of regret at the deceit she was planning. The self-recrimination only lasted for a moment, but it was long enough to make a tear well in the corner of her eye. She glanced unhappily down at the cabin floor as Vincent left the room.

Her sadness did not last long. She waited until she heard his footsteps trail away then reminded herself that she was alone below deck. It was enough of an incentive to get her off her feet. Emily rushed to the door of her cabin and sneaked a glance outside.

Through the open door at the end of the corridor she could see Vincent climbing the companionway. 'Fantastic,' she whispered to herself. She was alone. She moved quickly to the captain's cabin and pushed the door open.

It was empty.

Closing the door quietly behind her she made her way to his desk. The contract was still taking pride of place amid the cluttered pile of papers and she grabbed it gratefully. She would have preferred to study the document at her leisure. The meat of the agreement was sandwiched between thirty pages of legal waffle, littered with 'herein's, 'pertaining to's and 'party of the first part's. Flicking quickly through the papers, Emily made a series of brisk mental notes about details she had previously missed and tried to correlate them with the plans she had already put in action.

The contract was not as bad as she had initially thought, but she realised there was a lot of room for improvement. Her own proposal would easily appear more attractive than this one.

She was just reading the clause concerning account management when the sound of nearing footsteps disturbed her concentration. She glanced up from the desk, certain that the heavy footfalls approaching belonged to the captain. Hurriedly replacing the contract, she stepped away from the desk and glanced around the room. Her mind quickly selected and discounted reasons for her being there. She could think of no plausible explanation and panic did its best to squash her creative processes. She stood by the captain's bunk, breathless with fear, expecting the cabin door to burst open at any moment.

When the footsteps walked past, she breathed a heartfelt sigh of relief.

She rushed quickly to the door and glanced tentatively outside.

'Emily!'

She could see the captain standing outside her cabin door. He had his back to her and was calling her name, expecting her to answer. As she watched, he pushed his way into the room. The door swung closed behind him.

Emily moved quickly out of his room and stepped into the corridor.

He burst from her cabin, his face a cloud of thunder. 'Where the hell have you been hiding?' he demanded. 'Why weren't you in your room?'

She remained calm beneath his furious tirade. 'I didn't realise I was confined to my quarters,' she said coolly.

'Why weren't you in your cabin?'

'There's no en suite in there,' she said carefully. 'And the porthole isn't wide enough for me to stick my –'

'All right!' he broke in. 'I get the picture.' He glared angrily at her and ran his fingers through his hair. 'You don't make it easy to talk to you, do you?'

She shrugged. 'You find it easy enough to shout at me. Why don't you lower the volume and see if we can communicate on that level?'

'I have a better idea,' he said suddenly. He grabbed her wrist and twisted it sharply. 'I came down here to be pleasant to you,' he told her. 'I was going to invite you to join Laura and me for dinner this evening. She and I have some business to discuss, but I thought we could all celebrate the end of an enjoyable cruise together.'

'That sounds like a good idea,' Emily said tersely. 'But you're hurting my wrist.'

His grin was as treacherous as black ice. 'That's just a start.'

Emily stared uncertainly into the captain's menacing gaze. 'What the hell do you think you're doing to me?'

His grin broadened. Still holding her arm he pushed her roughly towards his cabin. 'I'm going to give you a lesson in manners that you've been needing for a long time,' he told her meaningfully.

'I've already had one of your lessons,' she reminded him. As she spoke she was backtracking along the corridor. 'That first night, when you tied me to your mast and caned my tits. Don't you think that was enough?'

He pushed her through his cabin door. 'Apparently not,' he said darkly. He slammed the door closed behind them.

When he turned around, Emily saw that he was carrying his cane. She glared at the hateful instrument, then turned her resentful stare on the captain. 'What the hell do you think you're going to do with that?'

'I'm going to beat some manners into you,' he replied sharply. 'I think we're both agreed that you need it.' He sliced the cane sharply through the air. It whistled mercilessly.

Emily walked backwards trying to get away from him. 'I won't let you,' she gasped.

'You came on board willing to accept my terms,' he reminded her. He whipped the cane through the air a second time. The whistling sound brought a smile to his lips. 'And these are my terms.'

Emily found herself pressed against the cabin wall. Her hand bumped against the captain's desk and she glanced down at it nervously.

Captain Wilde followed her gaze and he frowned. 'I never left that contract like that,' he said. He turned his puzzled expression to Emily, the threat of retribution building in the murky waters of his eyes.

She swallowed unhappily, aware that she had little in the way of options. If he discovered she had been looking at his paperwork, she knew she would be in trouble. The situation she faced now was bad enough. If he found out about her plans . . .

Emily dared not think about the recriminations that ensue her. Turning her back to him, she placed one hand on either side of the desk. Her body was hiding the contract from his sight, and hopefully keeping it from his thoughts. Taking a deep breath and bracing herself, she thrust her backside out for him. 'All right then,' she said calmly. 'If you want to punish me, then go ahead and do it.' She lifted the back panel of her blouse, displaying the peach-like cheeks of her arse for him. Glancing over her shoulder she stared at him defiantly. 'Make the most of it though,' she told him. 'After tonight, I'll be out of your life forever.'

He grinned at her, his dark eyes and unreadable smile masking thoughts that she knew would be disturbing. She watched him raise the cane and turned away before it began its descent. Bracing herself against the impact, she squeezed the edges of the desk tightly between her fingers.

A welt of pain soared through the cheeks of her arse. She bit back a cry in response to the blow, reluctant to give him the satisfaction of hearing her moan. Perhaps she had no option other than to let him do it, but she was damned if she was going to make it easy for him. Her fingers squeezed hard against the edge of the desk.

A second and third swipe of the cane bit her backside in rapid succession.

Emily inhaled deeply through her nostrils. Her teeth were ground tightly together and her lips were pressed into a single thin line. She steeled herself for another blow, aware of the dull pulse of her arousal. The distant throb between her legs was becoming more noticeable and she hated herself for enjoying such feelings. The man was hurting and humiliating her. She despised the pleasure that his punishment inspired.

At the same time, she could not deny enjoying it.

Tingling waves of joy began to spread slowly through her body, electrifying every pore. She kept her fingers pressed against the edges of the desk, aware that her fingernails were marking the grain of the wood.

The cane whistled through the air, biting her left cheek, then her right. Brilliant flares of pain, breathtakingly deep in intensity, erupted from her arse.

Unable to contain herself any longer, Emily groaned. She shifted her hands on the desk, knocking some of the captain's papers to the floor as she moved. She noticed his contract spill to the top of the pile and she smiled, confident that she had covered her tracks.

Moving her hand downwards, she pressed her fingers against the warm swell of her sex. Her arousal was growing stronger with each blow, as was her need to be satisfied. The tips of her fingers touched the nub of her clitoris and she released a second groan of delight. The excited flesh was so responsive she could feel the mounting rush of an orgasm build as soon as her fingers brushed against it. Using one hand to separate her labia, she employed her other to tease the pearl of pleasure. Her appetite for orgasm was stronger than ever. Moistening the tips of her fingers with the juice of her arousal, she teased the flesh with urgent haste.

Captain Wilde brought the cane against her arse with a passionate fury. Emily could feel the length of wood striping her backside, each blow leaving a brandished ember of pain in its wake.

With only the slightest pressure against her clit, she felt the orgasm begin to tear through her. Her breathing deepened, and she suppressed a cry of exultation. The sensation was exciting and exquisite, but she did not want Captain Wilde to know he had pleased her so greatly.

In spite of her efforts to conceal her pleasure, she realised he had witnessed her fulfilment. His dark laughter rang in her ears and she glanced over her shoulder to stare coldly at him. Her lip was curled into a sneer of contempt.

Smiling into her hate-filled eyes, he laid his cane gently down on the bed. 'You don't look as though you've learnt anything from that,' he noted wryly.

Emily bit back a retort, knowing that this was neither the time nor the place to antagonise him. She panted softly, her breath heavy and laboured with the aftermath of her joy. 'What was I supposed to learn?'

'I was trying to beat some manners into you,' he reminded her. 'Perhaps I should be doing it harder.'

Emily closed her eyes, simultaneously chilled and warmed by the threat.

He moved closer to her and slapped the palm of his hand against her arse. The smack was not as hard as the cane, but his flat hand rekindled the burning welt of each blow that had been administered.

Emily gasped.

His hands moved to her shoulders and he turned her around. Pressing his mouth hard against hers, Emily allowed the man to kiss her with an eager desire. His tongue probed her mouth and his lips pressed cruelly hard against hers. If his cane had left marks on the cheeks of her arse she felt sure that his lips would be bruising her mouth.

He placed a hand against her neck; she almost choked as he squeezed the sides of her face. But his harsh manner and rough manipulation of her body only served to increase her excitement. Emily felt sickened by her body's eager, wanton response to him.

'Let's see you naked,' he growled, moving his lips away from hers.

Glancing unhappily into his cold hard face, Emily barely heard the words. She felt his hands reach for the front of her blouse and raised her own protectively. He waved them away and snatched angrily at the front of

221

the garment. With one vicious lunge he had ripped it open. Buttons flew from the front of the blouse, pinging loudly as they struck the walls and floor. Emily heard the silk tear as he pulled it from her body; her outrage clear, she glared at him.

'I could have just unfastened it,' she said sharply.

He hurled the rent silk to the floor and forcibly pushed her to the bed. 'Don't you ever learn?' he muttered, glaring angrily at her. His hand reached for the cane and he held it above her. 'I'll beat some manners into you if it takes from now until this river runs dry.'

Emily's gaze was fixed on the cane. 'I only said –'

He did not allow her to finish. The tip of his cane flew through the air and stung against the hard swell of her nipple. Emily howled. She tried to sit up on the bed, her hand going to the flaming hot source of her agony.

He pushed her down roughly, a grim smile twisting his lips. 'Stay where you are until I tell you to move,' he snapped crisply.

Emily stared at him, not daring to disobey. Her nipple felt like an explosion. Sharp shards of pain throbbed with sickening force from the aching tip. The sense of dark excitement that welled within her continued to rise. She snatched lungfuls of air with a short breath, then screamed ecstatically as he brought the cane down on her other nipple. 'You bastard!' she exclaimed in fury.

Her inner muscles pulsed with wanton desire. The throb of pleasured pain racked the hardened nubs of her breasts. She glared angrily up at him, aware that he was grinning excitedly at her.

'You don't know how to be submissive, do you?'

Emily dared not speak. She pressed her fingers between her legs and began to tease the swell of her sex. Her nipples were aflame with a burning desire. Determined to satisfy the pulse of her own arousal, she rubbed two stiff fingers against the swollen ridge of her clitoris.

His smile was broad and salacious. Kneeling on the bed beside her, he cast an appreciative glance up and down Emily's body.

Emily glared at him as she rubbed her fingers against the hot wetness of her sex. She could feel the eruption of a climax nearing again and she attacked her clitoris with renewed determination.

He placed a finger towards one bruised and aching nipple.

She tried to flinch away from his touch, but he grabbed her quickly. Holding her nipple between his forefinger and thumb, he rolled the nub gently to and fro.

Emily groaned loudly; his brutal caress stimulated the memory of the cane's wicked tip striking her. Fireworks of euphoric pleasure erupted in her chest, sending a tingling message of joy throughout her naked body. She pressed her fingers harder against the furious burning between her legs and squeezed the reluctant climax from the tip of her clit.

As she revelled in the breathless delight of joy, he pushed his mouth against her other breast and took the second aching nipple between his lips. His tongue darted harshly against it, and she felt a thrill of pain burst from her breast. The stimulation was enough to send a second cascading waterfall of joy to follow the one she was enduring. When she felt the gentle pressure of his teeth nibbling at the sensitive flesh, she screamed with elation.

'Anyone with manners would thank me for that sort of pleasure,' he said quietly. He was still rolling the nipple between his fingers as he spoke. His fingertips seemed to be emitting small electric shocks into her body that left her powerless.

Emily glanced into his face and tested a faltering smile. 'Thank you,' she whispered.

He shook his head, his frown proving his dark unhappiness. 'You still require training,' he told her. 'If I'd trained you properly, you would have thanked me without the need for my prompting.'

Emily stared unhappily at him. She considered raising a protest, then realised she could not find the energy. Her fingers had moved away from the heated wetness of her cleft and she raised a hand to his chest.

He moved away from her before she could touch him. Grabbing her ankles, he pulled her to the edge of his bunk, then turned her over.

Emily gasped as she felt her face being pushed into the mattress. Her legs fell heavily down and she felt her knees connect with the hardwood decking on the floor of the cabin. 'What are you doing?' she demanded.

He grunted humourless laughter. 'One last caning, then you can please me,' he said coldly.

Emily shivered. Hating herself for enjoying his savagery, she heard herself whisper the words, 'Thank you, Captain.'

'That's more like it,' he said, not bothering to hide the satisfaction in his voice. 'Say it some more.'

With her knees on the floor and her face pushed into the mattress, Emily knew her arse was high in the air, available for whatever he wanted. She began to whisper words of gratitude as she lay there, dully relishing the taste of her newly acquired servility.

When she felt the first blow of his cane, she groaned loudly. A furious weal of excitement ignited in her arse cheeks. She continued to thank him as he punished her mercilessly. He struck her arse with his cane again and again, inspiring wave after wave of dizzying pain so intense it produced a draining wealth of pleasure. She could feel the onset of another orgasm, and she braced herself for its impact. The vehemence of her climaxes had become so strong she trembled at the prospect of enduring another. The heights of joy were too great for her to contemplate.

She continued to mumble her words of thanks, interspersing them occasionally with the words 'Please, no more'.

'Have you had enough?'

'More than enough,' she whispered. Before he could reproach her for insolence, she added the words, 'Thank you, Captain.'

He grinned down at her. 'I should have done this to you on the first night we met,' he reflected. 'I think it's just what you've been needing.'

Shivering, Emily tried to stop herself from nodding agreement. Regardless of how she felt about the man, she could not deny that he had taught her about new boundaries of pleasure. He had taken her to the threshold of a joy she could never have known in her previous life. Because of this, Emily realised she was indebted to him. If he had punished her like this on her first night aboard the *Amazon Maiden*, she knew things would have been different.

His hands grasped her hips and she felt the hard thrust of his cock pressing against her hot wet flesh.

She groaned excitedly, darkly aware of her urgent need for his length. Eager to accept his huge cock, she bit her lower lip and raised her sex for him.

He prodded the tip against the slick wet folds of her labia, nuzzling the head gently along their entire length.

Emily moaned.

Continuing to tease her, he placed his finger on the rim of her anus and pressed it roughly into the dark canal. The sensation was so thrilling and exquisite that she bit hard against her lip, drawing blood.

Still holding her hips with one hand, he pulled her against his hardness and slowly entered her. The finger at her anus probed deeper as his cock slid into her sex. She could feel him filling both clefts with slow deliberation. As he rode slowly into her, she realised her body was preparing for a tumultuous explosion of joy that would shame her previous climaxes to insignificance.

The position tightened the muscles of her inner sex naturally. She could feel his cock pressing hard against the eager confines of her pussy with furious desire.

He slid the finger slowly in and out of her anus as he rode her. Each time his cock filled her, he tugged the finger gently from her. Each time his cock made its slow egress from her wet velvet confines, he pushed the finger back inside.

Her moans, soft to begin with, quickly turned to urgent, demanding groans. She pressed her fingers into the mattress and squeezed the fabric hard, bracing herself for a gargantuan climax. Her body was drenched with a sweat too warm to properly cool her. Every muscle ached with burning longing.

When she felt his length begin to pulse inside her, her own orgasm was given furious release.

He groaned with the strength of his climax, his fingers pressing hard against her hip. He pulled her tightly against him, forcing her to feel the twitching tip of his length teasing the deepest recesses of her sex. Their groans became a spiralling crescendo, filling the cabin with the joyous sounds of their passionate abandon.

She pushed herself hard against him as he buried his length deep inside her warmth. Her satisfaction was so total she felt a tremor shivering throughout her body.

Without removing his cock, he leant over her. His mouth was pressed against her ear and she felt the soft whisper of his laughing breath as it tickled her neck. 'You enjoyed that, didn't you?'

She nodded into the pillow. 'It wasn't totally unbearable,' she admitted. 'Why do you ask?'

His laughter darkened and he slid his cock from the confines of her pussy. 'It could be like that all the time,' he told her. 'Laura's already made the offer. All you have to do is say yes.'

She considered his words carefully, wondering what to say for the best. She had still not come to a decision concerning Laura's offer, and she knew she was in no position to decide anything right now.

Glancing warily into his face, she placed a hesitant kiss on his mouth. 'That was wonderful,' she told him earnestly. 'And I appreciate your offer. I need to think about it though,' she told him. 'And I believe that you and Laura should give it a little more thought.'

'We've thought about it and discussed it,' he growled slowly, his patience wearing thin already. 'We know our own minds and we don't need to think about it again.'

She silenced his tirade with a second kiss. 'Humour me,' she whispered. 'Give it another day's thought.' She glanced at her watch and saw the time was nearly six o'clock. 'If you still think it's a good idea, ask me this time tomorrow.'

He glanced doubtfully at her. 'Just to humour you?'

She shrugged. 'People have been known to change their minds within twenty-four hours.'

He smiled confidently into her face. 'I'm set on the idea, but if you want me to ask you tomorrow, then I'll ask you tomorrow.' He shook his head disparagingly. 'Not that it's going to make a scrap of difference,' he added arrogantly.

Emily returned his smile. She had her own thoughts about how he would feel towards her by then.

Nine

John Masters stared at the contract coolly. He glanced at his colleague, gracing him with a speculative expression, then turned his attention back to Emily. 'This is why you brought us here?'

Emily exercised her warmest smile. 'I don't think you'll be disappointed once you've read it.'

He was a tall man with broad shoulders and a barrel chest ensconced in a well-tailored Saville Row suit. His sullen frown and sombre disposition were blatantly intimidating but Emily was unperturbed. She had spent the last week dealing with Captain Wilde. After him, John Masters and Alan Thomas would need to do a lot more than frown before she would feel unsettled.

Alan walked to his colleague's side and glanced over his shoulder. He watched the man flick casually through the pages of the neatly bound contract, then turned his suspicious gaze on Emily. 'Is this a corporate finance package for our current project?' he demanded. 'How did you know we required external finance?'

'That's why you're here in Havalaña, isn't it?' she replied evenly. 'You're wanting to negotiate an appropriate finance deal.' She leant back against the wall beside the door and idly fanned her neck with a lazy hand. It was a gesture designed to draw their attention to the excess of cleavage she was displaying. Emily watched the tactic work like a charm. Encouraged by their response, she unfastened the top button of her blouse and smiled knowingly at the two men. 'Amongst other things on your agenda, I assume you were discussing a similar package with Captain Wilde this morning.'

'You seem to know an awful lot about us and our movements,' John said, taking a step closer to her. 'But, if you'll pardon my French, we know fuck all about you.'

Emily remained calm beneath his fiery gaze. 'I didn't think you'd want to deal with an ignoramus,' she told him. 'As for my credentials, you'll notice there are lists of referees and contacts at the back of the contract. Any one of them will vouch for my capabilities in the management of corporate finance.' She smiled, a disarmingly confident gesture. 'And if there's anything else you want to know about me, you only have to ask.'

John took another step towards her. He was standing so close she doubted there was a hair's breadth between their bodies. She could sense the subtle fragrance of his cologne from beneath his jacket and she found the scent exciting.

'Did Wilde put you up to this?' he asked quietly. 'Are you another of his incentives?'

She dared to laugh, shaking her head by way of explanation. 'I learnt about your requirements through my association with Captain Wilde,' she explained carefully. 'But I don't think he knows I've prepared a competitive proposal.'

She graced John Masters with an alluring smile and placed her fingers against his chest. 'As for incentives,' she whispered. 'I think I can be quite competitive in that sphere as well.' She glanced past his broad shoulders and nodded towards Roderick and Judy. 'As you can see, I have two willing assistants. The three of us are prepared to make our offer just as appealing as anything Captain Wilde can put forward.'

Watching quietly, Roderick and Judy nodded meekly. They had followed her instructions to the letter. When

Emily arrived in Havalaña that morning, they were waiting for her at the port. After a brief visit to the British Consul, they had escorted her back to their hotel suite and presented her with copies of all the documents she needed for her business meeting.

Emily had not bothered to thank them and neither Roderick nor Judy had mentioned this. They had stood in attendance as she dressed for the meeting and listened to her attentively. Dictating orders like a military general, Emily had explained how the negotiations were going to go. She had told Roderick and Judy that they were to obey every instruction she gave them without question.

Knowing there would be repercussions if they disobeyed, the pair had happily agreed.

John Masters did not bother to acknowledge Roderick and Judy. He kept his gaze fixed on Emily. 'What if you're the incentive that I want?' His hand moved and brushed against her. The tips of his fingers rubbed against the fabric of her jacket, sending a soft tingle of warmth through the bud of her hardened nipple.

Emily released a soft breath of excitement. She smiled at him and raised her eyebrows suggestively. 'Perhaps that was what I had hoped for,' she replied. Her fingers were still on his chest and she moved them over his white shirt, tracing the swell of his impressive pectorals.

He placed his mouth over hers, kissing her with a forceful passion that revealed his innate arrogance.

It would have felt natural to succumb to such a kiss, Emily realised. The easiest thing in the world would have been to melt beneath his embrace and allow him to dominate her. Instead, she kissed him back. She pressed her mouth against his with all the fury of her avaricious sexual hunger. Her tongue probed between his lips and her teeth gently chewed against the sensitive flesh of his broad, lower lip. Embracing him as they kissed, she pressed her eager body against his and was encouraged to feel the hardness of his arousal.

Behind John's shoulder she saw Alan Thomas move toward Roderick and Judy and she said a silent prayer. She had tried to warn the couple what to expect and she had given them explicit instruction about what they should do and how they should behave. Though she did not doubt they were obedient, her heart beat rapidly as she realised this was the one part of the negotiations that was outside her control.

'And how do you fit into this?' Alan asked Roderick.

His gaze briefly incorporated Judy, but he was talking directly to Roderick.

From her place by the door, Emily watched nervously. She saw Roderick's adam's apple bob sharply up and down as he swallowed nervously. Because apprehension had lowered his voice, she strained to hear his reply.

'Judy and I have helped Emily to prepare the contract,' Roderick told Alan. He moistened his lips suddenly and said, 'Would you care for a drink?'

Alan smiled broadly at him. It was the hungry grin of a predatory animal. 'The girl can get the drinks,' he told Roderick, placing a hand on his arm. 'I'm sure that you and I can talk while she's preparing them.'

Roderick, allowing the arm to remain where it was, nodded and forced an easy grin to surface on his lips.

Emily held her breath. She knew that Roderick was neither stupid nor naive; he would realise exactly what Alan was implying. The man was being alarmingly intimate, and she wondered if Roderick found the prospect unnerving or darkly exciting. She had made threats of retribution if he did not behave himself, but she did not know how far he was willing to go to comply with her demands.

'You look nervous,' Alan remarked calmly. He brushed the back of his hand against Roderick's cheek. His fingers trailed almost casually against the sensitive flesh.

231

Roderick shivered. 'I suppose I am, a little,' he conceded. He studied the man's pale grey eyes, smiling softly.

Emily could see the growing bulge at the front of his pants and she stifled an exclamation. She had always believed Roderick to be one hundred per cent heterosexual. The sight of him being aroused by a man was totally unprecedented.

Roderick's cheeks flushed with embarrassment and he tugged the lapel of his jacket so his arousal was hidden. His crimson cheeks burnt darker when he saw the smile on Alan's face. It was obvious that the man knew why he had moved his jacket, or he had already seen Roderick's blatant excitement.

By the door, Emily eventually relented to the power of John's kisses. His hands traversed the swells and contours of her frame and she heard herself gasp excitedly. When his hands cupped her buttocks through the flimsy fabric of her short skirt, she winced softly. The cheeks of her arse were still tender from the beating Captain Wilde had administered the day before.

John's hands continued to brush unconsciously against her bruised flesh, exciting the memory of each weal and welt. Emily suddenly felt breathless with the pent-up yearning of her arousal. She smiled excitedly into John's face, her eyes shiny with desire. It had been her intention just to tease him to begin with. She had thought it would help her chances if his mind repeatedly strayed back to an allusion of intimacy while he studied the contract. Considering her own febrile desires, she realised she had not accounted for the effect he was having on her. The eagerness of his erection pushed forcefully against the flat of her stomach; she shivered happily at its nearness. Glancing over John's shoulder, she watched Roderick place a tentative hand on Alan Thomas's cheek.

A moment later, the two men were kissing.

The sight was so remarkable, she felt her own excitement intensify with voyeuristic delight.

Alan had his hands splayed through Roderick's long hair. Roderick was holding the back of Alan's neck as their mouths shared one another. From her position, Emily could see the pair rub their bodies closely together.

John Masters released her from his embrace and took a reluctant step away. He seemed surprised to find Judy standing next to him, offering him a glass of champagne from a tray. He thanked her and took a fluted goblet before testing the bouquet. 'An excellent vintage,' he told Emily approvingly.

She nodded her thanks. 'I thought you'd want to celebrate after you got my proposal in your hands,' she explained arrogantly. With a knowing smile, she added, 'Champagne was one of the ways that I thought we could celebrate.'

He returned her smile and drained his glass in one. Glancing around the room, he caught sight of his colleague, then discreetly turned away. After giving an apologetic cough, he said, 'Are you ready, Alan?'

Alan moved his lips from Roderick's. A reluctant smile of desire lit his expression.

Roderick studied the man, looking painfully unsure about the feelings he was experiencing. Emily could see that he had already succumbed to Alan's exciting mesmerism, but she doubted Roderick had ever been attracted to a man before. She wondered how he was dealing with the new experience. The intimacy the two men shared had been thrilling to watch.

Alan grinned at Roderick. A line of understanding etched his lips. 'You'll be at the business meeting tonight, I trust?' he asked quietly.

Roderick nodded. He swallowed, the sound seeming to resonate in the quiet room.

'We'll study this, along with Wilde's,' John Masters

told Emily, waving the proposal at her. 'You're invited to dine with us all this evening,' he added. 'Alan and I will have made a decision by then.'

Hesitation clouded Emily's brow. 'I thought you were dining on board the *Amazon Maiden* this evening,' she began.

'We are,' John told her. 'Wilde will have no objections to you being there.' A knowing smile broke his lips. 'He wants this contract so badly he' wouldn't dare to object to my inviting someone else on board his ship.'

Emily considered telling John Masters that the *Amazon Maiden* was a boat, not a ship. The fact had been repeated to her so many times it was almost automatic to correct the error. Wisely, she kept the thought to herself and graced him with a confident grin. 'I can't wait,' she said softly. 'I was already looking forward to tonight. Now I'm anticipating it more than ever.'

He nodded understanding, a broad grin splitting his lips. 'Come on, Alan,' he called brusquely. 'We have work to do.'

Together, the two men walked briskly from the room. John paused, before closing the door and gave Emily an appreciative glance. 'Until tonight.'

She nodded and smiled in response. His passionate kisses had bruised her lips, but they were not so badly damaged that she could not taste the sweet flavour of victory. She grinned triumphantly at Roderick and Judy and was pleased to see them smile back at her. There was only one cloud looming on the horizon now, she realised. Over dinner this evening she would have to face Captain Wilde again. The thought sent a shiver running down her spine. If she never had to set eyes on him again, it would be too soon. The prospect chilled her.

Realising her hands were shaking nervously, she snatched a glass of champagne from Judy's tray and sipped tentatively at the liquid. There was no doubt in her mind that when she next the saw captain, he would not be happy with her.

The door shook beneath the pummelling it was receiving. The hammering fist on the other side caused an echo to reverberate around the entire suite. It was a noise so loud and unexpected the three of them all jolted in their seats.

'Open up, you sneaky fucking BITCH! Open up, NOW!' The torrent of blows stopped long enough for the words to be shouted. Then they started again. Emily had no difficulty recognising the captain's voice. She was used to him delivering commands and orders at a deafening volume. Even though his shouts now transcended anything she had heard before, she knew it was him. It was unsettling to hear the note of anger that coloured his tone. Before, she thought she had heard anger in his voice. Now she realised this was the first time she had heard it. The thought was darkly unsettling. Emily tested a reassuring smile against the concerned faces of Roderick and Judy. The pair each held a flute of champagne and she saw that they were both trembling slightly. The sparkling liquid in their glasses fizzed and shook with the nervous tremor of their hands.

'I'm warning you, EMILY! If you don't open this door, I'll kick the damned thing OPEN!'

The door began to shake beneath a barrage of blows and kicks so forceful they were actually visible. Staring nervously, Emily wondered if it was possible he was trying to make good the threat. The door pushed hard against the jamb, groaning and bowing beneath the relentless pounding of his fists. The force of his rage seemed more than sufficient to destroy it. Emily could picture him bursting into the room in an explosion of splinters, shavings and mangled wooden debris.

'I think that will be for me,' she told Roderick quietly. 'Would you mind getting it for me?'

Roderick glanced at her doubtfully.

'Now,' she told him firmly.

He nodded and after placing his glass on a table, made his way to the door. It burst open as soon as he had unlocked it.

Captain Wilde stormed into the room, his face as dark as the underbelly of a thundercloud. His eyes were alight with malicious intent and his hands were balled into fists. His breath was a broken pant that exploded in soft, menacing growls. He glared threateningly at Roderick until the younger man took a reluctant step backwards. Casting his gaze furiously around the room, he caught sight of Emily and stamped angrily towards her.

Emily remained in her seat, maintaining a mask of cool control.

'I should snap your deceitful little neck like a fucking pencil.'

She raised her eyebrows slightly, as though she was considering the idea. 'I don't think that would be wise,' she told him eventually. 'Even over here, they do have some laws that forbid that sort of behaviour. I doubt you'd even be able to get away with it on board the *Amazon Maiden*.'

'You've stolen my contract,' he growled angrily. 'Don't you dare try and make shitty jokes with me after that. I ought to . . .' He raised his open hand high in the air and glared furiously down at her. His anger was so great he was lost for words

'Don't even think about hitting her,' Roderick said stiffly.

Captain Wilde turned to face him. His eyes were black coals of passionate hatred.

'Hit her, and you'll have to deal with me,' Roderick said, trying to hide the nervousness from his voice.

A malevolent smile broke the captain's lips. 'That's not a threat, son,' he growled. 'It sounds more like a tempting invitation.'

Roderick took a reluctant step backwards. 'I'll call the hotel manager,' he threatened desperately.

'You'll have to call his replacement,' Captain Wilde explained dully. 'The manager's in the corridor, nursing a broken nose.'

'Thank you, Roderick,' Emily broke in. She eased herself from her chair and walked boldly past the captain. Speaking carefully to Roderick and Judy, she said, 'I want the pair of you to go to the bedroom for a while. Captain Wilde and I have some things to discuss.'

Judy had remained silent throughout the captain's entrance. She had stared at the man, not bothering to hide her fear of his anger. Still holding him with a wary gaze, she asked Emily, 'Will you be all right, alone with him?'

'I'll be fine,' Emily assured her.

'I'll take good care of her,' Captain Wilde said, the implication of a threat obvious in both his words and the way he said them.

Roderick stared unhappily at the captain, then at Emily. He could see the resolution in her face and knew there was no point arguing with her. 'If you need us, we'll be in the bedroom,' he said slowly. He stared defiantly at the captain. 'You'd probably defeat me in a fight –'

'There's no 'probably' about it,' Captain Wilde said arrogantly.

Roderick sniffed unhappily and began again. 'You'd probably beat me in a fight. But if Emily calls me back in here, I'll make sure I hurt you.' He held the captain's gaze levelly.

'Take Judy to the bedroom,' Emily told him calmly. 'And thank you.'

With a reluctant air, Roderick made his way out of the suite, Judy leaning against his arm for support. As they moved, they both kept their gaze fixed on Captain Wilde. The entire suite remained in silence until they had vanished into the bedroom.

'You certainly know how to make an entrance, don't you?' Emily said sarcastically.

He reached for her hair and grabbed a fistful of her long tresses in one hand. Wrapping the hair around his fist like a rope he tugged hard and pulled her down to her knees.

Emily stifled a gasp of surprise, fearful that Roderick would come bursting back into the room, trying to be heroic. 'That hurts,' she told him tersely.

'It's meant to,' he replied in the same strangled voice. 'This is a prelude to my snapping your neck.'

She glared defiantly up at him. 'If you're going to hurt me, get it over and done with, then fuck off. I'm getting a little fed with up with the pathetic threats now.'

He struggled to contain his rage and she could see a reflection of the battleground on his face. He dragged her to her feet, using the length of hair he still held. Emily grimaced but remained silent. She was determined that whatever happened in this room, it was going to be between her and the captain. She was also adamant that she was going to be the one in control, regardless of the captain's methods.

'Why did you do it?' he demanded.

She tugged her hair free from his grip and started to move away from him. He stopped her with powerful hands on her arms and she stared defiantly back at him. 'I'm getting my drink first,' she told him. 'Would you care for a glass?'

He released her slowly, and nodded. With a glass in his hand, he repeated the question. 'Come on, tell me. Why did you do it?'

She smiled softly to herself. The expression did not reach her eyes. 'If you must know,' she began, 'I did it for three reasons. Firstly, I did it because I could. Back in England, I'm an executive with a company that specialises in corporate finance. Deals like this are how I make a living.'

'You never said,' he told her.

'You never asked,' she replied. 'My second reason was for the money. My bonus is earnings related. If I secure this deal, the bonus will equal five year's salary. I'm sure you'll agree, that's a powerful motive.'

He sipped at his glass and studied her carefully. 'And the third reason?'

She smiled into his questioning eyes. 'That's the main one. The other two were just icing on the cake. The real reason why I did it was because I wanted to have my revenge against you. I wanted revenge and this contract was the best way I could think of hurting you.'

He shook his head and swallowed the remainder of his champagne. 'Revenge,' he repeated slowly.

'I never forgave you for beating me on that first night,' she explained. 'I vowed then to make you pay for it. If they award me the contract, then I'll consider it a fair exchange.'

'You've done all of this because I tied to you to the mast and caned you?' he repeated. He seemed to be having difficulty understanding the words. 'But you enjoyed that,' he reminded her.

Emily turned away, her cheeks colouring suddenly. 'I don't recall –'

He grabbed her arm, his fingers pressing tightly into the flesh.

Emily gasped, unsure if the sound was a reaction to the stinging pain he inflicted or the arousal he caused. She could feel her nipples hardening in the confines of her bra. The familiar tingle of excitement was building between her legs, and she dared not look at the captain for fear that he would see the obvious signs in her eyes.

'You enjoyed it,' he repeated.

'I didn't want to,' she gasped, aware that her breath was ragged with excitement. 'You made me enjoy it. I had to make you pay.'

He pulled her close to his chest.

She glanced up into his face and he kissed her. His mouth devoured hers with a brutal disregard for tenderness or caring. As they kissed, his fingers pressed tighter against her arms, inspiring a wealth of agonised delight. When he finally released her, it was only so that his hands could go to her breasts. His fingers stroked and caressed the orbs through the fabric of her blouse, forcing rivulets of pleasure to trickle slowly throughout her body.

Emily did not bother to stop him.

'I honestly don't believe you,' he said, when their kiss eventually broke. 'You don't just enjoy being servile, you love it, don't you?'

Reluctantly, she nodded.

'So, why did you feel the need to avenge yourself?' His temper, always on a short fuse, was burning at a furious pace.

'I prefer being in control,' she told him simply.

'Bullshit!' he snorted.

She ignored his expletive. 'I've tried both sides of the coin,' she explained. 'I've had my arse whipped and I've drunk piss at your command. Admittedly, I loved both of those things. But I've also held the cane. I've tasted the power and I loved that even more.'

He considered her doubtfully. 'You're not the type to be dominant,' he said, not sounding certain of the words even as he spoke them.

She grunted dry laughter. 'Really? I've managed to get you in a rage over three dozen sheets of paper. I was in control when I did that.'

His sullen glare was not enough to mask the dull light of admiration that began to grow in his eyes. 'But you enjoy submitting,' he reminded her. 'Aren't you going to miss that?'

She shrugged, feigning nonchalance. 'I think I can live without it. If I win this contract, I'll be going back to England a wealthy woman. Roderick and Judy will continue to do exactly as I say. I think I'll have everything I want in life.'

'I doubt it,' he said bitterly.

She turned on him with a questioning expression. 'And what do you think I'll be missing?'

'This,' he replied flatly. He grabbed her arms again and pushed her down, towards the chair. She fell awkwardly but managed to remain silent, save for a shocked gasp. Even though it was only a small sound, she glanced nervously at the bedroom door, fearful that Roderick would come bursting through.

With her attention distracted, the captain grabbed twin fistful's of her hair. He pulled her head back sharply before releasing the tresses.

This time it took a lot more effort for Emily to stifle her cries. Her fingernails pressed into the soft pad of flesh above the ball of her thumb. As the desire to cry out increased, she pressed her fingers harder, wilfully resisting the urge.

He was pressing himself forcefully against her. She could feel the hardness of his erection and she knew he was as excited as she was. His fingers went to her breasts and he squeezed the orbs roughly.

With his mouth close to her ear he whispered softly. His warm breath tickling the flesh of her neck as he spoke. 'Without me,' he told her, 'you're going to miss the thrill of being properly dominated.'

'I'll learn to live without it,' she told him defiantly.

He released her angrily, a frown of foreboding contempt creasing his brow. 'I doubt you'll think of it as living,' he replied. 'But it's your choice. We can say our goodbyes over dinner this evening.' He climbed from the chair and moved towards the door. 'I think it will be the last meal we share together,' he said calmly.

Emily glared at him as he stamped towards the door. 'I hope it is,' she said thickly as he disappeared from sight. Easing herself from the chair she went to the door and called after him. 'I hope I never have to see you again after tonight, you lousy bastard. I hope I never see you again.' Echoing along the empty corridor behind him, the words had a hollow ring.

'Are you all right?' Roderick asked, appearing by her side.

She grinned unhappily at him. 'I'll be all right after tonight.'

The words occurred to her again later that evening as she was about to board the *Amazon Maiden*. The party was in full swing by the time the three of them arrived at the boat. An angry blood-orange sun was slowly falling beyond the horizon. The sky was a kaleidoscope of rich vibrant colours, ranging from midnight blue in the east to pastel shades of lemon in the west. The handful of clouds that speckled the sky were huge boulders of dusky amaranth granite. Against this backdrop, the stiff white sails and thrusting prow of the *Amazon Maiden* looked more majestic than ever.

I'll be all right after this evening, Emily told herself. She hoped it was true.

The melodic strains of a gay Tchaikovsky waltz, intermingled with chattering and laughter, bubbled merrily from the open door of the main hatch.

'Emily! You're here at last!'

Emily turned to the voice and was pleased to see Dawn rushing along the deck to greet her. She was dressed only in a loose wraparound blouse and a pair of cripplingly high stilettos. Her long tresses were held up this evening, giving her appearance an air of elegance that truly suited her. She rushed towards Emily and embraced her with warm welcoming arms.

'The Captain's furious with you,' she whispered softly. 'I don't know what you did, but you've put him in the foulest mood ever.'

As though it was done to deliberately contradict her,

the sound of the captain's laughter echoed heartily above the music.

'He sounds like he's hiding it well,' Emily observed wryly. She kissed Dawn chastely on the cheek and made quick introductions for the benefit of Roderick and Judy. Linking arms with the two women, she told Judy, 'Dawn has the most amazing jewellery I've ever seen. When we return to England, I'll be getting something similar for you.'

Judy whispered a quiet thank you, puzzled by Dawn's muffled giggles.

The three women made their way towards the main hatch with Roderick in their wake. Before they could start on the companionway, Captain Wilde appeared from the pilothouse.

He looked as though he had started the evening in full black tie. However, the heat, and his disregard for formality, had helped his outfit to disintegrate into a pair of long dark trousers and an open shirt. An unfastened bow tie dangled from the open collar.

'You've come full circle now, haven't you?' he growled, his stony gaze resting firmly on Emily.

Emily smiled courteously back at him. 'Good evening, Captain,' she said softly.

He held a glass in one hand and drained the amber contents with one long swallow. He casually tossed the glass overboard where it splashed into the river's fast-flowing waters. 'You came on board as stowaway to begin with,' he recalled loudly. 'Then you came back as member of the crew. Now you're here as a bloody pirate.'

Emily tried to ignore his words, wishing she wasn't blushing so profusely. 'Are John and Alan here yet?'

He nodded. 'Laura and Vincent are entertaining them in the saloon. I trust you'll go down below and join them.' He walked past the three women, his baleful glare fixed passionately on Emily.

243

'Where are you going?' she asked him sharply.

The captain placed his hand over Roderick's wary shoulders. 'Your friend and I are going to spend a moment out here to make our peace before we join you,' he explained. 'In spite of you being invited, I'd like this evening to go well, and that's not going to happen if Roderick and I are squaring up to one another every two minutes.'

Emily nodded her approval and took another step towards the companionway. She paused and fixed him with a steely expression. 'Have they awarded the contract yet?'

'They're waiting for your arrival,' he replied briskly. 'But I wouldn't get overconfident because of that. I'm sure John's got something up his sleeve.'

Emily considered him warily. 'And, do I have the Captain's permission to go below deck?'

He grunted dark laughter. 'You have the Captain's permission. And this time, Dawn and Vincent are under strict instructions to count the silverware once you've left.'

Emily ignored the sleight and walked confidently towards the main hatch. If John was waiting for her arrival before announcing who had won the contract, it had to bode well. She allowed Dawn and Judy to climb down to the saloon before she followed them.

The Tchaikovsy waltz had given way to Rimsky-Korsakov's *Sheherazade*. The heady pulsating rhythm of a powerful orchestra filled the room. All four of the occupants were either undressed or as close to as made no difference. John Masters and Laura were locked in a passionate embrace, their hands and fingers exploring one another fully.

Alan Thomas sat in one of the chairs, a glass of wine in one hand, a canapé in the other, and Vincent's head buried between his legs.

As she climbed into the room, Emily was afforded a

view of Vincent's tongue trailing along the entire length of Alan's cock. A broad grin of satisfaction had spread across Alan's face and he rubbed his fingers fondly through the blond man's hair. He waved acknowledgement to Emily and her companions with his glass of wine.

'Would you like drinks?' Dawn asked. She directed the question between Emily and Judy.

'Judy will organise them for us,' Emily said carefully. 'I'm sure you have duties to attend to.'

Dawn grinned and nodded. She moved forward and kissed Emily, her small mouth pressing gently against her lips. Blushing softly, she backed away and whispered the words 'thank you'. Emily watched as Dawn moved towards John and Laura, slipping out of the robe she wore as she neared them. She pressed her naked body against John's back and stroked her hands along his hips and thighs.

Sandwiched between the two women, Emily saw a grin of delight twisting John Master's face. He moved one hand from Laura's breast and reached behind himself, cupping Dawn's arse. For the first time, he noticed Emily and a smile of recognition lit his lips. 'We've been waiting for you! Where's Captain Wilde?'

She returned his smile. 'He's on deck, with Roderick.' She noticed Alan glance at her when she mentioned Roderick's name. Her smile broadened.

'We need to talk when he gets here,' John said.

'Should I fetch him?' Emily asked.

He shook his head. His lips brushed softly against Laura's before speaking. 'No. We can let the evening take its own course.'

Laura eased herself from John's arms, whispering a promise of return in his ear. She moved to Emily's side and placed a friendly kiss on her cheek. 'You've certainly got my husband in a rage,' she said, a trace of amusement colouring her tone. 'Although that's nothing new for you, is it?'

Emily glanced at Judy. 'Why don't you slip out of that blouse and see if John needs you?' she suggested quietly. There was enough force in her tone to make Judy realise the words were a command – not a request. She moved quickly towards John Masters, unfastening her blouse as she walked.

'You aren't mad at me, are you?'

Laura laughed softly. 'How on earth could I be mad at you?' She linked her arm with Emily's and pressed her naked body close. The swell of her breast touched Emily's bare arm, triggering a small thrill of pleasure. 'The Captain and I have been married for fifteen years now,' she explained quietly. 'We started playing games like this to spice up our love life, and it's worked brilliantly. Sex between us has never been better. The only thing that improves it is when my husband gets passionate about something.' She glanced knowingly at Emily. 'You've managed to make him more passionate than I could ever have believed.'

Emily grinned. She felt Laura's hand touching her breast through the flimsy fabric of the body she wore. 'You're not angry about the contract then?'

Laura smiled and shook her head. 'We won't collapse into penury if we lose it,' she explained. 'The chances are, we'd have more time for sailing, and other such things.' A wistful smile touched her lips. Speaking as though it was the first time she had considered the idea, she added, 'In a way, I hope you do win. It would make him so furious he'd be an absolute joy to live with.'

Emily allowed the woman to kiss her. She felt Laura's fingers traverse her body with measured curiosity. Her touch was electric, sending shivers of pleasure throughout Emily's body. The heady pulse of *Sheherazade* continued from the CD player, cocooning her in a warm, luxuriant world of hedonistic opulence.

Normally, she would have closed her eyes and enjoyed the tactile experiences from the solitary world behind

246

her eyelids. This evening, because there were so many exciting things to see, she glanced around the saloon and watched the others enjoying themselves.

The sights proved to be a powerful stimulant.

Alan and Vincent had moved from the chair to the floor. They were both naked, Vincent laying down with Alan kneeling over him. As she watched, Emily saw Alan take Vincent's length in his mouth. He sucked gently on the swollen purple end, his tongue trailing slowly around the sensitive flesh of Vincent's fraenum.

Moaning excitedly, Vincent thrust his mouth forward. He delivered a series of soft kisses to Alan's arsehole, his tongue sliding purposefully around the puckered rim. Moving upwards, he put his mouth over Alan's balls and tongued them carefully, before placing his lips at the base of the man's shaft.

Excited, the pair groaned in unison.

Emily felt a thrill of delight as she studied them. She was aware that her arousal was hastened by the sultry touch of Laura's fingers working their way up her legs. To allow the woman easier access, she parted them slightly. The tingling spark of excitement that stirred the lips of her labia was quickly becoming a demanding pulse that craved satisfaction.

She switched her gaze from Alan and Vincent, drawn by John's moans of mounting excitement.

As she had instructed, Judy had joined John and Dawn. With her pert breasts bared, she knelt before the man and took his length in her mouth. Her tongue worked eagerly on his long shaft, coating the hard erection with a glistening layer of wetness. As she licked him, she stared meekly upwards with her large green eyes.

Watching her, Emily realised something had changed in the woman's expression. Before she had boarded the *Amazon Maiden*, Emily had been aware of a hint of cunning in those emerald eyes. Seeing Judy now, she realised the assertive rebelliousness had gone. It had been replaced by a look of meek servility. Aware that she had brought about that change in the woman, Emily smiled happily to herself.

John Masters placed his hand firmly on her head and forced her to take his length between her lips. Judy smiled around his cock as she did this. Her gaze remained upturned, as she studied his face for signs of approval.

Behind John, Dawn was also kneeling. Her hands were gently stroking his legs and abdomen in long, languid caresses. At the same time, she had her mouth pressed between the cheeks of his arse. Although she could not see it, Emily knew the woman would have her tongue buried deep up John's anus. Her excited moans of enjoyment were muted by his backside, but Emily was close enough to hear them.

Laura's fingers teased at the heat between her legs and Emily finally closed her eyes. The excitement of watching the others was too powerful for her to indulge in it for too long. As much as she wanted to share their enjoyment by watching, she realised the urgency of her own arousal needed more practical satisfaction.

Laura's mouth went to her breasts and Emily thrilled to the pleasure of having her nipples sucked. The woman teased the sensitive buds of flesh with a careful tongue, inspiring waves of pleasure that seemed to carry on forever. Hardly realising she had moved, Emily felt Laura's tongue travelling downwards. The skirt she wore was brushed casually aside. Then she felt the intimate exploration of Laura's eager mouth against the hot, wet cleft of her sex.

She murmured a soft word of appreciation, keeping her eyes closed as the eruption of joy grew within her. A mouth pressed against hers and she kissed it happily, not knowing or caring who it was. A hand cupped her breast, the thumb brushing roughly against the hard bud of her nipple. She felt a second hand touching her, then a third and a fourth.

With her eyes closed, Emily was lost in a blissful world of sexual adulation. Fingers, hands, mouths and lips touched, stroked, kissed and caressed her. She could feel the pressure of a cock forcing against her thigh and reached a hand down to carelessly stroke it.

As Laura continued to tongue the cleft between her legs, Emily sighed happily, indulging herself completely in the experience. She felt the stirrings of an orgasm rise inside her, triggered by myriad touches and caresses. Her breath deepened as a pair of hands touched her buttocks then pushed softly at the forbidden rim of her anus.

'Wilde! I'm pleased you could join us at last!' John said cheerfully.

Emily opened her eyes suddenly. She was not surprised to see Captain Wilde standing over her. His hand cupped her breast and his lips were a whisper away from hers. She studied him calmly, determined that he would see neither contempt nor adulation on her face. 'I thought it was you,' she said coolly.

He raised his eyebrows. 'Yet you let me continue?'

She shrugged. 'You can try to please me all night long if you like. I'll allow you to do that.'

Still licking between Emily's legs, Laura smiled softly as her tongue probed the tender pink flesh.

Ignoring the darkening frown that crossed the captain's brow, Emily glanced at Roderick. He too had been caressing her as she stood with her eyes closed. His fingers rested against her buttocks and he pressed soft kisses against her neck. She kissed him softly on the cheek, then pushed him gently away. 'Why don't you go and renew your acquaintance with Alan?' she suggested. She glanced to where Alan and Vincent lay and saw the pair grinning broadly at one another. Their arms lay easily over each other's shoulders. Rivulets of Alan's thick white cream coated Vincent's mouth and lips. Alan was tracing patterns in the wetness with one long, careful finger. In spite of the fact that he had just climaxed, his cock was standing proud.

Emily heard Roderick swallow nervously. She would have been concerned for him if she had not seen the broad smile of anticipation that crossed his lips.

He placed a last kiss on her neck and studied her face. 'Is that what you want me to do?'

She nodded and grinned at him.

Without another word, Roderick moved towards Alan and Vincent.

As Roderick left her, John Masters joined the three of them. His cock was raging hard and Emily saw it was still coated with the wetness Judy had caused. She placed a finger against the swollen tip and stroked it softly. The length twitched appreciatively beneath her touch.

Judy watched her doing this and frowned slightly. Her unhappiness was quickly forgotten when Dawn knelt on the floor in front of her. After a tentative kiss and a hesitant caress, the pair quickly grew bolder. Within seconds, the two women were intertwined.

Laura moved her mouth from Emily's sex and eased herself from the floor. She glanced at Dawn and Judy then graced Emily with a soft smile. 'I'll leave the three of you to discuss business,' she said, before going to join the two women.

Emily stared carefully at John. 'Are you going to put the Captain and I out of our misery? Or are you still in the mood for other things?'

His smile was broad. 'I'm in the mood for a lot of other things,' he told her. 'But I could never keep you in misery, unless you wanted me to.'

She laughed softly. 'So who are you awarding the contract to?'

Beside her, she felt the captain's hand tighten

nervously against her buttock. It was comforting to realise he was just as tense about this decision as she was, and Emily took strength from his disquiet.

'Alan and I discussed it quite thoroughly,' he began. 'We've made a decision and I hope it's one that you'll both be happy with.'

Emily frowned. 'Go on,' she encouraged him. 'You've intrigued me.'

'We're awarding the contract to the good captain here,' John said quickly.

Emily felt her hopes plummet like a stone. She stared dully at John, dimly aware that Captain Wilde was grinning beside her.

'You're a shrewd fellow, John,' he said, clapping the man heartily on the shoulder. 'I've always said, you're one of the sharpest in the business.'

'Sharper than you may realise,' John Masters said quietly. 'We're prepared to accept your contract on one condition.'

In victory, Captain Wilde had the grace to be magnanimous. 'Name it,' he said simply.

As he spoke, John stared at Emily. 'We'll accept your proposal, Captain, on the condition that you get Emily to manage the contract.'

In spite of the raging melody of the CD orchestra, a silence fell between the three of them.

Night fell over the Amazon like a switch. When Emily had climbed aboard the boat the sky had been painted with more colours than an artist's palate. Now, the heavens were a dusty black, interspersed with shiny glittering diamonds. A silver moon broke the ebony night, tainting the world with pale slivers of light and darkening the shadows.

Emily stood alone at the bow, leaning against the pulpit and staring out into the blackness. A light breeze cooled her arms and legs, reminding her of her first night aboard the *Amazon Maiden*. Her thoughts were a whirlwind of doubts and questions, all spiralling through her mind in a tumultuous rage.

John had clarified his proposition before she came on to the deck. He wanted her to manage the financial arrangements that Captain Wilde had instigated. He was willing to offer a lucrative retainer for her services – a very lucrative retainer she thought distantly – and all she had to do was liaise with the appropriate people in order to get the whole package up and running. Her own proposal had convinced John of her abilities, but the captain's had offered a more secure prospect. She had noted all of the technicalities he pointed out, and was busy trying not to think of them.

The crux of her dilemma lay with John's final statement on the subject. 'If you want the job, Emily, it's all yours. You'll be your own boss, in charge of all the arrangements. The only person you'll have to answer to is Captain Wilde.'

She had told him she needed a moment to think about it. Taking a glass of wine and covering her modesty with a robe, she fled to the sanctuary of solitude on the empty deck. 'What do I do?' she whispered into the night. She had believed herself on the verge of being rid of Captain Wilde forever. Now she looked like being tied to him for the next three years. Either that, or throw away the chance of a lifetime.

'What do you want do?'

She whirled round on hearing the captain's voice. He stood disturbingly close to her. In one hand he held a bottle of wine.

'Are you spying on my thoughts now?' she asked angrily.

'You said the question aloud. Now, please, can we try not to argue for the next five minutes. You've got me trapped. You're in control now. What do you want to do about it?'

Emily stared at him, not bothering to mask the lack of comprehension from her face. 'I have you trapped?' she repeated, puzzled. 'What do you mean? And what do you mean by saying I'm in control?'

He shook his head dourly. 'Don't try playing games of innocence,' he cautioned. 'You're not in a position to carry them off.'

Emily started to say something in her own defence, then stopped as he continued.

'Unless I have you as my contract manager, I don't have this contract. It's as simple as that. Now, I'm supposed to do whatever you want to make you work with me. Like I said,' he repeated bitterly. 'You're in control.'

Emily could not stop herself from grinning as she heard his words. Her fear and anxieties were suddenly forgotten as she realised how strong her position was. Sipping at her wine, she walked past him, trailing a finger over his bare chest as she moved. 'Follow me,' she said quietly, employing a cool authority in her tone. She held her glass for him to take and he accepted it with numb fingers.

He glared dully after her, resentment curling his lips. But he followed.

Emily walked to the boat's mast and pressed her back against the cool length of wood. She placed her hands behind herself and held them tightly together.

'What do you want me to do now?' Captain Wilde asked curiously.

Emily smiled confidently into his puzzled frown. 'After you've tied my hands,' she said carefully, 'I want you to fetch your cane.'

He did not bother to hide his lack of understanding. 'My cane?'

'After you've tied my hands,' she said patiently.

He did as she asked, fastening her wrists tightly and securing her to the boat's mast. When he returned with the cane, he stood hesitantly in front of her. 'And what do you want me to do now?'

'I think you know what I want now,' she told him firmly.

'You know what I deserve for trying to steal your contract. You know what you want to do. Just remember, this time, we're doing it because I want to.'

His puzzled frown was replaced by a broad grin of understanding. With a sharp whistle, his cane sliced through the night air.

Emily groaned happily.

NEXUS NEW BOOKS

To be published in January 2005:

PETTING GIRLS
Penny Birch

Amber Oakley is suspicious when dominant couple Morris and Melody Rathwell invite her to judge their fetish club's puppy-girl show; but what could go wrong? It's not as if they're asking her to compete. She goes, little suspecting that the event will lead her into the clutches of a fanatic for treating girls as pets, to strip-wrestling in baked beans, and an encounter with an over-endowed puppy-boy!

£6.99   ISBN 0 352 33957 8

BELINDA BARES UP
Yolanda Celbridge

Britain, 1947. Schoolteacher Belinda Beaucul relishes exhibitionism, and caning lustful conscripts on the bare, while her own body wriggles under a sensuous nurse's discipline. She enters a twilight world of spivs, stolen nylons and flagellant parties and soon learns that post-war England is anything but austere. Teaching sultry girls in British Somaliland, meanwhile, requires rule by the cane. But when Belinda's prince enslaves her, she finds it is really her that craves a master's rod.

£6.99   ISBN 0 352 33926 8

FAIRGROUND ATTRACTIONS
Lisette Ashton

Beyond the bright lights of the fairground there is a mysterious world, hidden from the visiting crowds. Operating outside of the restrictions of the towns they entertain, the fairground's owners insist on indulging their lewd and base appetites whenever and however they please. Georgia and Holly are reluctant recruits to the fairground and they soon discover the pains and pleasures of this perverse regime, as both women endure a painful lesson in its strict rules. It's a lesson they'll never forget.

£6.99   ISBN 0 352 33927 6

If you would like more information about Nexus titles, please visit our website at www.nexus-books.co.uk, or send a stamped addressed envelope to:

Nexus, Thames Wharf Studios,
Rainville Road, London W6 9HA

NEXUS BACKLIST

This information is correct at time of printing. For up-to-date information, please visit our website at www.nexus-books.co.uk

All books are priced at £6.99 unless another price is given.

✂ -

Please send me the books I have ticked above.

Name ....

Address ....

....

....

.... Post code....................

Send to: **Virgin Books Cash Sales, Thames Wharf Studios, Rainville Road, London W6 9HA**

US customers: for prices and details of how to order books for delivery by mail, call 1-800-343-4499.

Please enclose a cheque or postal order, made payable to **Nexus Books Ltd**, to the value of the books you have ordered plus postage and packing costs as follows:

UK and BFPO – £1.00 for the first book, 50p for each subsequent book.

Overseas (including Republic of Ireland) – £2.00 for the first book, £1.00 for each subsequent book.

If you would prefer to pay by VISA, ACCESS/MASTERCARD, AMEX, DINERS CLUB or SWITCH, please write your card number and expiry date here:

....

Please allow up to 28 days for delivery.

Signature ....

Our privacy policy

We will not disclose information you supply us to any other parties. We will not disclose any information which identifies you personally to any person without your express consent.

From time to time we may send out information about Nexus books and special offers. Please tick here if you do *not* wish to receive Nexus information. ☐

✂ -